Rhapsody Suite

Model Student Book Two

Welcome to Model Student!

RHAPSODY SUITE IS the second in the *Model Student Series* by Devon Layne. The series comprises six books and is now available for order or pre-order. All beautifully designed and reasonably priced, Elder Road Books can be displayed with pride.

And for those who look inside, the characters and storyline will captivate as much as Devon's sensitive and sensuous sex scenes. Here's what readers have said:

A multi-part longer story, the characters feel like real people even though they are in a pretty rare type of arrangement.
They each struggle and fail and try again.
Great long read with fantastic sex scenes throughout.

An engaging and well-written story. But some of the writing, when describing Tony producing his masterpieces, is absolutely sublime.

It includes one of the most incredible sex scenes I've ever read.
Not the typical "insert tab A into slot B" nor
the bizarre "masturbatory fantasy played out with wooden models".

To order additional copies, see
https://www.createspace.com/6504352.
For more information and dealer discounts, contact
ElderRoadBooks@outlook.com or visit www.DevonLayne.com.

First paperback edition
ISBN 978-1-939275-45-5

Devon Layne

Rhapsody Suite

Model Student Book Two

ELDER ROAD BOOKS
BELLEVUE WA

One

"**FUCKFUCKFUCKFUCKFUCK!**"

It might have been an appropriate sentiment if I'd been balls deep in Lissa or Melody. Unfortunately, I was walking into my Art History midterm on Monday morning.

Melody and Lissa had carted me out of the Admin building at ten last night and fed me. Then, the two of them took me to my dorm room, stripped me, put me in bed, and kissed me goodnight. I was already so exhausted I couldn't stay awake till they left the room. I barely made it to my exam on time in the morning and when I looked at the basket full of papers at the door I realized I hadn't finished writing the Art History paper that was due today. I couldn't afford a fail on a paper in this class. Even though I loved the subject, I couldn't stay awake in the classes, so I wasn't doing that well on the tests. The papers were the only thing keeping me afloat. I couldn't cut Concepts because it was the last class before the midterm on Wednesday. *Damn it!*

I pulled out my Daytimer and looked at my schedule. After Concepts I had court time for two hours and I couldn't skip that because my coach was also my lover. She definitely wouldn't approve. If I got out of the Club by half past six, I could grab a sandwich at the cafeteria just before it closed and start working on my paper by seven. There was nothing in my schedule that said I was meeting with Melody, so I would have four hours to write the paper. *Damn! Do I have to have 'meeting my lover for dinner' on my calendar?* This paper had to be in the office by midnight. Brian, our TA, was a born enforcer and I'd heard stories about guys getting to the office at a minute past midnight and being told their papers wouldn't be accepted. When the midterm exams were handed out, I managed to block out everything else and answered the four essay questions in record time. I didn't think I'd done badly, and I picked up an hour that I could go to the library and work on the stupid paper.

I was typing like mad to get the research done that I had barely touched in the past two weeks. It wasn't like I didn't know this was due. We got a schedule of assignments at the first of the term and a paper was due every three weeks. The subjects were even spelled out along with the requirements for the paper. I could have done this anytime I wanted to forgo a few hours of hot sex with my girlfriends. *Shit!*

I didn't eat lunch and headed straight to Concepts class. After an hour of lecturing on the properties of three-dimensional art—a lecture that we'd already heard last week, but Ms. Brock insisted on reviewing for the upcoming exam—we were each given a lump of clay.

"Okay, people. This is the project portion of your midterm. The written portion is on Wednesday. You should think of this as a portfolio piece. Here is your model." Ms. Brock uncovered an object comprising a bunch of triangles and diamonds on a pedestal in front of us. "It's a very subjective test, but most of art is. Don't try to duplicate the model. You don't have the right materials for that. Try to capture the feel of the piece. Show me what the sculptor wanted to communicate with the shape and balance."

I sat at my workbench staring at the lump in front of me. It was supposed to be a geometrically perfect study in balance and contrast. My lump seemed dedicated to remaining a lump while my head continued to process the information I'd been researching for Art History. I didn't even have a decent view of the model.

Everyone else seemed to be busy mashing, folding, and shaping their lumps. I finally got up and walked to the front of the room. Ms. Brock watched me closely, but didn't say anything, as I approached the model and looked at it. I'm not really into modern and abstract forms, but this *was* an elegant piece. I wondered who the sculptor was. Balance and contrast was a good reference point for looking at it. The diamonds and triangles weren't all interconnected once you looked at all the sides of the sculpture. The connectedness was a two-dimensional illusion. And the illusion changed as you walked around it. Some pieces looked like they were floating, even though when you walked around the piece you would find a different shape connecting them back together. It wasn't just the interlinking of individual shapes that got to me, though. When you stood back and looked at the overall balance of the piece, different shapes emerged. It was cool to just look from different angles and see different triangles and diamonds evolve. I must have spent twenty minutes just wandering around the piece and looking at it from all directions.

I went back to my desk and stared at my lump, trying to see in it anything that approached the balance and contrast that the piece in the front had. I dug my hands into the moist clay and started squishing it together. As soon as my fingers touched the clay, I was in a different world. I'm not much on sculpture in general, but I love the sensual feel of pushing and molding clay. It felt so cool to have my hands in the medium. There's something 'elementary school' about it. I wasn't really paying attention to the model anymore. I was content just to push the clay around with my fingers. I'm not sure I even had my eyes open. The next thing I knew the class was over and Ms. Brock was standing beside me looking at my not-so-lumpish-looking lump of clay. I kind of liked it.

"Not bad," Ms. Brock said.

"Thank you."

"I know you were concentrating, but did you notice how many students went up and really looked at the model?"

"No. Didn't everyone?"

"Not one. Except you. Why did you get up and come to the pedestal?"

"I couldn't really get a good feel for it from where I was. I mean, it's three-dimensional. Sitting here I could only see one side. I'm sorry I disrupted the class. I didn't mean to." She must have been pissed at me for getting in front of other kids as they worked. I guess it was selfish of me or something. God, I hate this fucking school. Why can't I do anything right?

"There's no need to apologize. I'd like you to take Intro to 3-D art in the fall. Do you think you could fit it into your schedule?"

"I don't know. I'm doing a double degree between here and SCU. I just don't know how the schedules are going to work out. I really want the 2D Studio Art class that Dr. Henredon is teaching."

"I know painting is your first love, but I think that more exposure to sculpture could help your painting as well. This is really a fine bit of work you did." I looked at the lump of clay again. It was nothing at all like the model. It wasn't open and airy. It was just a couple of triangles linked together to form a sort of... bird.

"I asked you to capture the balance and contrast of the piece. Look around the classroom. Every single one tried to copy the model, seeing only one side of it. You walked around the model and created a piece that captures balance and contrast. It's good work, Tony. Not gallery work, mind you, but it shows a lot of potential in working in multidimensional media. Consider the course as you put together your schedule. I'd like to see you there. This will make a good addition to your end of year portfolio."

"Thank you," I said as I gathered up all my bags. I glanced at the clock in the room and realized I had to hustle if I wanted to make my court time—and I did.

"Good luck in your tournament," she said as she walked away.

———————◄◆►———————

I SENT A text to Melody as I was walking to the gym. It just said, "Got a paper due by midnight. Can't meet for dinner tonight. Love u." My phone vibrated just as I got to the gym. The return message said. ":-(Miss you. <3" I got into my shorts and T and headed for the court. Lissa was already there warming up. I stepped through the door and the moment it closed a ball whizzed past my ear.

"You're late!"

"Only a minute. I got stopped by my prof after class."

"More praise for your work? I don't have time for it. Play!" With that she sent another hard low ball toward me and I scooped it up and into the front wall. What was wrong with Lissa? She seemed angry. Geez. I wasn't more than a minute late and she's clobbering me with kill shots. I wasn't even warmed up yet. I missed the next shot.

"Stay low! You can always come up if needed. It's easier than scooping down if you are too high. Now watch for it." She started another rally and we kept going over and over. When you are in a club tournament, there usually isn't a rally that goes more than four or five hits. One guy or the other flubs a shot or can't pick up the return. The higher up in real competition you go, the more evenly matched the players are, and the less likely they are to make a mistake. Lissa was playing at the level she was when she won her championship. All I could do was try to keep up. We hadn't been playing for more than five minutes when everything else just faded away and all I could see was where the ball was about to be.

"Water!" she shouted. We were both doubled over and panting. I don't think either of us had any idea how long we'd been at it until we walked through the door to get our water bottles and take a drink. I glanced at the clock. We'd been going for almost 90 minutes. Lissa rinsed her mouth out and spit in the water cooler. "That part was for you. I need work on my backhand. Get in and serve to me."

This wasn't going to be anywhere near the free-for-all we just had. I was going to serve every kind of serve I could make into her backhand. But she was ready for them all. She nailed every serve. I was getting pissed off, but I was also seeing something else. I got low and served a hard spike right up the middle of the court. She automatically spun and tried to pick it off the back wall but she was a fraction too late and didn't get a square hit on the ball. It fell to the floor just short of the front wall.

"I said backhand! I need work on my backhand." Now I was really pissed. I sent another one sailing by her on the right and she didn't come close to picking this one up. "Can't you place a serve now?"

"I put it right where I intended to." I shouted back at her. "What kind of work on your backhand are you going to get when you're sitting there waiting for it? You're cocked three-quarters to the left. Of course you can return everything I serve there. You're ready for it. Square yourself up for a real serve and I'll decide when it's going to be a backhand and when it isn't. You focus on returning the ball."

I don't know where that came from. For a minute she looked like she was going to tell me off, then she squared herself up and waited for the next serve. I served two to her forehand and then she missed one to her backhand. I came back with the same serve and she nailed it. She was cheating left and I put another one so far to the right that I had to flatten myself against the side wall to keep from getting hit by my own serve. She almost didn't reach it in time and scowled at me. She moved further to the right and I skimmed one along the left wall. She pulled her backhand and took it off the back wall with so much force it almost knocked me over. All right. If that's the way she wants to play, we'll play tough. We didn't say another word to each other for the rest of the lesson. I just kept peppering her with serves moving back and forth across the court. There were about twice as many backhands as forehands, but she was too proud to let me slip one past her because she was in a bad position. We were drenched in sweat when we heard the next guys with a court reservation pounding on the door to let us know our time on the court was up.

Lissa brushed past me on the way out the door and grabbed her bottle and towel. Then turned and headed for the locker room without a word to me. I ran to catch up with her.

"Lissa! What's wrong?" She pulled to a stop and spun to face me.

"What's wrong? I signed a model release for a figure painting class. I didn't know my tits would be displayed two feet wide in the busiest corridor of the campus. Shit! What do you think is wrong? It's like having your naked picture on the Internet."

"I thought you liked the picture."

"I did. It's beautiful. It's just… I can't… I always…"

I wrapped her in my arms and she heaved a sob into my sopping wet t-shirt. She pulled back with a look of disgust.

"Go shower. I don't want to talk about it." She walked into the ladies' locker room and I couldn't do anything else. After my shower I hung around the lobby for half an hour but she had either already gone home or she was waiting till I left before she came out. I couldn't wait any longer. I couldn't get any food now anyway. The cafeteria was closed. I headed back to the library and started in on my Art History paper again.

I WAS STANDING in front of Dr. Bychkova's office at 11:45 p.m. with six pages of analysis of the conflict between Picasso and Dali. I knocked and pushed the door open to see Brian sitting there with his hand out. I placed my paper in it.

"Just in time." He looked up. "Tony?"

"Yeah. Sorry I didn't get this in earlier. I was pretty busy this weekend."

"So I saw. Henredon is hauling everyone he can collar down to that hall. Nice work. Why didn't you just take a pass on this one?" I just stood and looked at him. What the hell was he talking about?

"What do you mean?"

"Dr. Bychkova assigned six papers and the grading will be based on the best five of the six. He does it so students can skip one if they need to. You've done fine on the last three and there's only two left. Why bother with this one?"

Fuckfuckfuckfuckfuck! Of all the stupid, asinine, fucked up rules to have. I'd just spent an entire evening working on a paper I could have skipped. It wasn't that great a paper and would probably be the lowest score of the six anyway. *I hate this fucking school. I hate my life. I hate myself.* I walked away from the office swearing at myself. I'd skipped dinner with Melody. Lissa was pissed off at me because of the painting. I was exhausted and I didn't know what to do. And my back hurt. I'd spent thirteen hours yesterday painting on a vertical surface in front of me. There is no way to get comfortable when you're working in that position. Lissa worked my ass off on the court and I cut my spa time so I'd catch her before she left. That was unsuccessful and for all I knew she'd never speak to me again.

When I got to my room I was so tired I didn't even bother to turn on the light when I entered my room. I just stripped, walked across the room and fell onto my bed. There was a loud squeak as I landed on something considerably different than my mattress.

"Ow."

"What the...?"

I jumped up and snapped the light on. Melody was lying in my bed and it looked like she was very naked.

9

"Brush your teeth and come to bed."

"What are you doing here? How did you get into my dorm room?" I was just shocked. I certainly wasn't disappointed.

"I met your roommate, Ryan, at lunch today. He's moved out. He and Arlene found an apartment and decided to take it now instead of waiting for summer. I convinced him to give me his key."

"And you thought you would just move in?"

"Not yet. But I thought you might like some company tonight."

I did. I kissed her and all the tension seemed to melt out of my body.

"It would be okay if you did," I said. She looked a question at me. "Move in." She didn't answer, but cuddled up closer.

"How'd the paper go?"

"I really don't want to talk about that. It was another waste of time." I headed into the bathroom and brushed my teeth. Should have done that anyway, but I was so tired I just collapsed. When I got back to the bed she held the covers up and I slid in feeling her soft skin against me. She wrapped me in her arms and I was so contented I almost drifted off to sleep. A thought occurred to me and I struggled up out of darkness to ask her, "Does Lissa know you're here?"

"We talked about it this weekend. We can't live with her and she doesn't want us not to be together just because she can't be with us. We agreed that we all expected each other to be with whichever of us and we'd trust that no one was intentionally left out. I had a really good weekend with her, Tony. And it wasn't just sex." She kissed me softly, but I wasn't ready to settle down yet.

"When we played racquetball today, she was upset. She wasn't happy about the mural. Said it was like having her naked picture posted on the Internet. I hung around to talk to her, but she never came out of the locker room as far as I could tell."

"That doesn't sound right. She loved the painting. I love the painting and it's my ass sticking out." I put my hand on the body part she mentioned and squeezed her cheek lightly.

"No one knows that."

"Ha! Sandra and Amy were all over me about it today. But I don't care. I love it." This time, the kiss she planted on me was enthusiastic and for a minute I was lost in it. I didn't think we'd make love tonight. It was just being together that was important.

"I'm still worried about Lissa. Why can't she be with us this week?"

"She's got the kids. I think she's a little nervous about having them around us."

"I'd like to meet them. They are part of the woman we love. Have you met them yet?"

"She picked them up Saturday morning after she dropped you off. We didn't spend anywhere near as much time naked this weekend as you imagined."

"She seemed so pleased with the painting Sunday night. But it was just a whole different Lissa this afternoon."

"Let's tell her we love her and miss her. Get your phone." I grabbed my cell phone and we both typed in a text message and sent it to her. "Lissa love, miss you. Love you!" I quickly tapped out a second message and sent it to Melody. She grinned when her phone chimed. We waited there a minute for a response from Lissa, but none came, so we put our phones on the desk and settled back into bed.

It was wonderful to settle into Melody's arms and have her spoon up behind me. Her face rubbed against my shoulders and every so often she would kiss a spot. I could just stay like this forever.

"What was that with Kate about?"

"What?" I'd almost drifted off to sleep. Kate?

"About changing her mind and anytime you want. Were you propositioning someone behind our backs?"

"No. I wouldn't do that!" I turned in bed and faced her. It was a lot more cramped in my dorm single bed than in Lissa's king size bed. "I wouldn't, Melody."

"I know that. I'm teasing. So what was it?"

"It took me a while before I figured it out. It seemed like it came out of the blue. But when we were working Saturday, she struck some kind of pose and I told her she should model. It was a big joke to her and she went on about how it wasn't going to happen. I think what she was saying was she changed her mind and would model for me."

"That figures. She'd be a good model. I like the shape of her face, and she's tall. I could see her in one of those shadowy scenes that Sandra paints."

"Why'd she run away?"

"Probably had to run home and change her panties." Melody was thoughtful for a moment. "On second thought I don't think she was wearing any."

"How could you tell that?"

"If she had panties on she'd have taken them off and thrown them at you—my rock star boyfriend." She giggled.

"As if. Why would she want to model for me anyway?"

"That's easy." Melody kissed me again. "After seeing that mural, there probably isn't a girl in school who wouldn't model for you. She just wants to see herself through your eyes."

I've read some sex stories—online—and it seems like they all talk about guys waking up in the morning with a girlfriend blowing their morning wood. I woke up on the edge of the little bed with a faceful of hair. Melody was still peacefully sleeping. I've got one of those clocks that projects the time on the ceiling so I know if I can go back to sleep. My alarm would ring in about five minutes. But I thought the whole blowjob idea wasn't bad and maybe it would work the other way as well.

I worked my way down Melody's body under the covers and managed to get her legs pushed apart far enough to get between them. I'd had my face down here before and we both really enjoyed it. The difference was I was under the sheet and blanket and her scent mingled with mine was trapped all night and pretty intense. It wasn't unpleasant. It was like opening a fresh can of coffee and getting a concentrated dose of that heady aroma. I started licking her labia lightly—not trying to probe or anything, just caressing her with my tongue. She squirmed a little and her petals began to unfold until her inner lips opened and I dipped my tongue deep enough to get a clean fresh taste of her. I couldn't see much in the dark, but I played my tongue over her smooth shaved mound and dipped back down to drag it over her clitoris. The little bud hardened and seemed to poke out further. I was sure I heard her moan and I suspected she'd woken up. Her hand was tangled in my hair. Her hips started moving, pushing her nubbin harder into my mouth. It was so cool to feel her passion rising and I could hardly wait to feel her come. She was moving toward it fast.

I could feel her stomach pulsing up and down as I pushed a finger into her and looked for that spot along the top Lissa had shown me. Her pussy clamped down on me hard. Just as she came, my alarm clock rang. She shrieked and sat straight up, almost snapping my head back. But apparently the alarm didn't stop her orgasm because her juices were flowing all over my face and she kept gasping out squeaks as she panted. As soon as I was released from her grip, I struggled out from under the bedclothes and silenced the alarm. Melody was still sitting in the bed gasping for air with the sheet covering nothing but her feet. As she caught her breath, her breasts were bobbing up and down and were so incredible to watch I was mesmerized. I wished that I could really capture movement when I paint. That image was incredible. She was incredible.

She looked up at me, her eyes refocusing.

"That was interesting. I don't even know how to describe it."

"A four alarm orgasm?" She burst out laughing and I hugged her.

"God, no! I couldn't take four of them! Let's shower. We've got to get to class. Maybe I can take care of that while we're at it." She pushed my erection down and it sprang back with force. It was a good morning.

Two

WE WERE LAUGHING by the time we got to Fundamentals. We'd each received a text from Lissa, but it was just a smiley. Then Melody started trying to figure out what the emoticon was for cunnilingus. :p(|) That degenerated into us sending texts back and forth about the kinds of boobs you could represent (o)(o), an erection 8===, fellatio :-O=8, and asshole (*). We were still trying to figure out threesome when we walked into class looking at our phones and giggling.

Everyone was quiet and staring at us. Obviously, Doc had been saying something about the painting since he had a slide of it displayed on the screen when people entered the classroom.

"Oh geez," I whispered. "Are we late?"

"No."

"You are not late, Tony. I called the rest of the class yesterday and asked them to come fifteen minutes early. Everyone will get out fifteen minutes early as well."

"I didn't get a message."

"No, I wanted to discuss this piece with the class without you for a few minutes. Now, if you'll join us, I was just asking, what is it about this painting that makes it so special?" There was a general murmur and a suggestion of technique, freedom, composition. Doc kept shaking them off. Finally, Melody stood up and walked to the front of the class. I could see Doc begin to smile as she got to the front of the room.

"All right," she said, facing the class. "I confess. It's my ass." She turned around and bent over. For a second I thought she was going to moon the class, but she kept her jeans on. Everyone started clapping. Melody turned around, bowed, and came back to sit beside me. I was blushing. She was giggling. When the commotion died down a bit, Doc started speaking again.

"Lovely as your ass is, I'm looking for something else. Kate, you were there. You watched most of it take shape. What do you think?"

"It's the connection between the artist and the model," she said firmly. "When you look at some of the great portraits we've studied, those that touch the viewer most... it's always about the interaction between the model and the artist."

"Yes. The connection is there. It is seldom a conscious decision. You can't walk into the studio and just say, 'I'm going to connect with this model.' But sometimes something magical happens and the link is there. That is when art speaks to us."

"What about abstract art?" Sandra asked.

"You mean the kind of art that you look at and ask yourself, 'what is it'? If you are in doubt, there is probably a weak connection. But it doesn't have to be that way. Artists can connect with many things. Everyone who paints has to paint a still life or landscape at one point or another. Most are mere exercises in technique, rendering, and lighting. But then you come to that sublime connection, like with Monet's *Water Lilies*, and suddenly you are lost in the simplicity of the connection. But not in all of his paintings. Of the 250 Water Lily paintings by Monet, scarcely half a dozen draw the viewer into the connection between artist and subject. The same is true of abstraction. If the artist has connected with the subject, it is likely that the viewer will as well. But it is rare. The artist must be in a unique frame of mind. The model or subject must have a deep connection—real or imagined. The skill must be there to reveal it. The rest of the time, we rely on technique, composition, lighting… all the things you have mentioned this morning."

I was a bit embarrassed and Doc never did mention what he'd talked to the rest of the class about before Melody and I got there. Mercifully, he moved on to normal topics and we discussed the techniques and paint choices for doing large scale murals. It seems that doing a dry plaster piece like the one in the Admin Building was really different than doing an outdoor mural on a building. Doc showed slides of several paintings on the walls of buildings and talked about how the surface was prepared. He rewarded everyone for showing up fifteen minutes early with an extra fifteen off at the end and the promise of a short midterm on Thursday. It was nice getting out of Fundies half an hour early. That meant we had time to get lunch before I went to Art Orientation and Melody went to her textiles class. Sandra fell into step beside us.

"I can't believe you did that, you tramp!"

"I'm not a tramp! But did Doc Henredon really just say I had a cute ass?"

"A lovely ass. Now that everyone knows it's yours, you're going to get asked out a lot. Better put a leash on her, Tony."

"I don't think that's a problem," I answered. Amy was just coming into the cafeteria from her Advertising Fundamentals class when we got there. Sandra immediately started telling her about Melody's comment in our Studio Fundamentals class.

That set them off and I easily excused myself to go to class before they had finished discussing exactly how close I'd been to the ass in question.

THE WEEK PROGRESSED with minimal hassle and I did okay on my midterms. Having Melody in my bed every night was a definite plus. We pushed the two beds together and aside from falling through the crack in the middle once, we were able to pretend they were one bed and still be able to get a decent night's sleep. I slept in Wednesday morning since we'd had the Art History exam on Monday and there was no class on Wednesday. Unfortunately, the only contact I had with Lissa was a call that said she had a business function to attend to on Wednesday and that she'd asked Rod to work with me during my practice time. I was disappointed, but said I loved her and we needed to get together. She just said she'd see us on Friday.

Rod is huge. He's easily 6'7" and weighs about 250. The thing is, he's also fast. He can stand in the middle of the court and pretty much reach all the walls. It's hard to get anything past him. It was a good workout and I thanked him. He wished me luck in the tournament.

Finally, Friday came. Our last midterm was a life painting to be rendered in watercolor pencils while the model posed. That was a challenge, but I like watercolor and the pencils give you really fine control over detail. With that over, we said good-bye to our friends going home for spring break and raced from lunch to the gym. Lissa and I were teaching Melody a bit of racquetball before we started our workouts. But when we got there, we found Lissa already in the middle of her warmup. She was doing the same thing I'd done a few weeks ago when I'd beaten myself into exhaustion. Lissa was dripping and the ball was taking a punishment.

"She's amazing, isn't she?" Melody asked.

"Yeah. I love her."

"So do I."

"Does that make us weird?"

"Not unless you don't love me."

"I do love you, Melody. I can't believe how much I love both of you. I couldn't do the painting without having both of you in it."

"What do you think is bothering her?"

"I don't know, but I think we're about to find out." Lissa let the ball dribble past her and roll across the floor as she sank down on her knees. Melody and I went through the door into the court.

"Hello, sweetheart," Melody said as we approached.

"Hello, love," I echoed as we both bent down to kiss her. Her hands went to our heads and held us to her. She was gasping for air, almost sobbing. Then I realized some of the water running off her face wasn't sweat. "Lissa…"

"We need to work first, and then talk," she said quickly. "Tony, work with Melody on her serves for a few minutes while I get some water." With that she rushed out the door. Melody and I looked at each other and decided the best bet was to show her we were listening and do what she said. We'd been working for more than twenty minutes before she came back. She'd changed into dry clothes and might have even taken a shower, but she walked onto the court with an air of authority that only the coach has. She gave a couple of instructions to us as we worked on Melody's serve and then said it was time to work on competition. Melody left the court and sat to watch through the Plexiglas wall.

"Three games in the match, just like the tournament. I'll serve first. This is your test run for the Intercollegiate Championships, Tony. Don't hold back."

———————<><>———————

"CONTROL!" LISSA SCREAMED at me as another of my serves hit the back wall before the floor. "You can't just power your way past me. You have to control what you're doing." Was she talking about racquetball or us? There was no question that I was trying to serve hard to her, taking out my own frustrations on the ball. But I knew that wouldn't win any tournaments. In fact, it wouldn't even test Lissa's playing. I set the next serve straight down the center. Lissa didn't even wait for the bounce before she sent it back at me. I saw it coming before it ever reached the wall. Six feet off the scuff in the wall, headed right back against the left edge. I didn't wait for it, either. I charged the wall and sent the ball across court from about three feet away. It was all I could do to keep from smashing my face into the wall, but Lissa stood no chance of returning that one.

Then we started to play in earnest. I couldn't close the gap on the lead she had over me in the first game. I made her work to keep it, but it was a foregone conclusion that she had me wrapped by the time I got my head in the game. The second game was a different matter. We didn't talk to each other during our two-minute break between games. I saw John watching with Melody and there were a couple of other players I recognized there. Lissa stepped back into the court and I started the first serve. From then, the battle was on and it was all about control. Lissa moved me all over the court with perfectly placed returns trying to keep me off balance.

20

An open or pro division player comes into a game with a strategy and executes her plan throughout the game. The only way I was going to overcome her strategy was to force her to change it. I placed two consecutive shots right into her backhand. Monday she wanted work on her backhand, but I knew from experience that those hits were just as powerful and accurate as her forehand. But I'd seen a weakness there on Monday. My next shot came in close on her forehand and she couldn't swing back far enough to get the ball. It glanced off the side wall and hit the floor. I had my game strategy and started playing it.

Life's like that. You keep taking your best shots, but success depends on the reactions of other people. If you're good, you can control their reactions, keep them off-balance, and force them to move to your beat. But there's always a player who is just as good as or better than you are. That player will control you and your moves.

I felt like the court was the only place I was ever in control. I kept running from one side of life to the other trying to return other people's serves. That had to stop and it had to stop now. Lissa and I took a five-minute break with the match tied at one game each. We left the court to get a drink of water and stepped in opposite directions, just as if we were in tournament play. Poor Melody didn't know which way to follow and wisely didn't try to talk to or approach either of us. She stayed in front of the glass wall where a couple dozen other people had gathered to watch our match. Someone at the club had posted a small sign on the door into the court that said "National Women's Open Champion Lissa Grant vs. Intercollegiate Competitor Tony Ames."

When we stepped back into the court, our eyes met for the first time this afternoon. Lissa had a predatory sneer on her face. *My god! No wonder she was the national champ. I bet her opponents wilted under that look.* My eyes closed to slits as I stared right back at her. I didn't smile. There was a flicker of recognition in her eyes. She hadn't won yet.

We were connected.

In the instant before her first serve hit the front wall, I recognized what we were doing and it thrilled me. We weren't just playing racquetball. We weren't just having sex. We weren't just competing. We were connecting on a level I'd never imagined possible. I knew what she was doing as if my own muscles were swinging her racquet and she knew my moves just as well. We tested each other through the first three rallies and then things heated up. At the end of a dozen rallies the score was tied one to one. This was going to be a long game.

A player enters a game with a strategy, but has to be adept at changing and adapting the game plan as it progresses. I saw the shift in Lissa's strategy with the first lob serve. It came down in the crotch of the back wall and died for a point. I lost two more points before I adjusted to her new style of play.

Trying to describe every rally in a racquetball tournament would be like describing every lick and suck in making love. It's exciting as hell when it's happening, but it loses something in the telling. Lissa and I were both exhausted and dripping with the score tied at ten to ten. The next point would win the game and the match. My goggles were dripping and the bandana I had tied around my head had exceeded its capacity to absorb my sweat. As I looked at Lissa, getting ready to serve for the last point, my heart was wrenched inside out. I could feel her desire as she bounced the ball. It wasn't just desire. She *needed* this point. I had two-tenths of a second to understand what I was doing when I sent the ball straight into her backhand. If I'd been standing in front of her return with my racquet directly in the path of the ball, I couldn't have hit it. It had so much spin coming off two walls that it rolled down the guts and hit the frame of my racquet. I flicked it back the direction it came from, but it didn't make the front wall before it touched the floor. I'd lost. Lissa won. I dropped my racquet and just ran to her and hugged her.

Outside the court, about 30 observers were applauding. They'd seen a game they wouldn't soon forget. I couldn't care less.

—————◁◆▷—————

THE THREE OF us were sitting in Lissa's van. When we came out of the court, the crowd was all trying to talk about the game and I saw Lissa slip away toward the locker room. I grabbed Melody and quickly whispered to her not to let Lissa out of her sight. I was afraid she'd try to leave without talking to us. Melody hurried after her into the locker room. I was waiting in the lobby when they came out and we walked together to her van. Lissa seemed resigned, but nothing would have prepared us for what she said once we were in the car.

"My loves, I have to break up with you."

We all sat there in silence taking in what she had just said. Melody was sobbing. I was stunned. Lissa sat quietly behind the steering wheel with tears running down her face. I could hear the echo still playing in the back of my mind ever since Sunday night.

I love you. I'll kill you. But I'll love you forever.

Three

"**W**as it the painting?" I asked. Lissa had just stunned us—no, broken our hearts—by saying she was breaking up with us. I wanted to scream at her. Shake her. Plead with her. It had to be something I'd done and the mural was the only thing I could blame.

"No," she answered. "Yes. The painting is wonderful, Tony. It's beautiful. I couldn't be prouder to be in anything. I'm sorry I blew up at you about it. It wasn't the painting; it's what I saw in the painting. It's what I saw about all three of us. It was so beautiful and so frightening."

Tears were flowing freely among all three of us now and I reached to touch Lissa and found Melody's hand there with me. Lissa grasped both of our hands and pulled them to her lips, then leaned her cheek against them.

"I saw what you see, and I can't be that. I'm a single mother with two kids. I have a career. I'm seven years older than you are. I don't even know how these kinds of relationships work."

"Neither do we, but we'll make it work," I said. "Lissa, you are a part of Melody and me. It breaks both of our hearts to see you like this."

"I thought it would be fun. I liked you both and I was lonely. I thought I'd put some excitement in all our lives. I've never done anything like this before. I didn't intend to fall in love."

"Darling, none of us intended to fall in love. We thought we were just experimenting—finding out about sex and things we hadn't done before," Melody said. I remembered her using almost those same words when we first decided to go to Lissa's house with her. Melody and I were barely more than friends when we started. The last five weeks had been an emotional roller coaster. "I'll never be able to play racquetball like you, Lissa," Melody continued, "I'll never be able to paint like Tony does. Shhh… it's true. But my darlings, never in your wildest imaginings will you ever be able to love me more than I love you."

"Let's go home and talk some more," I suggested. I said "home." It didn't really make a difference where that was, as long as I was with Melody and Lissa.

"We can't go to my place," Lissa said with finality.

"No problem," Melody replied. "We wanted to show you Tony's redecorated dorm room. It's three blocks away."

Lissa looked at us and nodded. We got out of the car and walked to the dorm.

———◁◆▷———

"Oh, my!"

We'd just walked into my room and Lissa was taking in the makeshift king-size bed we made by pushing the two singles together. We'd gone to Bed Bath & Beyond and bought a king-size mattress pad and "bed in a bag" sheets, pillows, and bedspread. Now it wasn't bad to sleep on. We'd pushed the desks together on one side and raised the adjustable height beds on their legs so we could fit the dressers under them. Melody brought the braided rug she had in her room and my dorm room now resembled a nice farmhouse bedroom.

25

"Take you back to your wild and carefree college days?" I asked.

"Tony, I didn't start college until I was married and Damon was a toddler. I never had wild and carefree. I'd never done any of this, before you."

"Here I thought you were teaching us," I blurted out.

"I thought models were…" Melody started at the same time and stopped. Lissa had never looked so vulnerable. I pulled her into an embrace and Melody was right there with me.

"There were lots of opportunities as a model and I experimented a little—mostly kissing and a little petting. Jack became my manager and agent when I was thirteen. He guarded me like a mother hen when I was traveling—which was most of the time. I didn't have that many opportunities to socialize with other models."

"That sounds kind of predatory," I accused. "Where were your parents? They let you be with this guy when you were thirteen?"

"Shh… Don't speak ill of Jack. He was a perfect guardian. I would have done anything for him, but he refused every juvenile advance I made—kindly and respectfully—until I was eighteen. I guess he couldn't resist me any longer." Lissa paused, struggling with her own demons. I willed her to go on, but let her take her time without pressuring her. "You need to know. It's only fair." she said finally. "My parents were killed in an auto accident when I was twelve and I went to live with my father's sister. Jack was her husband. They became my legal guardians. Aunt Jane got uterine cancer the next year. It was fast and devastated Jack. In just a few weeks, she was gone and it was just Jack and me. After the first time I won a modeling competition, he threw himself into making my career successful and I became the center of his universe, and he of mine. I wanted to be everything to Jack that he was missing since Jane had died."

"Wait! You married Jack? Your guardian?" Melody asked. "They don't allow that, do they?"

"When Jack found out I was pregnant, we went to France for a year and got married. Damon was born in Paris. When we came back, we were husband and wife and parents of a beautiful boy."

"What happened?" I asked quietly.

"Life. Jack is thirty years older than me. He loves me and absolutely dotes on his kids, but when I finished my associates' degree and started working in the industry, he started to withdraw. He said he didn't want to tie me down. The thoughts had already crossed my mind, though. I know if he hadn't started the proceeding, I would have eventually. We were divorced a little more than a year ago."

"All the experience you've had, though," I held the question in my voice. "All that you've taught us."

"The blind leading the blind. Tony, you are the only man I've been with other than Jack. Melody, you are the only woman I ever… loved. I'm such a fraud."

"Um… you know…," Melody said, "if that was supposed to make us love you less, you just failed big-time."

"I'd take you faking over someone with real experience any day of the week," I said.

"You guys! Don't you see?" Lissa sobbed. "I lied to you. I used you. I'm so sorry! I don't want to get between you two. I almost drove you apart last week because I was so selfish."

We'd all talked last weekend about how we'd have to learn to share and not be jealous of each other, no matter what combination we were in, but Lissa was still blaming herself for something that, as far as Melody and I were concerned, just didn't exist. I looked at Melody and could tell we were in agreement; this was all about Lissa.

"Lissa, you and Melody saved my life," I started, still holding on to Lissa's hands. "A few weeks ago, I was nearly suicidal. I hated everything about my life. I was drowning. You'd pull me out long enough for a gasp of fresh air on the court and then I'd slide right back under water when we finished. Melody rocked my world when we gave each other our virginity—in *your* basement. But as soon as school pressures hit me again, I was right back in a funk. I'm not cured yet. On Monday this week, I was right back in the shitter. But you needed me on the court and Melody was in my bed when I got home. I'm way too much trouble for either of you, but together… Oh god! … Together, I'm filled with so much love that the hope is sticking with me even when I'm down. It's not just sex, it's the whole American dream—two kids, two cars, and two wives. How can I be depressed?"

At last, both Melody and Lissa looked at me and broke out laughing. We sprawled out on the bed just holding and hugging each other. I thought—I hoped—that just maybe, we'd saved our relationship. Lissa seemed to be thinking hard, but she was cuddled between Melody and me and not letting go.

"You let me win that last rally," Lissa accused, poking my chest. "You can't ever let an opponent win like that. People will walk all over you."

"I didn't *let* you win it. When I saw you prepare to serve, I realized there was no way you could lose. I tried to return that shot. I could have been a world champion player, and it wouldn't have made a difference. Sometimes you just know the outcome before you make the play."

We lay there holding each other, not doing anything. We might even have dozed off together for a few minutes. For those few minutes, Lissa seemed content to lie in the arms of her lovers, but she stretched and sat up between us.

"I have to go home. The kids are with their nanny. I have them this weekend." She looked at us. I could tell she was still sad and if we let her walk out the door we might never see her again. "I just don't know how to make this work," she continued. "You think I'm older and wiser and more experienced. I think I'm a kid who has kids. How could I explain us to them? Or to my ex-husband? I'm just overwhelmed."

"Hey. Let a professional at being overwhelmed help," I said, standing beside her.

"And a professional at being overwhelming," Melody laughed jumping up with us.

"I think it's time your kids met the rest of the family," I said decisively.

Lissa's eyes got big as she looked at us.

"Really?" We nodded. At last she smiled. "You have no idea what you're in for."

<hr>

Wow! Was that statement ever correct! When we got to Lissa's house, two small hurricanes went tearing past us. One was on a blue and yellow scooter with his legs pumping as fast as they'd go as he circled through the living room, kitchen and down the hallway. The other was running behind, switched directions abruptly and nearly caught his brother as he squealed around the corner. A door slammed at the end of the hall and the voices were silenced.

Lissa's house had always been immaculate when we were there. Outside of the kids' bedroom, there wasn't a sign that children lived in the house. This time, there were various toys, trucks, and building blocks scattered everywhere. Legos were hooked together to form tunnels and ramps for an auto racing track. Half a dozen books were scattered on and around the sofa. It was like a different house.

"Molly, I'm home," Lissa called into the house. In a moment, a plump young woman about my age came out from the boys' room and greeted us in the kitchen. She was even shorter than Melody and had big eyes that looked like they were used to laughing a lot.

"They are little terrors today!" she laughed. "Oh! Sorry, Lissa. I didn't realize you had guests. I'd have made them put the toys away."

"Don't worry, Molly. Sounds like you were having fun. These are my friends, Tony and Melody. We're hanging out tonight. Guys, this is the most wonderful nanny in the world, Molly."

"Do you want me to get the monsters ready for bed before I leave?"

"No," Lissa answered. "We'll take care of it. Don't you have a date tonight?" Molly blushed.

"Sort of. But Steve's not picking me up till eight, so I've got time."

"Baloney! Go get yourself beautiful and wash the gravy off your face before you see him," Lissa teased. "Unless you want to serve Steve dinner off your cheeks."

Molly was beet red as she reached to where a splatter of gravy decorated one side of her face.

"Those boys! We were one step away from an all-out food fight. If you're sure, I'll run. Nice to meet you Tony, Melody. Good luck!"

As much as she'd protested and volunteered to help, as soon as she was dismissed Molly wasted no time grabbing her keys and bag and heading for the door.

"I'm going home, Damon and Drew! Mommy's home," she called from the door. The bedroom door opened and the two boys ran to Molly to hug her before she left. Then they turned and seemed to notice their mother for the first time. Both boys' faces split into wide grins and they wrapped their arms around Lissa's legs yelling, "Mommy!"

"It looks like you boys had a good time with Molly today. Did you learn anything in school?" Damon, the older boy, stuck his lower lip out in a pout while Drew ran back down the hall to their room.

"School's dumb!" Damon declared. "Jimmy pushed me on the bars and I fell."

He pulled up his pants leg to show a series of Band-Aids on his shin. They had various dinosaurs and monsters decorating them, but I couldn't see any sign of scrapes or injury. Lissa lifted the edge of one to confirm the suspicion and patted it gently back into place.

"Well, look at the bright side. You got a lot of monsters out of it." Damon grinned and hugged Lissa just as Drew came back with a colorful sheet of paper that, as far as I could tell, had no resemblance to anything living or inanimate. He held it proudly in front of his mother. She squinted at the paper and I was about to ask, "What is it?" when she spoke.

"You are definitely improving," she smiled. "Did you use every crayon in the box?" Drew nodded proudly. "Boys, we have company. You remember my girlfriend, Melody…"

We'd been watching this while standing aside and realized that we were holding hands and squeezing each other every time one of the boys did something cute—which was everything they did. Now we became the focus of their attention and Melody dropped my hand to catch both boys as they ran to hug her. They were certainly outgoing. I remembered hiding behind my mother whenever I was introduced to another adult.

"Meddy!" Drew exclaimed as if she was a long-lost friend. Damon immediately looked up to me and I kneeled down on the floor to get to the same height. I held out my hand.

"Are you Mommy's boyfriend?" he asked.

Before I could parse what he'd said I'd already answered, "Sure am."

He ignored my proffered hand and came straight to hug me. It was so cool. In a moment Drew was wrapped in my arms as well.

"I'm Tony," I said.

The greeting, though intense and affectionate, was short-lived. Within half a minute, the boys were headed out of the kitchen.

"All toys to your room, boys!" Lissa called. "Storytime as soon as you're ready for bed!"

———⊲◆▷———

I WAS SURPRISED at how fast the boys got their toys back in their room. It wasn't long before they were ready for bed and I discovered I was the designated story reader. I settled in the middle of the sofa with a boy on either side. Melody sat next to Damon on my right. Lissa said she was going to get something going for dinner, but that didn't seem right. I asked her to please come and sit with us, so she got comfy on my left and Drew shifted so he was leaning against her instead of me. I read *Go Dog! Go!* and *Hop on Pop* for Drew while Damon patiently waited with *Horton Hears a Who*. I had to laugh when I thought that the same books were probably still in the back of my closet at home in Nebraska. I had the stories mostly memorized since I'd read them so many times growing up.

I thought about home for the first time in a long time that night. I missed home, but I hadn't really thought about why. The feeling was so overwhelming that I couldn't think about it rationally. I missed my mom and dad. I missed my friends from school, and especially my art teacher, Lillian Stone and my best friend, Beth. I'd always loved drawing and I guess I showed some talent for it when I was in middle school, but Ms. Stone taught me how to control it. It was sheer luck that when they built the new consolidated school district high school, they hired her to teach art. She turned what I loved into a passion. I was looking forward to visiting her this summer when I went back.

But that got me thinking about summer. The break was just two months away. What would happen to Lissa and Melody and me when school was out? I thought about being home again and realized that, as much as I missed home, it was hard to see myself *there* now. Something had shifted in the way I viewed things. I felt more like this room, Melody, Lissa, and even the two kids we were carrying to bed were where I was anchored. I wasn't even torn. I wanted to go visit my family and friends, but I didn't want to go back to Nebraska—not to stay.

Just a few months ago, I'd applied to transfer to the University. I expected I'd hear from them sometime in June telling me when to arrive and what my financial aid package was. But I was no longer interested in transferring.

I can't say I led a sheltered life. Mom and Dad gave me a lot of freedom. We lived in a farmhouse, but we didn't farm. The property was rented out to a neighbor. Dad always talked about building an airstrip out in back. We had a barn that was used for storing hay and straw in the winter, but Dad had sold all Granddad's farm equipment except a small tractor mower at auction after Granddad died a few years ago.

Dad taught in the elementary school and loved it. He had no desire to become a farmer. Mom was a dabbler. She worked at the local bookstore as a part-time clerk, but most of her paycheck seemed to go right back in the till to pay for the books she brought home. At home, she had a sewing studio in the spare room where she made cloth bags and purses and explored a variety of fabric art creations that ended up on shelves in the studio and were never seen by the public. *Melody would love it*, I thought. The one exception was that every newborn baby in the area received a "Grimp." They were huge stuffed dolls with a fat soft body and really long legs and arms. You couldn't walk into a grocery store without seeing some kid dragging one of them along behind. Mine still sat on my bed back home. I wondered if maybe I should bring it for Damon and Drew.

Being with the boys just brought out that feeling of nostalgia and I started thinking about how I was going to tell my folks about my new family.

$\mathcal{F}$our

"**Y**ou two can use the spa if you want to before bed," Lissa said. "I've put clean towels in your room." She was nervous. It was different than being with her before. She was ready to go to bed alone and send us to the guest room because of the boys. I could understand. Gosh. You don't want your kids seeing an endless parade of sex partners staying in your bedroom overnight. But we weren't an endless parade, and sex wasn't strictly necessary for us to be together. This wasn't going to work.

"Lissa, do your kids have friends?" I asked.

"Of course."

"Do they ever have sleepovers?" I continued.

"Yes."

"Do you make the other kids stay in the guestroom?"

"No," she answered, grasping my line of thinking.

"We're your boyfriend and girlfriend. The boys already know that. We're having a sleepover. We don't intend to leave you alone tonight."

"I can't go in the spa while the boys are here," Lissa persisted. "I need to be able to hear them."

"Why don't you and Melody relax in the tub for a while," I said. "I've got some planning work to do in my Daytimer that I don't want to put off until after break. I have to figure out what needs to be completed before I take time off for the championships. I can listen for the boys."

Lissa looked at me with her mouth open, making little movements that looked like a fish. Melody took her hand and led her away while I spread my things out on the breakfast bar. I don't know if Lissa was more surprised at being relieved of child duty for an hour or that I was working ahead on my schedule.

An hour later, Melody padded out in her bare feet, wearing nothing but a towel. She kissed me soundly and then whispered in my ear. I closed my books and turned off the kitchen light. When I got to the bedroom, I found Lissa sprawled on her stomach in the middle of the bed. One lamp lit the corner of the room, shedding a soft glow. Melody had begun stroking Lissa's head, massaging her scalp. I contemplated sketching the scene, but instead I undressed and crawled up to join them on Lissa's other side. Melody handed me a bottle of body oil. While she continued to work on Lissa's scalp, I warmed oil in my hands and went to work on her shoulders.

She was tight. Even after the long soak in the tub, Lissa was carrying tension that she just couldn't let go. I kneaded her muscles, alternating between deep pressure to work out the kinks, and gentle long strokes to simply soothe and relax her. Pretty soon, Melody had oil on her hands and together we worked from her shoulders down both arms at once. Melody and I watched each other carefully. Neither of us is a trained massage therapist, but we just figured out what would feel good if we were in that position and as one of us tried something, the other would mimic it. We seemed to be doing a pretty good job, based on the sighs and little moans that came from Lissa and the lessening tension in the muscles we touched.

It was good almond oil and before long Lissa's skin was glistening. Melody worked high on Lissa's back as I moved into her lower back where she was just as tight as her shoulders had been. As we moved together, Melody and I were touching each other as well, our sides and arms pressed together above Lissa. As I ran my hands up Lissa's sides, they slipped under Melody's hands and Melody stroked up my arms, then back down onto Lissa's back as I slid down toward her butt. As Melody followed my hands down the curve of her back, she turned and gave me a kiss and we continued our massage.

I think we found a hundred ways to massage the spectacular globes of Lissa's butt—palms caressing, fingers probing, jiggling, tapping, pressing, stroking. And eventually kissing each beautiful cheek as we moved down to her legs.

I could make love to Lissa's legs for hours. By the look in her eyes, so could Melody. From the sounds we were hearing, I didn't think Lissa would object. I've always loved legs, but watching a cute girl in a short skirt couldn't even compare to putting both hands around a Lissa's thighs and letting my thumbs follow the line of her muscles to her ankles. Lissa's body is so tight there's pretty much no butt-ledge. It was a clean, unbroken line as our hands took long strokes from her waist to her ankles. The calves that guys appreciate so much when they see them in a pair of high heels are so delicate beneath the fingers that I wanted to cradle them gently, not just rub.

I was acutely aware of Melody's body pressing against mine as we worked on our lover together. She reached across to put a hand on each cheek and drag her fingertips sensuously down Lissa's sculpted legs. To get a better angle, she knelt between Lissa's legs. I moved behind her and reached over her to follow her hands with my own. When Melody reached to start the stroke again, I let my oily hands flow from Lissa's legs onto Melody's, stroking upward from where she knelt and moving across her tummy and breasts. Melody's breath caught and she ground her butt into my erection for a moment before we both moved back and each lifted one of Lissa's feet to massage.

Lissa once joked to me that she was a classic runway model—tall, skinny, and big feet. True, since at 5'10" she was as tall as me, and her size-ten feet were as big as mine. There was nothing clunky or out of proportion, though. Her feet were long and thin, with high arches. Her toes were as delicate as her fingers and it made me just want to suck them into my mouth. Melody caught my eye and winked. Then we both lowered our mouths and bathed her toes with our tongues. Her feet aren't very ticklish, which was a good thing. I'd have had a paroxysm if they'd been doing to me what we were doing to Lissa.

When we finally petted her feet for the last time, I reached under Lissa and gently rolled her over. A little smile played on her lips but she kept her eyes closed as we started the whole process over again. Maybe it was a little more interesting for us since this trip down included those beautiful breasts, but as sensuous as the massage was, it wasn't overtly sexual. Oh, Melody and I were certainly teasing each other with stray strokes and we sure didn't ignore Lissa's breasts. Melody couldn't resist a little lick of each of Lissa's nipples. I was always between half-hard and hard. There was enough sexual edge just because we were enjoying ourselves and each other so much.

When I started rubbing circles on Lissa's tummy, Melody linked her fingers through mine so it was like two hands and twenty fingers. Lissa was quaking as we moved down, carefully avoiding her plump labia and working the last of the tension out of her quads. I glanced over at the bedside clock and realized with a shock that we'd been massaging Lissa for an hour and a half. Little trembles kept going through her body and she kept moaning in a high-pitched whine. Melody and I linked hands once again as we settled down on either side of Lissa and with our joined fingers, we reached down and stroked Lissa's pussy from bottom to top one time.

We didn't penetrate anything, didn't part her folds or try to find her clit, but with that one stroke, Lissa came up off the bed arching her back so that only her shoulders and heels were touching the sheets. The scream was ear-piercing. Not only was there a flood of juices from her pussy, but an equal flood sprang from her eyes as they flew open looking wildly around. They fixed first on me and then on Melody. Lissa's arms came around the two of us and hugged us close to her as she sobbed.

"I love you. I love you both," she gasped. "Oh god, I love you so much. And I'm so scared. Tony, Melody—please don't ever let me leave you. Please. Oh god, I love you! Please. Please."

The sobs diminished as we kissed her eyes, her cheeks, and her lips, whispering words of comfort and assuring her that we would always be with her. We settled down and in a few minutes Lissa was sleeping, cradled in our arms. Melody looked at me. I whispered, "I love you." She smiled and slipped out of bed. She put on a robe and padded down the hall to check on the boys and make sure that our lovemaking hadn't woken them. She slipped back into bed with a smile on her face and put both hands on one side of her face to show me they were asleep.

Soon, we were too.

———◁◆▷———

SPRING BREAK WENT way too quickly. We spent the entire week at Lissa's house. Lissa still had to work, but we put more time in at the club, practicing every day. I was feeling strong and my game was the best it's ever been. Sam Jacobson came by and went over the registration information for the championships in Tempe. He gave Lissa our tickets and hotel reservations.

Melody and I went downtown to the Market one day. I'd lived in Seattle for seven months, just ten blocks from Pike Place Market, and had never visited. We picked up some fresh vegetables and fish, found some really good orange coated almonds, and tried on silly hats. We were sitting at a little café on the second floor when Melody suddenly pointed down the stairs. I had to shift my position around a little before I saw Kate taking an order from the counter and leaving the restaurant.

"I didn't know she was staying in town," I said. "Where does she live?"

"I don't know, but she's always alone. I suppose we should be more friendly."

We met Lissa at the club at three that afternoon and Melody took the car to go get dinner started. It was an odd practice. John brought in a doubles team and I played against both of them. By the time they finished kicking my butt, I was exhausted. I wanted nothing more than a long hot soak. I had to cut it short to be out front when Melody picked us up. Dinner was delicious.

I spent a lot of time with my planner, figuring out what I was going to have to finish in order to go to the championships in April. Once I saw it, I surprised both Melody and Lissa by actually researching and writing my next Art History paper in advance. It was a good paper, too. I was really going to make this work.

I got inspired one evening as I saw Lissa running hot steamy water in the Jacuzzi in the master bath. All of a sudden I could see her in a painting. She was expecting me to undress and join her since we'd had another hard practice, but instead I asked if I could draw her. What an unbelievable model. She sat quietly on the edge of the tub with her feet in the water for twenty minutes while I drew. When I asked her to turn her head and look at me over her left shoulder, the image was perfect. We had to run more hot water before we actually got in the tub. By that time, Melody had joined us, too, and we just soaked for an hour, laughing and talking. Life was so good.

————⊲◆▷————

WHEN CLASSES STARTED again, I thought the buzz about the mural would die down. Instead, the work of finishing it kept the Fundies class busy with Doc Henredon and there seemed to be a lot of students who came to watch. I got a couple of notes handed to me by girls I'd never spoken to before, volunteering to model for me. Apparently Melody was right about girls wanting to see themselves through my eyes or something. Of course, Sandra was right, too. Melody was asked out four times the first week we were back at school. She smirked when she told them all she'd have to ask her girlfriend.

When one guy saw us holding hands, he stopped us in the hall and said, "I thought you had a girlfriend. What are you doing with him?"

"She said it was all right to sleep with Tony as long as I shared with her," Melody promptly replied. "And there's enough of him to keep us both happy." The guy stared at us all the way down the hall.

By midweek, it seemed like everywhere I went there was a buzz about the mural and—to my surprise—the upcoming racquetball tournament. There was actually a poster in one of the halls that had the date of the tournament and a huge "Go Team PCAD" with my picture on it. I finally figured out that Amy and Sandra had put it together. After we turned in our projects for Ms. Brock on Monday, she announced there'd be no class Wednesday afternoon, so I found myself at a cafeteria table at noon with Melody, Amy, and Sandra, able to relax and shoot the bull. We were laughing like crazy at lunch and it felt good to be surrounded by my friends. Friends. It was a concept I was beginning to accept.

"So, don't be offended, but I gotta ask," Amy said. She leaned across the table to Melody and me conspiratorially. "How's it work? You know, with you guys?" She waved three fingers in the air. I was in way too good a mood to be offended. It was a little personal, but I decided to amp it up a notch.

"Well, Amy, I thought you knew about these things. It's pretty simple. You insert Tab A into Slot B." Amy choked on her drink, but she wasn't about to concede the point.

"But what about Slot C?" she persisted.

"Well, usually there's a Tab D for that."

"Wait," Sandra broke in. "You've only got one… thing… right? How can there be a Tab…" I stuck my tongue out at her. "Oh. Oh! Oh my god! I think I just wet my panties."

"Well at least you're wearing some today," Melody cracked. Sandra turned pink.

"Excuse me." We looked up and Kate was standing next to us with her lunch tray. "Can I join you?" We all scooted over and welcomed her to the table.

"Speaking of wet panties…" Melody whispered to me as she moved closer. I grimaced at her and raised my eyebrow. She giggled.

"Hi Kate," I said. "How's it going?"

"Um… pretty good. Not as good as it seems to be for you, but not bad. I… uh… wanted to wish you luck in the tournament. Wish I could come and watch you play."

"Yeah. Too bad there isn't a fan bus to Tempe," Amy said. "We could all go down."

"Are you going, Melody?" Kate asked.

"Nah. I wish. I can't afford to just go jetting off somewhere. I'm leaving him in Lissa's capable hands."

"Lissa? The model?" Kate was fumbling for words, but you could see the questions all over her face.

"Lissa's my racquetball coach," I said. "SCU is paying for one athlete and one coach to go to regionals."

"Wow!" Kate practically gushed. "So it's true you're transferring to SCU?"

"Not exactly. It's a new joint program. I'll be doing simultaneous degrees at both schools. They had to enroll me in one credit of PE practicum and accept all my PCAD credits in order to make it legal for me to compete. The PE class is strictly pass/fail." Everybody laughed at the thought that I was getting a Phys Ed credit while going to art school. Sometimes life is just too ridiculous for words.

"Two degrees?" Kate asked. "That sounds like an awful lot of work."

"Not so unusual at universities," I explained. "Lots of people do double majors or multiple degrees. This just takes it across school boundaries. A lot of the courses will count toward both degrees, but if it all works out I'll get a BFA in Studio Art and a BA in something. That still hasn't been finalized.I could take me an extra year, though."

"Yeah. It still sounds like a lot of work."

I've heard it said that there's a lull in conversation every fifteen minutes or something and that an entire room will go silent at the same time. It looked like we'd just hit that in the cafeteria, but I could tell there was something more on Kate's mind. She wasn't the most sociable girl in the school and most of us thought she was stuck up. But I was beginning to think that she was really just shy. Finally, she turned to Melody and whispered.

"Is it really you in the painting?"

Melody grinned.

"Yeah, that's my dimply ass sticking out in the admin hall."

"Did you… I mean… did he… really…?" Kate babbled, clearly unable to form a complete sentence.

"Did I pose?"

"Yeah."

"Mmm hmm. And it's not as easy as it looks."

"How did you ever get up the courage to… to undress… in front… oh god!" Kate's face was so flushed that I was afraid she'd pass out. She really wanted to know what went on!

"Somebody wants to get naked in front of your boyfriend, Melody," Sandra giggled.

I could have strangled her. I thought Kate was going to bolt right then and there. Instead, a tear escaped from one eye and Melody wrapped an arm around her to keep her from running.

"You're a fine one to talk," she snapped.

Sandra had the good graces to blush a little herself. I could still see those plump breasts and huge nipples in front of my face if I closed my eyes. Melody turned to Kate and gave her a squeeze.

"I know what you're feeling," Melody said. "And you're right. I actually considered getting drunk before I did it. Remember when we goaded Tony into posing in class? Did it turn you on?"

"No!" Kate almost shouted. There were clear smirks on all three girls' faces. Kate dropped her head a little and whispered, "Not at the time."

"Well," Melody continued, "I just kept thinking about what it must have been like for Tony to be on the other side of the easel."

"So you just… stripped and posed?"

"Wellllll…" Melody teased. "We got the sex thing out of the way first."

It was my turn to choke on my food. Kate's mouth was hanging open. I was afraid she'd pass out from hyperventilating. This was definitely more than I was prepared to listen to. I didn't know what Melody was up to, but I was superfluous to this discussion.

"I'm going over to the gym a little early and do some stretching before practice," I offered. "I'll see you guys later on."

"See you later, Tony," they all chorused.

"Sure. See you." I took off. *Sorry, Kate, but I'm leaving you to the wolves!*

Five

SCHOOL WAS SCHOOL. I was finding it more tolerable now, partly because I was playing racquetball almost every day, and partly because Melody had moved into my dorm room. Twice, we'd managed to get Lissa to come and stay with us, and we were at her house all weekend.

We were seeing more of Kate now, too. She was joining our little group for lunch most days and was proving to be more sociable than I ever imagined. She was still pretty shy, but every once in a while, she'd catch one of us off guard with a zinger that showed she had a great sense of humor.

I stretched canvases, helped unload a huge block of marble for the sculpture studio, dabbled in different media, painted the new picture of Lissa at the bath, and went to class. On Monday, when I handed in my Art History paper two days early, Brian actually looked at me as if I had grown an extra head. I explained that I'd be missing class Wednesday to go to the tournament and he wished me luck.

Dr. Henredon had already given me a release from class for the week and Prof. McIntyre told me my final project was complete and graded as far as she was concerned and that attendance at the remaining classes for the year was optional. Not that I was going to take full advantage of that. Figure painting was my favorite class. I stopped to see Ms. Brock before class that afternoon and she said she had received word that I would be unavailable for the week and as far as she was concerned I didn't need to be there this afternoon. Suddenly, I had nothing to think about but the tournament, so I headed for the gym.

I was surprised to find Lissa already on the court when I got there. She was returning serves from John and battering each of them past him no matter where he served. He has a strong forehand, but he's nowhere near her level and she had no difficulty returning everything he served. Still, something looked odd. I stood there and studied the action through the glass wall. It finally hit me and as soon as John missed the next return I pounded on the glass. They turned to look and Lissa motioned me in. I slipped my shoes off and opened the door.

"Hey, guys," I said.

"You're here early," Lissa answered.

"Yeah. I was just watching. Do you mind if I make a suggestion?"

"Shoot," Lissa said.

"Lissa, you can return anything John serves. No offense, John; it's the way she is. But you've got a gap in your stance, Lissa. We've talked about this before. You can't let yourself get sloppy just because John isn't as good as you. You're supposed to be preparing for Opens. You're leaning into your backhand to your left before he ever serves. You know you can switch back to the right to catch anything he serves. But a power-serve low at the stretch of your forehand would leave you watching the ball go by. You've got to square yourself up while you're waiting for the serve. We talked about that once before."

"Wow," John said.

"No kidding, wow," Lissa responded. "It was a strange day when we had that practice, but I see what you're saying. Let's run a few more serves. Tony, make sure I'm on target. If I'm developing a bad habit, I need to correct it now. And thanks."

She smiled at me and gave me a little kissy face as I backed out of the court. I watched a few more rallies and then Lissa turned to look at me and raised an eyebrow. I went back in.

"Better?" she asked.

"Definitely better, but you've got to get up on your toes more when he brings his racquet back to serve," I explained. "You're delaying because you know he doesn't have the power. Stop thinking of him as John your trainer and start thinking of him as Yuri Gedov. You can't let him slip one by on you."

She absolutely beamed at me and turned back to the game as I went back outside to watch. About every five to ten rallies, I'd pop back in and tell them what I saw. I gave a couple pointers to John on how he was serving, too. By the end of an hour, they'd both broken a sweat and were working hard. They came off the court talking about how it had gone.

"That was so helpful, Tony!" Lissa said. "There's no way I could see that on the court."

"Thanks for the pointers on my serve, too," John said.

"Is there anything else, coach?" Lissa asked. I looked at her blankly.

"Umm… You're *my* coach," I stated the obvious.

"It's a fair trade," she said. "Go get ready and I'll get you a partner to warm up with."

John raised his hands in surrender and shook his head. They were discussing who they could get to warm me up as I entered the locker room to change.

FOR ME, PRACTICE was light. Tomorrow, Lissa and I would fly down to Tempe and sign in. Competition started Wednesday at 9:00 a.m. I knew some of the competitors would be coming from farther away than me, so I hoped everyone was planning to get there on Tuesday. There was a welcome banquet that night and I wanted to get a first look at the competition. I worked on form and Lissa kept pacing back and forth on the court behind me as I returned serves from Rod and tried to get my serves past the big guy. It was a good practice.

A small crowd was outside the court when we quit. I knew Melody and the girls would be there—they'd said they wanted to cheer me on to Tempe—but Sam Jacobson and Dean Peterson were there, too. So were a bunch of other kids from school and a few that I didn't recognize. They called Lissa and me over to face the gathering.

"We're happy to have Tony Ames representing the combined student bodies of Pacific College of the Arts and Design and Seattle Cascades University at the USAR National Intercollegiate Championships in Tempe this week," Dean Peterson addressed the crowd. "We want to make some introductions so you'll all know who you're cheering for. I'm Nathan Peterson, Dean of Students at PCAD. On my right is Sam Jacobson, Athletic Director at SCU. On my left is Coach Lissa Grant, the reigning Women's US Open Racquetball Champion. And finally, this is Tony Ames, representing our schools on the court." There was a quick shuffle and Melody led Amy, Sandra, and Kate out in front of us. They were dressed in black leggings and sweaters and did a little jump then yelled.

"T-O-N-Y. Goooooo Tony!" They were waving black pom-poms. I cracked up.

"And that is the self-appointed PCAD cheerleading squad," Dean laughed. "Is there anyone at SCU who can give them some pointers?"

Everyone was laughing and applauded the effort.

"Tony, we want you to know that we're behind you on this and wish you well in the tournament. But win or lose, we know you will represent our schools with good sportsmanship and your best efforts. Now I think Coach Jacobson has something for you."

Sam Jacobson motioned me over to stand beside him.

"We've never had a racquetball club at SCU. I have a feeling, though, that you may have some others on the court with you next fall. This is an unusual way to launch a new sport at the university, but we want you to know that SCU is also behind you. I'd like to introduce Tim Kost, a senior, captain of SCU's basketball team, and president of the student athletic association. Tim."

I had to crane my head up to look at the guy. He's easily a foot taller than me.

"The teams at SCU want to welcome you, Tony. We rummaged around in the locker room and finally found a warmup for you that we thought was small enough to fit."

Everyone laughed at that. We must have made quite a picture standing there together. He handed me an obviously brand new warmup jacket and pants in SCU's Maroon and Gold colors with the school's lion mascot embroidered on the back. I slipped on the jacket and modeled it for the group, which had grown since the little impromptu ceremony started.

"Welcome to SCU Athletics," Tim said, shaking my hand.

Everyone applauded and there was another disturbance as two *really* cute girls from SCU ran forward in maroon and gold cheerleader outfits, did a flip and landed in the splits in front of me with their hands raised. Everyone cheered. Then the girls sprang to their feet and each took one of my arms.

"Tony, I'm Sonia," the blonde on my right said.

"And I'm Bree," the redhead on my left chimed in. "We really aren't here to upstage the new PCAD cheer squad, but they said we could welcome you to the team, too."

"The girls from PCAD have a gift for you, Tony," Sonia continued. "I guess you get to wear the PCAD school colors, too."

I bit on the lead-in. Melody, Amy, Sandra, and Kate were approaching.

"What are the PCAD school colors," I asked.

"Black and black, of course," Melody answered as she presented a package to me. "Tony, we'll all be thinking of you on the court this weekend. And we'll all be waiting for you when you get back. You're the only athlete any of us know who could invite a girl up to see his sketches and be serious about it."

That got everyone laughing. I ripped open the package and found a complete set of black Ektelon shorts, t-shirt, and socks. At the bottom of the package there was even a black jockstrap.

"I suppose this is for next time I model for you?" I asked, lifting the jock for everyone to see.

All four of them opened their mouths in surprise. It was the most synchronized movement of their improvised cheers so far. The girls all arranged themselves around me. I was going to reach for Melody, but Sonia and Bree weren't relinquishing their hold on my arms. Sam and the dean were looking expectantly at me. I guessed I was supposed to say something.

"Gosh. I'm kinda overwhelmed. I know some of you here from the club, and some from PCAD. I'm guessing that some of you are from SCU, too. It's good to meet all of you and I'm looking forward to getting to know you all over the next year."

There was a cheer that told me there were probably a couple dozen SCU people here. There was a little squeeze on my left arm and the redhead's tits pushed firmly into my side. For a moment I lost my train of thought.

"Anyway. Uh…I'll do my best to represent both schools at the championships this week. I've never competed at this level before, but my coach has and with her beside me, I'll try not to be too nervous. I just…" I stammered, getting choked up.

Damn! All these people—some that I didn't even know—came out to wish me well. And I really hadn't even done anything yet. Somebody flashed a picture of me surrounded by the 'cheerleaders.' I could feel tears of embarrassment forming behind my eyelids. I cut it short. "Thank you. Thanks to all of you," I said quickly.

I shut up. This time all six girls jumped up in the air. And everyone joined in the cheer.

"T-O-N-Y. Tony!" cheered the whole crowd.

———◁◆▷———

LISSA AND MELODY were both in my bed in the dorm that night. We'd made love together. We all thought it would feel more like college to sneak into the dorm together than to just go off to Lissa's house. Lissa's packed bag was in her car and mine was sitting by the door, ready to go in the morning.

I was still feeling overwhelmed. I'd talked about the trip, the impromptu pep rally, the game, Lissa's workout, the new uniforms—I was a regular motor mouth until Lissa and Melody both shut me up by covering my mouth with various body parts. Then we just lay there cuddling with each other, enjoying the afterglow.

"Looks like Tony's got a couple more modeling candidates, if you ask me," Melody said.

"Oh, go on," I said. "They were just there to promote school spirit."

"What promotes school spirit better than a cheerleader having sex with a star athlete?" she persisted.

"Well, if I come back in the bottom tier, nobody's going to think I'm a star athlete. Those girls won't even know who I am once football season starts."

"I wouldn't be too sure of that," Lissa said. "If the coaches and Dean hadn't been standing right behind you, they'd have had their hands on your ass instead of your arms."

"They sure didn't want to let go of you when we showed up," Melody added. "We're going to have to figure out a schedule for all the girls who want to get naked for you. With the two of us, I think that makes seven who are standing in line."

"What? Who?"

"Tony, don't be dense," Melody said. "There's me. And you know Lissa, right? Do you need me to introduce you? Then there's Amy, Sandra, Kate, Sonia, and Bree. And yes, I'm sure."

"I don't know how I feel about that," I said slowly. "I'd rather just be with you two and not deal with any complications."

"Sweetheart, complications are going to arise," Lissa said. "I love you and I need you. But I don't feel jealous of Melody."

"But you love Melody, too."

"Yes. But it's more than that," Lissa continued. "We're not going to be jealous of you."

Melody nodded against my chest. Her hand was playing with my balls and I'd never really softened completely after I came in Lissa a few minutes ago.

"Speaking of things arising," Melody said. "I feel a situation coming up."

"We should take it in hand right away," Lissa said. I felt her hand join Melody's and groaned. "Oh. He's in pain. I think suction therapy is in order." Both girls disappeared beneath the sheets and I felt the most exquisite sensation I'd ever known. They were kissing each other. Kissing with a lot of tongue. And my cockhead was right in the middle of their tongue fight.

"Okay," Lissa said, raising her head. "Last one until the end of competition."

"What?" I managed, still dazed.

"No wasting strength and no late nights when we're in Tempe," she explained. "We have to maintain a strict athlete/ coach relationship while we're on the road."

"Suddenly I'm not looking forward to this trip anywhere near as much," I complained.

Then I gasped. The dueling tongues slid down my shaft to lick my balls and then slid back up to the top.

If this was the last one till after competition, at least it was going to be memorable.

Six

TEMPE WAS AWESOME—awesomely hot! It was close to ninety degrees when we landed and it was not going down. Fortunately, every place we went was air conditioned. Unfortunately, it was a real shock to walk into a cold room after being in the heat. I spent my time alternately sweating and shivering. We checked into our hotel and I was pleased that Lissa and I were next door to each other, though there wasn't a connecting door like I'd hoped. I was wound so tight by the time we'd tossed our bags in the rooms that I was bouncing around and just wished she'd hold me before I exploded.

But Lissa was all business. She told me to change into my workout clothes and my school warmups, bring my court shoes and be ready in ten minutes. I did as ordered, and was ready when she knocked on my door. We drove over to the University Student Recreation Complex and I was blown away. The place has thirteen racquetball courts! Number fourteen is configured for squash. As soon as we signed in, I was assigned a court time for practice. We got our credentials and headed for our court. A guy smaller than me was running around the court chasing his coach's serves. We watched and Lissa gave me a running commentary on what she saw. It helped me get focused. I was bouncing again when Lissa pounded on the court door at the stroke of the hour.

Lissa got me settled down pretty good. We worked up from basic exercises to a short scrimmage so we could get loosened up. It was only thirty minutes, but by the time we were finished I was more relaxed than I'd been all day.

There was a huge dinner that evening for all the coaches and competitors. There were thirty men's singles competitors in the Gold Division that I'd play in, but there were around two hundred total competitors in the various divisions with men, women, and doubles, gold, blue, red, and white. The schedule was packed. My first round on Wednesday morning would be at nine. It was a double elimination tournament, so there would be eight matches on eight different courts at the same time. The other five courts would be used for warm-ups and training. I would be on court four facing a guy from LSU. After the first flight of men's singles, there'd be a women's flight and a doubles flight, then the second first round flight would go. The winners of the first flight would take on the next eight players.

Friday afternoon at 4:30, sixteen losers would play to see which eight players would be the first ones eliminated. I just didn't want to be in that group.

Lissa and I went back to our rooms and I lay in bed texting Melody for an hour. Then Melody and I got to texting Lissa and she laughed about us being next door and told me to go to sleep. I sent an "I love you" message to both girls and eventually dozed off.

———◁◆▷———

YANNI, *LIVE AT the Acropolis*. I'm embarrassed to say I even have the piece, but it was my dad's from someplace back at the dawning of the Age of Aquarius and I liked the energy. It blocked everything else around me out as I stretched and warmed up. Lissa tapped me on the shoulder and I pulled the headset off as the announcer was giving the pairings for the first round. I got the first look at my opponent.

Shit!

The guy reminded me of Rod at the club. He had a good six or eight inches on me and arms like an orangutan. All he had to do was stand in the middle of the court and he could reach anything. He won the toss and served first. The game was on.

The less time I spend talking about this match, the better. His first serve came skidding down the right wall and he was only barely out of the way far enough to keep from being called for a hinder fault. It went downhill from there. It's not that I didn't score, but I couldn't hold a rally against him. I lost in two straight games and was one of the first losers on the board. Thank god, it's double elimination. Every player is guaranteed at least two matches. There were other matches going on, but I was done until the first elimination round at 4:30.

"Hey. Go watch the cute girls play in the next flight," Lissa said. "Don't be upset. It's your first collegiate tournament."

"But Lissa, if I don't do well they'll take my scholarship away." God! I sounded like a whiny baby. I just didn't want to be embarrassed when we went back home. I imagined that everything good that had happened to me in the last month would suddenly evaporate. And I'd already started concocting a fantasy about coming home with a medal and invitation to the National Singles Tournament.

"Who told you that?"

"I just assumed. They give me an athletic scholarship, they expect me to perform, you know?"

"Tony, nobody is judging you by your first college tournament. Be realistic. You're a freshman. The guy who just beat you is a senior and is seeded fourth in the country. It was a bad draw. Relax."

I could think of one great way to relax, but she shoved me toward the bleachers and I plopped down to watch the women's first flight. I just stayed in front of the same court I'd played on. I pulled a sketchbook out of my bag and a piece of charcoal. I caught a couple people in the crowd who held still for a few minutes while they talked and I quickly sketched them. I flipped to another page.

Sketching action is difficult. You have to put your brain where the action is and freeze the scene in your mind. Then you've got about thirty seconds to draw before the scene evaporates and you have to pick a new one. We used to do exercises back in high school. Ms. Stone had us go to various events and we had to come back with at least three sketches of what went on. I'd sketched basketball games, school plays, the PTA meeting, and a horse show. Now that one was a challenge. Nothing like sketching a horse turning barrels. The trick was to ignore any of the extraneous stuff like shadows, saddles, and costumes. You had to just focus on the line of action. I started sketching the girls as they played.

I put down half a dozen sketches and moved to the next court. I had a soundtrack from Cirque du Soleil's *Allegria* playing in my ears as I spent an hour just plopping down in front of each court, making half a dozen quick action sketches, and then moving on. By noon, I'd sketched some of the doubles and was ready to work on the second flight of men. Lissa brought me a sandwich and a cup of coffee and stayed as we ate. She didn't say much, but looked through my sketches, occasionally making a comment on one of the competitors.

Everything was about racquetball. We were in an incredible sports facility. I was watching people play. I was even occasionally cheering a great shot. But I wasn't thinking about *playing* racquetball. With my sketchbook and charcoal in hand, I was able to separate myself from the game. When the second flight of men's singles started, I parked myself in front of court eight to watch most of the match. I'd be playing the loser of this match in a few hours. I sketched the two guys as they went back and forth. They were beautiful. I was way into *Deep Forest* when I felt a tap on my shoulder. I pulled my headset off and turned to see a tall brunette with flashing eyes and a great figure smiling at me. Her hair was pulled back into a ponytail and her brown eyes looked like they went down into some shadowy depth that mere humans couldn't fathom.

"Hi. I'm Allison Perkins. Couldn't help but notice you drawing. Did you do a sketch of me while I was playing?"

"Oh. Tony Ames. Um… probably. I hope you don't mind. I just do it while I'm watching."

"Can I see?"

"Sure. What court were you on?"

"Six. One of the shortest matches in history. If you weren't there early you probably missed it."

"I hear you. I got whipped good in straight games. My first collegiate competition and I didn't last a full hour." I started flipping through the pages of my sketchbook until I saw the court number and time that I wrote at the bottom of each drawing.

"Who were you up against?" she asked while I found her court.

"Rob Snyder, LSU."

"He's an asshole." She snorted as if she'd had personal experience with the guy. "You're lucky you lasted long enough to get on the court with him. Did he try that thing where he almost gets called for a hinder on the first serve? I swear a receiver can't see where that ball is coming from."

"Yeah. Took me right out of my game. Here it is." I held up my sketchbook to show her the page with her sketch on it. It wasn't bad. She looked at it intently.

"Uh… Tony. Where are my clothes? I did not play that game naked."

"Didn't have time to draw them. I'm just sketching the action, not really doing portraits."

"What about my right leg?"

"You moved. Look, if you want a detailed drawing, take off your clothes and stand in the middle of the court for fifteen minutes in a good action pose. I'll put in all the detail you want."

"Kinky."

"Naw. I'm just an art student."

"Kinky." She insisted, still giggling. We watch the game for a while and I turned back to a blank page. She watched as I did a thirty-second sketch of one of the guys. "He needs a cock."

"Can't see it, can't draw it," I said, pointing first to the court and then to my drawing.

"Is Lissa Grant really your coach?"

"Yeah. You know her?"

"Like my idol. I saw her at Opens last year. I'll be watching you."

"Allison!" A voice barked at her from off to our side. "Let's get loosened up. Your flight starts in thirty minutes. You need to get focused on the ball."

"Instead of the balls," Allison whispered. "Coach calls. Hope I'll see you later."

I waved at her as she bounced down the stairs. *That girl needs a stronger sports bra.*

I watched the first consolation round for the women. It looked like Allison was out to set a record for least time on the courts. She lost eleven-two and eleven-one in twenty minutes. I didn't get to say anything to her, though, because Lissa called to have me start warming up for my 4:30 match.

I CAN DRAW with almost any music playing, so I'd had my player set on shuffle. If something I didn't like at the time came up, I touched a button on my headset and moved to the next song. When I'm painting, I prefer to work to classics and a selection of highly charged electronica. But getting ready to play racquet-ball, I was discovering I really like the energy of classic rock. Creedence Clearwater Revival was 'Lookin' Out My Back Door' while I warmed up for my match. I was rockin'. Just before I stepped onto the court, Lissa stopped me and took my headset and music player, handing me my goggles.

"Tony, I know you want to go home a champion—maybe even go to the Ektelon National Singles, but the most important thing right now is this game. Not even this match. Just this game. Put your head in it and forget about everything else."

I nodded and went in to meet my new opponent. As much a giant as my last opponent was, this kid was littler than me. I'd seen him practicing with his coach just before my court time when I got here and again in a match this afternoon. I knew he was pretty fast, but he was way overmatched when I saw him play earlier today. We shook hands and each batted a ball around a bit to get warmed up until the ref called attention and came in to flip the coin. He won the toss and I prepared to receive.

I was still grooving to CCR in my head thirty minutes later when I walked off the court with my first match victory of the tournament. It was a little sad, because that meant that Jim, my opponent, was done. Man that sucked. I played hard, but not over-aggressively. The poor guy just couldn't return anything I served him. I've had days like that. I just kept pumping serves across the short line and he kept bobbling them. I wasn't even trying to make him run the way his coach did. We shook hands as we left the court.

"Glad you got a chance to practice your serve so much," he joked. "You should be warmed up for your next match now."

"Hey, everybody has days when things go wrong. Should have seen me get slaughtered in my first match."

"It's great just being here, though, isn't it? I never thought I'd even make the team. Good luck."

Nice guy. Lissa hooked my arm and told me to get a shower and change and then we'd grab a bite to eat. She wanted my uniform dried out before my next match at 8:30. We were down to twenty-four players in the tournament now and after the flight tonight there would only be sixteen.

I HAD TO work for it, but by 9:40 I was still in the hunt. I called Mom and Dad to tell them that I was still playing and my next match would be at nine in the morning. They wished me luck. When I talked to them last week, I was a little disappointed that they wouldn't be coming to the tournament, but I didn't really make a big deal about it. Dad said they'd been following the results on the Internet and that made me feel kind of proud.

Then Lissa and I called Melody while we waited for my uniform to finish in the hotel's coin-op laundry. At 10:30 Lissa checked up and down the hall and then leaned in to give me a luscious goodnight kiss.

I hadn't done more than pull my shirt off when there was a knock on my door. I just assumed it was Lissa, so I didn't even look out the peep-hole before I swung the door open. When the girl with flaming red hair and hot tight body pushed past me into the room, I was speechless.

Seven

"**T**ony! **You** wouldn't believe what happened." She tossed an overnight bag on the floor and turned to give me a big hug.

"Um… uh… Bree?" I asked, completely lost.

"Well, at least you remembered my name. I came down this afternoon to cheer you on. I got so caught up in your match this evening that I never got to the hotel to check in. Can you believe they gave my room away? I am so miffed."

"What are you doing here?" I asked, still clueless.

"I just explained. Sonia and I flipped a coin to see who would represent the cheer squad in learning about our newest school sport. I won, so I caught a flight this afternoon with Coach Jacobson. Well, not exactly *with* him, but we were on the same flight. I don't think he even knew I was there."

"Sam came down?" I was such a great conversationalist. I was sounding dumber and dumberer.

"Yeah. Didn't you know? He was watching your last match with your coach. Who, by the way, is one of the hottest chicks I've ever seen. So we're trying to figure out if racquetball is a sport that will be good for cheerleading, but it seems kind of crowded. Are all the courts like that with just a glass wall at one end? You couldn't have more than a few dozen fans at a competition."

"Most courts are like that until you get to The Ektelon Nationals. They set up a glass cage in the middle of an arena for the final rounds at least. I went to watch Opens a couple of years ago and there were almost a thousand competitors. But it's not really an NCAA sport, so I don't think there are cheerleaders." I lost my train of thought for a moment as Bree was taking off her sweater and shoes. "What are you doing here?"

"I told you…"

"No. I mean here," I insisted, waving at the walls. "In my room."

"Oh. Well, since they gave away my room and we're sort of teammates, I was hoping that you wouldn't mind company tonight. I thought it would be a great way to get to know you better."

"I've got to get to bed and get sleep. I've got a match at nine tomorrow morning and I can't be staying up all night."

"Oh, I understand the athlete during competition thing. I won't keep you awake or make any crippling sexual demands on you—though personally I think the whole thing about abstaining from sex before a game is stupid. But I'll wait till you're finished for that. I can sleep on the couch."

"There's no waiting for *that*," I said. "I've got… uh… a girlfriend."

"Really? Who?"

I almost answered that question and caught myself just in time. I would have regretted that, I was sure. I was so thrown by this little redhead prancing into my room and making like she was going to sleep with me that I wasn't thinking straight.

"A cute cheerleader from PCAD," I said vaguely.

"Which one? Let's see. There was the dyke, the little chub, and two pretty cute girls. One was tall and skinny and the other one had sort of reddish hair and looked soft all over. That's the one, isn't it?"

"Yeah" I agreed. "That's Melody. But hey! Sandra's not a chub. She's a little Rubenesque but…"

"No offense. I was just trying to get to the right one. So, I'll clear it with your girlfriend before I fuck you. I'll tell her it's part of your initiation into the athletic department. Mind if I take the first shower? Since we're not doing anything tonight, there's no reason to shower together. Don't want you to have rubbery legs in the morning. Unless you'd rather…?"

With that, she grabbed her bag and disappeared into the bathroom. I heard the shower turn on as soon as the door closed.

I grabbed my phone and sent a text to Lissa and Melody that just said, "You wouldn't believe what just happened." My phone had just vibrated with a message when there was another knock at my door. I saw Melody had sent the return text asking "what?" and figured Lissa had just come next door to find out. I swung the door open as I started to text Melody back.

Allison Perkins breezed in the door, gave me a kiss on the cheek, strode straight to the bed, and started stripping her clothes off. She was only wearing sweatpants and a t-shirt, so it didn't take long before she was naked.

"I thought maybe you could fill in some of the details in your sketch," she said, striking a pose that was similar to the one I'd sketched of her on the court. She looked a whole lot better than she had in her shorts and t-shirt. The muscle definition I'd seen in her legs continued right up into her butt and her back. And I could see for sure now why her sports bra was having such a tough job. I was about to reach for my sketchbook.

"What are you doing?" I squeaked instead. "You can't just come into a guy's room and take your clothes off. I've got a girlfriend."

"Do you know how much I had to work myself up in order to do this? Just get out your sketchbook and draw me before I lose my nerve. God!"

She was definitely flushed and I was not going to let the opportunity to sketch her go to waste, so I started rummaging in my bag. Of course, that's when Bree walked out of the bathroom wrapped in a towel and stared at Allison.

"Tony!" Bree said. "You didn't tell me we were partying, tonight!"

"Is that your girlfriend?" Allison asked, mortified. "Oh god!"

Allison started scrambling to get to her sweats back on, but Bree just stripped off her towel so she was standing as naked as Allison. *Damn!* Bree looked good, too. She had the pale skin and scatter of freckles of a true redhead and if there was any doubt left, the triangle of hair above her pussy proved the carpet matched the drapes, as they say. Allison stopped dressing with one foot in her sweats and the other raised as Bree approached her. Allison towered over the redheaded cheerleader. Each time she hopped a little, those incredible breasts did incredible things. Bree definitely took control when she hauled Allison's head down with her hand and planted a searing kiss on her lips.

I still had my phone in my hand from my unfinished message to Melody and Lissa. I held it up and took a picture of the two naked girls standing next to my bed and sent it along with a message that just said "WTF! Help!"

"Tony, this will be so much fun! I like this one," Bree said.

"Honest, I didn't know his girlfriend was here," Allison scrambled. "I just wanted him to draw me. Like in the action sketches he was doing earlier."

"Oh yeah," Bree responded. "Let's give him some real action to draw." She was standing on her tiptoes so she could reach Allison's mouth with her own. She kept one foot on the ground and raised the other to wrap her left leg around Allison's hips and pull them together.

"Oh god, you're luscious," Allison whimpered as she lost her balance and the two fell back onto the bed.

Just then there was another knock on the door. I just opened it while I was staring at the two of them. For all I knew it could be another girl or both of their boyfriends. I was too dazed to care.

Lissa walked into the room. She looked at me with a little smirk on her face and then turned to the girls and cleared her throat. They looked over at her and then both jumped up off the bed and faced Lissa, looking terrified. That was amusing. Allison had a nicely trimmed landing strip above very pouty lips that were beginning to open and show her arousal. I wasn't sure how much of that she'd been sporting when she came into the room and how much was a result of Bree's steamy attack. And they both had tits to die for. Bree's nipples were a little bigger, and lighter in color than Allison's. For as big as Allison's boobs were, though, her areolae and nipples were delicate and perched high. Both girls stood straight at attention as they faced Lissa.

"Coach Grant," Bree said. Allison's mouth just worked up and down. I knew from our earlier conversation that she was in awe of Lissa already.

"Ma'am," she finally squeaked out. "I'm sorry. I didn't mean to… I only wanted to… I mean…"

"Ladies," Lissa said firmly, "I don't want to hear it. But there are rules. He's out of play with a match in the morning. You are free to stay here, but no room service, no liquor, and no pay per view movies. Do you understand?"

"Yes ma'am," Bree said. Her eyes were about as big around as saucers and Allison was still near tears at being caught like this by her idol.

Lissa didn't respond. She just grabbed my hand and dragged me out of the room before the girls could say anything else. In a heartbeat we were inside Lissa's room and she started giggling like a little girl.

"You have got to check the peep-hole before you open your door, Tony!" she laughed. "Did they come in together or one at a time?"

"One at a time. I'm sorry, Lissa. Bree just marched in and said she'd come to cheer at the match and the hotel gave her room away and that she was going to have to sleep on my couch. Then she went in to take a shower and Allison came in. She just stripped off her clothes, posed, and asked me to draw her. Then Bree…"

By that time Lissa was laughing so hard she had tears rolling down her cheeks. My phone had been chiming every thirty seconds since I sent the photo message. I finally looked at it and there were a dozen messages from Melody asking what was going on and if I was okay.

Lissa and I both started texting her back as fast as we could. Melody was sending back "LOL" and "ROFLMAO" messages. Finally, she sent one back that just said, "Please stop. In tears!"

I quit messaging and dialed her.

"Eight!" was the first thing she said when she answered the phone. I could hear voices laughing in the background. "I told you Bree wanted to get naked with you. I might have to kill her. I like that Allison, though. She's got balls!"

"Um… not that I could see. And I'm pretty sure I'd have noticed." Lissa signaled me to put it on speakerphone. She could hear the laughter at the other end.

"Who's with you, Little One?" she asked.

"Oh we're all here, sweetheart. Amy, Sandra, and Kate. I'm sorry, Tony and Lissa. I couldn't keep us a secret from them. Amy and Sandra knew and Kate…" Lissa looked at me and raised an eyebrow. I could tell she was a little worried. I was confident that Melody wouldn't have told them if there was any doubt that they'd keep our secret, but for Lissa's sake I had to say something after they'd chimed out their "Hi's" in the background.

"Ladies," I said, "you all know how difficult this could be on Melody and me. But it could be really hard on Lissa if people found out we were… you know… with my coach. You're our friends, though, and we don't want to be isolated from everyone we know. Just, please, treat our relationship in confidence, okay?"

"Hey, this is Amy. We're all for you and wouldn't do a thing to hurt you. If anything, we three are a little jealous. Just be our friends, okay?"

"You got it, Amy," I agreed.

"This is Kate. I just want to say thank you for including me. I like having friends. And, yeah. Ditto."

"You know me," Sandra said. "I'll just be hanging around waiting my turn. Seriously, we all love you three and won't tell a soul. You have our word. We're really happy for you."

"Thank you," Lissa said. "Would you all mind if we take this off speaker phone now so Tony and I can say goodnight to our sweetheart?" Everybody said goodnight and good luck tomorrow. We could hear the difference as Melody put the phone to her ear.

"You guys headed for bed now?" she asked.

"Yeah" I offered. "I've got a match at nine."

"I miss you. Wish I was there."

"Wish you were here, too, honey," Lissa said. "It's going to be hard sleeping with this guy when he can't fool around. Our boy needs his rest. We love you."

"I bet it will be hard," Melody giggled. "Cuddle each other for me, okay?"

"Love you, Melody. 'Night." I said. I breathed a big sigh and turned to Lissa after I disconnected. "Are you worried, lover?"

Lissa shook her head. "I don't think it's a good idea to make us general knowledge on the competition circuit or in the athletic department. Technically, I'm not faculty, so I don't think there'd be many questions from SCU. PCAD seems to allow a little more artistic license in relationships, but when word is out to a few, you've got to assume that everyone knows. I don't want you and Melody to suffer because of me, but I'm glad you've got friends."

"We've got friends, Lissa. Those girls will be just as good friends to you if you let them. Speaking of which, I hope you'll introduce us to some of your friends soon," I said. "You know, Lissa, it's not about Melody and me. It's about the three of us together."

"Let's take it slow, Tony. I want everything with you, but I'm just not ready to face the PTA, okay?" She kissed me gently and whispered, "Someday."

We just held each other, standing there in the middle of a hotel room a thousand miles from home. Right then I was ready to skip the rest of the tournament and just take her to bed with me.

"Look, it's almost midnight. Get yourself in bed."

"I'll sleep on the couch."

"Nonsense. Just because we're not having sex tonight doesn't mean we can't cuddle up and sleep together. Since it seems your bed is occupied, I couldn't stand it if you didn't sleep in my arms."

———◁◆▷———

LISSA AND I ordered room service breakfast in the morning. It was good and light. I was definitely ready for the challenge on the courts. We opened the door to my room next door cautiously after knocking lightly. I wasn't sure what to expect. It was quiet and the girls who invaded the night before were gone. The bed, however, showed signs of active use—very active. All the towels were wet, too. I guess they just got out early. I grabbed my bag and we headed for the rec hall.

That's where the shit hit the fan.

It was a neat display; I had to give them credit for that. They'd commandeered what used to be the message board where you could post notes for other people at the event. Now the board held a nice display of my drawings from yesterday. Over the top was a neatly printed sign that read "Action sketches from the competition by SCU/PCAD competitor Tony Ames."

I groaned and Lissa sent me to get ready while she went to find Bree and Allison. Her lips were set in a firm line as she left.

When I went to my locker, the entire bay cleared out. The other competitors just turned their backs and walked out of the locker room. I walked to my court for warmups and recognized my opponent as Wally Barnes. He was the same guy that sent me Jim yesterday afternoon. Apparently, Wally 'd been defeated last night. He was one of the few guys that I'd sketched.

I held out my hand to greet him and he turned his back on me. It was a quiet warm-up. The ref called attention and announced the game. Wally won the toss and took the ball to serve. Just as he bounced the ball for service, I heard him mutter, "Eat shit, faggot."

Eight

HE MUST HAVE said it louder than he intended because the ref's whistle was blowing before the ball hit the front wall.

"Technical foul. Poor sportsmanship. Deduction of one point. No serve."

Holy shit! In racquetball if you get called for a technical foul you lose a point, even if you don't have a point to lose. I didn't expect the refs here to be so hard on people. If he heard the comment, I figured it would merit a warning, but not a foul. We hadn't really started the game yet and I was leading zero to minus one. Wally was really going to be pissed if he lost by that point. I couldn't figure out why the hell he was so upset. Sure, there was a drawing of him posted on the board, but it was a good drawing, damn it. What's with the faggot shit?

He came back strong with his next serve and evened the score at zero-zero. I had to put his trash talk out of my head and get with it or this would be my last match. We played hard with the score rocking back and forth, but when he had me down ten to nine, I could tell he was regretting the point he lost with his profanity. I saw his muscles bunch as he went into his service motion and knew before the ball left his racquet exactly where it was going to come to me. The ref called "side out" and I stepped up to serve. I glanced over my shoulder to make sure he was ready and could see the sneer on his face. *Yeah? Well eat this.*

Two aces later I was up one game to none in the match.

Wally was good—the strongest I'd faced since my disastrous first round. He nailed me in the second game and after a five-minute break he was back in the service zone. He pushed off for a drive serve and I was right behind him, five feet back at the safety line. We played hard for over twenty minutes until my last serve came scooting back against the wall three feet away from me and he flubbed the return. He turned and argued with the ref for a hinder, but the line judge put thumbs down and the match was mine. He still ignored my offered hand and stormed off the court. I stepped out and Lissa grabbed me to head in the opposite direction. That's when I noticed I had a little fan section. Bree and Allison were cheering for me and chanting my name. Jim, the guy I beat yesterday afternoon was there, too. A couple of the other women I'd sketched yesterday who weren't playing in the morning match were clapping. What surprised me, though, was that beside Coach Jacobson, I saw my dad.

I ran up and gave him a hug.

"Dad! When did you get here? Did Mom…?"

"Just me. We looked up the scores and the competition clips last night and I decided to catch a plane down from Omaha early this morning. Sorry I didn't get here for the start of the match. I heard there were some fireworks."

"Yeah. It was nothing intentional. I think it did more to throw him off than me. It's just these two…" I pointed at Bree and Allison.

"We're sorry, Tony. I had no idea they'd create such a mess," Bree said.

"I told her about them and I just thought they were so cool that people should see them. But we took them down," Allison said. Both of them were looking up at Coach Jacobson and he nodded. I had a feeling he had something to do with the removal. Bree handed me my sketchbook with the loose drawings inside the cover. I introduced Lissa to my dad, and while Dad was congratulating her on my win, Sam pulled me aside.

"Tony, show me some good sportsmanship. You represent our school," he whispered.

I didn't have time to ask if I'd done something wrong when somebody cleared his throat behind me and said, "Excuse me." I turned to find Wally behind me. I might have cringed a little, not knowing what to expect, but if anything he looked contrite. Behind him I could see his coach with his arms folded glaring, not at me, but at Wally.

"I just wanted to say 'sorry', man. You're a good competitor and I lost my cool. There was a bunch of trash talk about you in the locker room and I let it get to me. Anyway. Congratulations." He held out his hand and I shook it gladly.

"It wasn't my idea to have any of that stuff displayed," I said. "I'm sorry if you were offended or if you took any crap because of it. I hope we'll meet on the court again." He nodded. Then I had a sudden inspiration. "Hey. Would you like the drawing? You can do whatever you want with it then and you won't have to worry about anyone else seeing it."

"Really?"

"Sure." I leafed through the loose pages in my book and pulled out the picture of him. He took it and looked at it closely. His eyes came up and met mine and he smiled. He pushed the page back at me and I thought he was refusing.

"Sign it?" he asked. We all laughed and I grabbed a pencil

out of my bag, scrawled my name on the bottom, and handed it back. "Thanks. Good luck for the rest of the tournament."

"Now," Dad said. "Come and tell me about how things are going and introduce me to all your fans here."

"How about if I shower and change first? I've got to rinse out my clothes and get them dry before my noon match."

"Here, Tony," Sam said. He handed me a bag. "With the schedule today I figured you might need a fresh change. Just put your dirty uniform in the bag and Bree will go wash it."

"What?" the cheerleader screamed.

Coach turned to her and said firmly, "And it had better not come back faded or shrunk, understand, Brianna?"

"Yes, father," she said.

"Wait. Coach Jacobson is your dad?" Bree nodded while Sam just laughed.

"And she can be quite a handful; but I think you already know that."

"Yeah. But… I mean, nothing happened, Coach. Really."

"So I've heard," he chuckled. He waved me off toward the showers and turned to talk to my dad.

————◁◆▷————

MY NEXT MATCH was with a guy who'd suffered his first loss that morning to the same Rob that had trounced me in my first match. We sized each other up on the court, but I didn't detect any antagonism. We'd both lost to the same guy, so it was like a race for second place between the two of us. The matches were getting longer as the competition got tougher. We played three games and were never more than two points apart. I felt like it was sheer luck that I nailed my last serve and pulled out the match. It seemed like there was less and less time between matches now as the field narrowed. Bree handed me a clean uniform on my way into the locker room and took my dirty one on the way out to lunch.

"I can do my own laundry, Bree," I said.

"No way. If dad found out I didn't comply, I'd never hear the end of it. He *is* the athletic director, you know." She leaned in close to me and whispered in my ear. "You are so going to owe me when this is over, though." I swear, the swivel in her hip when she turned and walked away from me could have knocked me over from across the room. Maybe if I left now, I could be back home before she knew I was missing.

We had a light lunch and dad was enthusiastic about my prospects. He obviously liked Lissa—who wouldn't?—and was amused by the unending line of girls who came by asking if they could have my sketch of them and if I'd sign it. Sam Jacobson was steering the conversation around to National Singles and said that if I was in the top tier the school would send me. "We want to see you in the final bracket, but whatever happens, we're glad to have you as a member of our team. The founding member, as it happens." I finished the last spoonful of the rich, meaty soup Lissa had ordered for me. All I had to drink was water. I was drinking like I'd never seen water. The Ektelon National Singles Tournament. Wow! It was really a possibility.

When Bree came to the table she brought Allison with her and both girls seemed a little less sexually aggressive toward me. I suppose that had to do with Lissa, Dad, and Sam all being there.

"You seem to have cheerleaders, too," Dad said, looking at Bree and Allison.

"Yeah. Much as I like 'em around, though, I don't think racquetball is really going to become a cheerleader sport." I joked.

"Just isn't enough room for their... uh... gymnastics." I grinned at Bree. I was willing to joke and tease them, but I was staying glued to Lissa's side. For some reason, I think Dad noticed.

———◁◆▷———

MY NEXT OPPONENT was a kid from SoCal. He was good, fast, and had a backhand that sizzled. Once you dropped to the lower bracket—as in having lost once—games were only to eleven points instead of fifteen until semifinals. We played three hard games and I ended up winning eleven to eight on the last game. He just sort of fizzled in the last ten minutes. It was like sudden death. One minute a guy's a contender and the next minute he's out of the competition. I had to figure out how to stop feeling so bad about those who lost. I was sure most of them wouldn't be that upset if *I* went down.

The next crisis appeared at seven o'clock that night in the form of my opponent in the semifinals. While I'd dealt with the guy from Memphis State, Rob Snyder had fallen to the defending National Intercollegiate Champion, Karl Higgendorfer. So the semifinal match was going to be a replay of my first match of the tournament. This was not going to be fun. Lissa led me away after last match and shower at five and just gave me water and a power bar for dinner. We talked strategy and she took my music player from me. After scanning through my playlists, she set one playing and put my headset over my ears. I was told to stay put until warmup time.

The music was mostly dubstep with a mix of grunge tossed in. It had an underlying edge and strength that just filled me up. She'd started the list with "Fire and Ice." By the time she called me to warm up, I was listening to Alice in Chains pounding out. "We pay our debt sometime."

Rob won the toss—I hadn't won one since the tournament began—and elected to serve. The ref called "first serve" and Rob looked over his shoulder to make sure I was ready. I had my racquet held up over my head as I scuffed at an imagined wet spot on the floor then stepped back across the receiving line while I slowly counted to five and lowered my racquet. When the ref calls the serve, the server has ten seconds to put the ball in play, but he has to wait for the receiver to be ready. Racquet held over the head is a sign to wait. If I took too long, I'd be called for a penalty, but waiting five seconds gave Rob only five seconds to center and serve. As soon as he turned away from me I moved to the right. I knew just where this ball was coming and when it whistled down the sidewall toward me, I sent it back so hard and so close to Rob's head that he ducked instinctively. Before he'd regained his balance, the ball came off the front wall and bounced off his foot. "Side out!" the ref called. I picked up the ball and moved to the service area.

"Now let's play racquetball," I said lowly as Rob passed me. He jerked toward me with a scowl on his face, but he didn't raise his racquet, so as soon as his toes were behind the receiving line, I made a driving serve to the left. He returned, but it was weak and I came back for the point.

Rob is a hell of a competitor and he adjusted fast to my more aggressive strategy. Before we'd finished the first game, it was beginning to get physical. You see action photos in magazines and the players are always diving across the court with racquet outstretched. Their bodies are parallel to the floor and you know that in less than a second that player is going to smash down on the hardwood and burn the skin off his whole body. Well, that's how our match was turning out. It wasn't just me diving, either. I was keeping the ball low and hard and Rob was spending a lot of time bending and scooping in order to keep the ball in play. I won the first game, he won the second. I was in control in the third leading by two points and only two points from victory when the unthinkable happened.

It was legit. There was no evidence that he was doing anything but going for the ball, but he took my legs out from under me when he hit me and I did an almost complete back-flip before I came down. Almost complete. My right ankle was turned awkwardly when I hit and I felt the pain lance up all the way into my hip. I screamed and heard the ref blow the whistle and yell "Time out!"

Lissa and Sam were on the court before Rob had managed to leave it. They were quickly followed by the tournament doctor and an ASU trainer who'd been assisting all athletes. The doctor pulled my shoe off and felt around my ankle. It was tender but I was determined to get back on it. Sam and the trainer hooked themselves under my arms and helped me off the court. I didn't put much weight on it as I moved off. Dad was there as soon as I was down on a bench with his hand on my shoulder asking me how I was. I couldn't focus on him, though. I had to listen to the doctor as he poked and prodded. I saw Lissa look at him and he sort of shrugged. She took my face in her hands and forced my head around to look her straight in the eyes.

"Tony, how badly do you want to go to Ektelon Nationals?" she asked.

"Lissa, I can do this. I want to do this. I can take him. I just want to get there. It's important." She looked deep into my eyes as if she could read how committed I was and then she looked up at Sam and motioned for him to follow her.

"Trust me, Tony," she said as she left.

"You should stay off of this," the doctor said, checking under the ice pack. "No tournament is worth permanent injury."

"It's okay, son," Dad said, but I shook them both off and turned to the trainer.

"Tape it," I said. He looked at the doctor and the doctor shrugged again. The trainer pulled out a roll of athletic tape and began quickly wrapping my ankle and crossing below my arch. The tightness of the tape would support the injury and hold the swelling down until I finished the match.

I was getting nervous. I could only catch glimpses of Lissa and Sam talking to the ref and line judge. They'd called a guy in a suit over who I recognized as the tournament director. In a match, you get a maximum of fifteen minutes to recover from an injury and resume play. I was fidgeting around trying to get my sock and shoe on so I could return to the court. I knew I only had a minute or two left. Dad was still touching my shoulder, trying to just pour his strength into me. I stood up and felt the twinge in my ankle as I put weight on it. The ref had returned to his microphone with Sam, Lissa, and the tournament director following him. I'd taken only one step toward the court when he spoke over the public address system. Almost 200 people gathered in front of the court for the semifinal went silent.

"Ladies and gentlemen, Competitor Tony Ames of Seattle Cascades University concedes the game because of injury. Game and match go to Rob Snyder of Louisiana State University."

The scream in my throat turned to a sob before it reached my mouth and I collapsed against my dad.

Nine

THAT WAS IT. It was over. I was trying to cram my swollen foot back into my shoe so I could get on the court and my coach was conceding the match for me. My coach. My lover. The one person in the world I trusted more than anyone else. She had asked me and knew I wanted to go to Nationals. But she threw it all out anyway. I guess I didn't mean as much to her as I thought. How could she do this to me?

Bree was leading my makeshift cheering section in a cheer of appreciation or something. My dad was saying something to me about pulling it together. Sam was repeating that he needed me to represent SCU and show great sportsmanship. And Lissa kept trying to touch me. I flinched away from her and mopped my eyes on Dad's shirt before I turned to face the crowd. I stepped out and winced as I put pressure on my ankle. Everyone cheered as I raised my hand and waved at them.

I've heard of bittersweet moments. I wanted to hear them cheer. It pounded in my heart. How can you be down when so many people are showing love? But they were cheering for my effort, not my victory. "The thrill of victory. The agony of defeat." ABC's *Wide World of Sports*. I could see that skier dude crashing off the jump every weekend.

I limped over to where Rob and his coach were talking to his own excited fans and held out my hand. He took it and smiled.

"You okay, man?" Rob asked. "After the first serve I thought I was a goner. I hope you know it was an accident." I looked into his eyes and nodded my head. I could see that it had been an accident. We were both playing crazy aggressively and I ended up on the short end of the stick. It could just as easily have been him who got injured.

"Congratulations, Rob. Good luck at The Ektelon."

"You keep playing like that and I'll need all the good luck I can get." Well, that was a compliment, but it didn't make much sense. I figured he must be talking about next year. "Hey, if you get a chance, I'd love one of those sketches you do. They're like the most popular keepsake here at the competition. You should be selling them."

"I'll try to knock one out during the final round tomorrow," I said. What a turn-around in opinions from this morning when the other guys seemed ready to crucify me for drawing pictures of them. "Just don't stop to pose on the court. It'll wreak havoc with your game." We bumped fists and I turned and headed toward the locker room. All I wanted now was a shower and bed where I could curl up in a ball and cry. I threw an arm around Dad as I walked for support. *Damn! That ankle hurt a lot more than I thought now that the adrenalin was seeping out of my system.*

Lissa put an arm around me from the other side. I had a jolt of fury at her. I couldn't snub my coach in front of the stands. I had just enough sense left to keep good sportsmanship and my scholarship in mind, but I wouldn't look at her and didn't put my arm around her. She kept talking to me in a low voice, but I was turned toward my dad and wouldn't listen. Sam had gathered up my equipment and met us at the locker room door.

Another player was standing next to the locker room door when we got there. Karl Higgendorfer, the guy I would have met in the finals.

"Hey, Ames. Tough luck tonight. I was really looking forward to playing you in the finals. Next time, eh?"

I shook his hand and wished him luck.

Dad let go of me because the locker rooms are limited to competitors and coaches only. I made to escape into the refuge and was surprised to find Lissa walking right in with me.

"You can't come in here," I said in surprise.

"I have an injured athlete. I can go anywhere I need to."

"I don't need you." That was harsh. It grated on my own ears. My voice caught and I couldn't get anything else out. I sure wasn't prepared for what came next.

Lissa practically threw me against a locker, grabbed my head, and turned me toward her. I thought, *This is really stupid. She's going to try to kiss me after that?* But kissing wasn't on her mind.

"Tony! Look at me! Darling, listen!"

"How can you 'darling' me? You just conceded my chances after you asked what I wanted."

"Exactly. I got you what you wanted."

"What?"

"You said the most important thing was to get to National Singles. So would you rather win this match or go to Nationals?"

"That doesn't make sense, Lissa. Sam said he'd send me if I was top tier. I can't afford to pay my own way."

"That's what I was talking to Sam and the Director about. I wanted a witness when Sam said that he considered 'on the podium' to be top tier. You won third. You are on the podium."

"So I got bronze. That isn't the final bracket."

"Tony! Wake up. Sam agreed you are qualified and he'll pay your way. You're going to the Nationals, Tony."

No. I must have hit my head when I fell on the court. I was hearing things—making up a fantasy. Sam had been specific about what he thought top tier was—final bracket. But there was Lissa, in my face, telling me that I was going to National Singles. Lissa, who I trusted. Lissa, who loved me. I was such an ass. She *did* love me. She did what I asked. I didn't know what to say. I didn't know how to say it. I just looked at her with tears flowing down my cheeks. I was totally overwhelmed.

Then she *did* kiss me. Boy, did she kiss me.

Fortunately, we heard the locker room door open before anyone saw us and when Rob and his coach entered the room, Lissa was helping me down on a bench. The coaches nodded to each other and then Sam came in with Dad. Sam got him a special pass so he could come in and help me. The trainer came in, too, and Lissa asked him to cut the tape off my ankle. *Damn, that hurt!* Usually if you're going to tape up like that, you shave the area first. Believe me; I wouldn't have to worry about shaving *that* area anytime soon.

"You want your chest hair waxed, too?" the trainer joked.

"No. Thanks. I think I'll keep both of them." Lissa left the locker room and Dad and Sam helped me get to the shower. No hot tub or steam tonight, even though that was what I wanted most. It would aggravate the swelling. As soon as I was mostly dressed, the trainer came back with elastic compression bandages and ice packs. Sam and Dad were talking about various things and I heard Dad mention that he was planning to bunk with me tonight. That brought my head up. I hadn't thought about what having Dad here tonight would mean to my love life.

And that brought me to another issue. I was going to have to tell my parents about my unusual relationship. This wasn't just a phase. Melody and I had spent all spring break with Lissa convincing her that we were in it for the long haul. I'd slept in Lissa's room last night and intended to tonight, too. But what was I going to tell my dad? I needed to talk to Lissa and make things right with her. I wasn't prepared for this.

———◁◆▷———

IT WAS ALMOST nine when I got out of the locker room. Dad suggested we get something to eat and Sam said there was a good Mexican restaurant just off campus. We were going to walk, but Lissa suggested that she drive me over so I wouldn't hurt the ankle any worse. Some unspoken communication passed between Lissa and Sam and Sam turned to my dad.

"Saul, why don't you and I escort Tony's cheerleaders over to the restaurant so they aren't accosted on the walk? We'll meet Tony and Lissa there." Dad glanced at me and I thought he tossed a quick look at Lissa, too. He nodded his head.

"Tony probably needs coaching in private," Dad said with a chuckle. "Don't want him embarrassed at his celebration dinner." He and Sam headed out with Bree and Allison. I was relieved as I wrapped my arm around Lissa and headed for the car.

———◁◆▷———

WE JUST SAT in the car with my phone on speaker as we quickly recapped the game with Melody, explaining that we were headed to dinner with my dad and Sam. That brought up the topic I really wanted to talk to them about.

"Hey, my loves," I started, "I really need to ask you something. I had a flash of anger after the match this evening because I thought Lissa had betrayed me. I'm sorry, Lissa. I should have known."

"I wish I could have explained before the ref announced the decision," Lissa said. "I know hearing it like that shook you up."

"Still, I'm in love with you. I shouldn't doubt that you care for me. Melody, that goes for you, too. I'm in love with you. I know that you are always on my side. So what I need to ask—and I'm sorry this is going to sound so dumb—but I need to know—are we really together now? I'm not asking for a lifelong commitment or to find a state or country where the three of us can get married, but this is more than a fling, right?"

"Honey, being away from you and Lissa tears me apart. I've been so lonely this weekend I can hardly stand it. As far as I'm concerned, I don't ever want to be without you. I know it's too early to figure out how it will work in the future, but I want to *have* a future with you. I love you both."

"I think you both know how I feel," Lissa picked up from Melody. "After I saw you with my boys, the last of my resistance crumbled. I don't know the *how*, but the *what* is real. I want us to be a family. We'll figure out a way to make it work."

"Why'd you ask, Tony? Didn't you know what we'd say?"

"I thought I knew," I answered Melody. "I just had to hear it explicitly from both of you. I want to tell my dad tonight."

"Tony!" They started giggling as they realized how they had responded—exactly the same.

"I know you might not be ready to do the same with your families," I continued. "We each have to approach it the way we think is best, and I know we have to be careful around school. But my folks have always supported me in everything I do and I've kept them too distant from what was happening in my life. My dad's here with us tonight and I know he's already picked up on Lissa and me. He might not know exactly how far it's gone, but he knows we're attracted to each other. I don't want to give him the wrong impression or mislead him. I want him to know that it's both of you. I want him to know I love you both."

"Tony, if you think the time is right, I'm with you," Lissa said. "I was kind of hoping you'd sleep in my room tonight and then figured there was no chance with your dad sharing your room."

"I only wish I could be there with you two when you tell him, Tony. If you want to introduce me over the phone, I'll be up." She paused. "Amy, Sandra, and Kate know. I told them without even asking you guys. It's really too exciting to me to keep a secret forever."

Ten

"**D**AD, I'd like to tell you about my girlfriends," I said, leaning over the seat to look at him. He'd jumped in the back of the car to give me room to stretch my swollen ankle.

Well, there it was. I'd started the conversation. Dinner had been nice and I was finally feeling like I'd come to grips with the outcome of the tournament. If I'd gone back in to play, I might have beaten Rob, but there was an equal chance that I'd have done serious—maybe even permanent—injury to my ankle. That would have put me out of competition and maybe out of my scholarship. Lissa and Sam figured it out. That's what coaches are for. So now that the three of us were in the car, I had to talk to Dad.

"Both those little cuties at dinner tonight? Tony, I'm proud of you, but don't you think it would be nice to share with the other guys? You don't have to take *all* the best girls." He was making light of it. Well, that was a good sign.

"Allison and Bree aren't my girlfriends, Dad."

"I know, son. I was trying to make a joke. Why don't you tell me about you and Lissa?" I think both of us snapped our heads around to look at Dad. "Sam said you had a unique relationship. I'm a little surprised that the school would allow that between a coach and athlete."

"We came as a package deal. I was involved with Lissa before I got the offer from SCU and PCAD. We've been friends for months and lovers for weeks."

"I understand, son. Lissa, I don't know too much of your background, but I could tell right away that you meant more to Tony than just being his coach."

"Tony's very important to me, Mr. Ames," Lissa said.

"Tony, your mom and I had a long, agonizing talk last fall. Remember when we dropped you off at school?"

"Yes. I didn't think Mom was going to hold it together without crying in the parking lot. Um... I didn't quite hold it together all the way to my room."

"Well, you were scarcely out of sight before she broke down. But we took a couple of extra days as we drove back to Nebraska—went down to Napa Valley and drank some wine. And we talked. A lot. We talked about the fact that you were truly a man now. We always want to be there for you when you need us, but you won't need us as much. We also decided that as much as we can, we will support your life decisions. As long as they are decent people, we won't reject any friend or girlfriend you have. Lissa, we might not understand why a woman who is a little older and probably more experienced than our son is so interested in him, but you showed tonight that you have his best interests at heart. Deborah and I will welcome you into our lives as long as you and Tony are together."

Lissa was crying. She kept wiping tears out of her eyes so she could see the road. I squeezed her thigh with my left hand and realized that my dad reached forward and had a hand on each of our shoulders.

"Thank you, Mr. Ames. Just from knowing Tony, I knew I'd love you and your wife, too."

"Please. Call me Saul and my wife is Deborah. We're all adults here. Speaking of which, I should call her and introduce you."

"Um… Dad… There's more."

"Oh?"

"I said girlfriends, remember?"

"Oh, dear. This is complicated."

"I guess so. Before you call Mom, I'd like to call Melody and introduce her to you, too. We're not exactly a couple. We're a trio."

"Ah. A *ménage à trois*. You are all involved with each other?"

"I love Melody every bit as much as I love Tony," Lissa said as she pulled into a parking spot at the hotel. "I never thought about using the French word. It's always used with such temporary connotations."

I dialed Melody and put her on speaker phone.

"Tony! I love you!" came clear across the connection.

"Guess what, sweetie. We just found out there's a word for us. *Ménage à trois*."

"French. What does it mean?"

"Literally, 'household of three,'" my dad answered automatically. Melody gasped.

"Tony, is that…?"

"My dad," I completed. "Lissa is here, too."

"Hi, darling. We miss you."

"Hi, Lissa. Uh… Mr. Ames, I guess that means Tony told you about us." Melody sounded so far away over the phone. I wished she was in the car with us.

"Yes. I'm happy to meet you, Melody. I wish we were all in one place so I could see you together."

"Oh, believe me, I wish I was there, too. Are you all right with us, Mr. Ames?"

"I just told Lissa to call me Saul. We're all adults here. As to being all right with you, I love my son and part of that is to love who he loves—even sight unseen."

"You sound just as wonderful as Tony, Mr... uh... Saul."

"Okay, stay on the line while I get Tony's mom, and that means Deborah to you both, on my phone."

"Wait, Dad. I've got three-way dialing."

"I'm sure *that* comes in handy." We all laughed. I put Melody on hold and connected with Mom.

"Congratulations, Tony," Mom said. "Dad told me you qualified for Ektelon National Singles. We're going to come to cheer for you."

"That's great, Mom. Hey, I called because I just introduced Dad to my girlfriends and I wanted to introduce you, too."

"Girlfriend? I didn't know you had one."

"Uh... two, Mom."

"Oh. How exciting. Saul?" You could hear the panic in her voice when she spoke Dad's name.

"Hang in there, Pumpkin. They're nice girls," Dad assured her.

"Mom, Melody is on the line with us. She's back at school."

"Hi, Mrs. Ames. It's nice to meet you." I could hear my mom take a deep breath.

"I'm sure Saul already gave you the lecture. Please call me Deborah. It's nice to meet you, Melody."

"And this is Lissa."

"Hi, Deborah. I'm so glad we get to meet you and Saul."

"Lissa? Tony's coach?"

"Yes. We were together before she became my coach. She didn't exercise any undue influence over me."

"In fact," Lissa said, "Tony is going to be acting as my coach as well. He's already helped my game. But that's just one part of our relationship."

"Are you classmates?"

"Not exactly, Mom. Melody's a classmate. Lissa is…" I wasn't sure how to phrase it.

"I'm a few years older," Lissa supplied. "Just enough to add some stability to these two wild ones."

"Hey!" both Melody and I exclaimed before we all broke out in giggles.

"*Who* adds stability to the wild ones?" Melody asked through her laughter. I thought of Lissa's boys, but decided that overwhelming my parents a little at a time was better than all at once.

"It's a shared responsibility," I said.

"Well, I hope all three of you plan to spend some time here in Nebraska this summer. I want to make sure my boy hasn't bitten off more than he can chew."

"Mom!"

———◁◆▷———

WE TALKED FOR about ten more minutes and Dad told Mom he'd call her back in a little while. We went up to the hotel rooms and I opened my room door and then handed the key to Dad.

"I suppose you'll be spending the night… elsewhere?" he said.

"Yeah. We're right next door."

"Well, it looks like a comfy room. I expect I'll be on the phone with your mother for quite a while. Breakfast?"

"Not too early, though," I said. "It's been a long day. I want to watch the finals at noon, so let's meet at ten." I started to leave when I thought about the fact that Bree and/or Allison probably still had my other room key. "Uh… Dad? Just for safety's sake, I'd suggest you put the security chain on the door. Strange things happen around here at night." I left before he could question me any further.

⊰◆⊱

"It was so wonderful, Tony! I can't wait to tell my mom and dad. But I'd be too scared if you weren't both right beside me when I do. They're… um… unpredictable. They never want me to grow up and Dad's kind of conservative. Just thinking about it makes my heart beat so fast I think I'm going to pass out." Melody's voice came through the speaker phone on the bed beside me. I'd had to plug it in because we'd used so much juice talking to my parents in the car. Lissa was putting a fresh ice pack on my ankle and I gasped. "What are you two doing?" Melody asked suspiciously.

"Just getting ready for bed, darling," Lissa said calmly.

"What was that gasp?"

"Lissa just put an ice pack on my ankle. It's cold."

"Yeah? Are you two naked?"

"Well, I kind of am," I said. I had a robe on when I lay down on the bed and it seemed like everything Lissa did as she was working on my ankle caused the robe to fall open a little more. "I think Lissa is trying to sneak peeks at me." I surprised myself when I realized that I wasn't self-conscious about Lissa or Melody seeing me when I wasn't aroused. I was no longer embarrassed about my lack of endowment.

"What about Lissa?"

"She just got out of the shower and is wrapped in a towel. It's pretty short, though. Every time she bends over, I see a little bit of paradise."

"Mmm. Pull it off of her."

"Hey!" Lissa exclaimed as I caught hold of the towel and it came loose from her. She laughed. "You win. We're naked."

"Lissa, is Tony hard yet?"

"No. He's got the cutest little prick, but… oh my!"

"Are you touching him?"

"I didn't have to. I'm just standing here watching. It's growing. It's like when your little clit comes out of its hood and gets big when I suck it. Only Tony's is getting a lot bigger than that."

"What's she doing, Tony?"

"Just standing here, like she said. But Melody, do you know how beautiful she is? I can't help myself when I look at her."

"Tell me."

"She's all scrubbed, right out of the shower. Her skin is practically glowing. She used one of those loofa things. Her skin looks so soft I just want to touch it. But I can't reach her from where I'm lying. She's staring at me and I'm getting hard just looking at her. She's breathing a little harder and those unbelievable breasts are rising and falling. Don't you wish you could just lick one of her hard little nipples?"

"I do. Are you hard, Tony?"

"Yeah."

"I'm so wet. My clit's throbbing, but I don't want to touch it yet. Lissa?"

"Yes, Sweetheart."

"Are you turned on?"

"Oh yes. My nipples are so hard and sensitive they almost hurt. I wish you were here to lick them while I ride Tony. I'm so wet, just watching him get hard."

"I'm going to dip my fingers in my pussy and taste them, Lissa. Will you do that with me?"

"Oh yes." I watched as Lissa stepped nearer to the bed and dipped her fingers into her wet opening. Then she slowly licked one of the fingers with her eyes closed, savoring it. When she was finished, she pressed the other finger against my lips and I opened to suck her in and clean the juices off her hand.

"Do I taste like you do, Lissa?" Melody's husky voice came through the phone.

"No, sweetheart. I taste like canned tuna."

"No you don't!" Melody and I both exclaimed at the comparison. Lissa ignored us.

"You, my love, taste like fresh-baked oatmeal cookies. I just want to eat you with a big glass of milk," Lissa said. Melody whined at the other end of the line.

"Tony, do you want to make love to Lissa?"

"Oh, yes. Melody, she gave me a taste of her nectar and it doesn't taste at all like tuna. But her pussy lips are just glistening with moisture and I can't wait to touch her with my cock. Are you ready for my cock, too, Melody?"

"I'm just dripping, darling. I want to slide down on you and hold Lissa while she rides your face. I'm just so horny for you both."

"I can't wait anymore, little one," Lissa breathed. "I have to get into bed with Tony."

"Oh, poor Tony," Melody giggled. "I'll bet he has to just lie there on his back so he doesn't reinjure himself, doesn't he?"

"That's right," Lissa said. She put a hand on my chest and pushed me down on my back. She let her fingers trail south along my torso until they just grazed my cock. I moaned.

"Oh, he must be in a lot of pain. Isn't there anything you can do for him, Lissa?"

"He seems to be losing some precious bodily fluids—all from his cock. It's all shiny with juice leaking out of the little slit."

"We taste tested our pussies, baby. It seems only fair that we should compare it with a taste of Tony. Tell me what it tastes like, Lissa." Lissa went down on my cock, first just licking up my precome and then sliding her lips along the entire length.

"Mmm. Yummy. Boy juice is a little saltier than girl juice. We could have it for a cocktail snack."

"Lissa, I can't wait any longer. You have to put him inside."

"That's just what I was thinking, love." Lissa straddled my thighs and began moving toward me.

"It's so amazing to watch Lissa come toward me on her hands and knees, crawling up the bed," I said. "Remember when Doc Henredon described her as a tigress? I feel like I'm going to be her next meal. She's dangerous and so exciting I'm shaking."

"Are you in her, Tony?"

"Just the head of my cock is pressed into her sweet folds. Her pussy has turned all pink and is open. So hot and wet. I can see her little bud just above where my cock is slipping into her. She's going so slowly."

"What do you see, Lissa?"

"I see my beautiful lover's face. I see his hands caressing my sides…, my breasts…, my tummy. Oh! Oh, and my clit. When I look at where we're joined, I see myself splitting to either side as his shaft opens me further and further. Oh, Melody, I wish you could share my pussy so we could both feel our lover entering us at the same time. I want to feel him enter you like he's moving into me."

"Oh, my love! How can you take it so slow? It's agonizing," Melody's voice was broken as she sobbed over the phone.

"Mel, Lissa has her eyes closed and is biting her lower lip. You know how she bites just one corner?" It was the exact same expression Lissa had on her face the first time she invited Melody and me to make love to her on the daybed setting for my painting.

"I love that expression on her face. She looks so innocent and so naughty at the same time. I don't think I can take much more. Tony, I wish I could share your cock so I could feel myself being buried in Lissa's pussy. I want to feel the pulses of come rocketing out of me like you do."

"I'm touching Lissa's thighs, Mel. She's so strong. She's holding all her weight and not letting herself go all the way down. She's so beautiful, Melody."

"I want to kiss you, Lissa—feel your tongue on my lips and my tongue. I want to hold your beautiful breasts against mine and know this is what it is to love a woman. And this is how we love our man." I could hear Melody gasping for breath over the phone and imagined her touching herself, listening to Lissa and me.

"Oh lovers! I'm holding so still, but I don't think I can hold back any longer," I whispered. "Lissa is all the way down on me and I feel her pussy pulsing. Can you come with us, Melody darling?"

The only answer I got was a scream over the phone beside my head and a gasping, "I love you I love you I love you." I couldn't make sense of much more because my hips were up off the bed as I tried to get as much of my body as possible inside Lissa. My thumb vibrated quickly against her clit with the flat of my palm pressing against her tummy above where we were joined, my left hand wrapped around her butt pulling her toward me. She started with a whine—her lips tightly pressed together—but as they opened, an unintelligible siren was raised in one long wail as I roared my orgasm into my lovers.

My lovers. Not just one, but both of them. Even though she was a thousand miles away, Melody was only a heartbeat from where Lissa and I were joined together.

Eleven

I RECEIVED a bronze medal at the awards ceremony Saturday afternoon and an official invitation to The Ektelon National Singles Competition. I had four weeks to heal, train, and pass all my classes.

There was a lot to do. I had final projects in three classes, exams in two. I would have my portfolio review to determine my overall progress for the year. I'd be working out every day. Sam and Lissa had already worked out a rehab schedule for my ankle. Not only did I have to recover, but I needed to maintain my strength and flexibility during the time I couldn't be on the court. The week of finals, I'd be gone to Nationals, so I had to cram four weeks of work into three at school and take my exams the week before. It made me tired just to think about it.

Dad, Sam, and my little cheer squad stayed with me through the day and applauded loudly when I got my medal. Allison was on her way to the airport before I got a chance to thank her, but Bree said she had all of the contact information I would ever need. Sam, Bree, Lissa, and I all boarded the same flight home. I was going to curl up with Lissa and kiss all the way back, but Sam asked if I'd trade seats so they could have a coach's conference. I ended up sitting with Bree. I braced for the interrogation.

"So what's with you and the Ice Queen?" Bree abruptly asked once the plane was off the ground.

"Huh?"

"Didn't you know that's her nickname on the circuit? Allison said she is absolutely cold to everyone. She never attends a party or social event, doesn't accept any dates or invitations, and never says more than a half-dozen words to any competitor. But with you, she's on fire. Anybody can see how she changes when you're in the room. She went to dinner with us last night and was laughing and joking with our fathers. But she wasn't flirting with them. She was flirting with you."

"Lissa didn't flirt with me at dinner."

"I don't think either of you were aware of it. You're so natural together. You ate part of her burrito, for god's sake."

"I was hungry and she had more than she could eat."

"I was sitting on the other side of you with more than half the food on my plate untouched. You didn't try to eat any of it."

"I've known Lissa a lot longer."

"And a lot better, I think. You said you had a girlfriend back at school."

"That's right. See?"

"So what's she think of you and Lissa? Or do you keep it from her better than from everyone else?"

"We're not keeping anything from anybody," I lied unconvincingly.

"You forget that Friday night you had two naked girls making out on your bed like mad and you left to go sleep with your coach," Bree said.

"How'd that go, by the way?" I asked. Maybe changing the subject would help.

"We got along fine, but if you've got visions of hot girl-on-girl action, forget it. I think she'd have gone along with it if I'd pushed and you were there, but the fire kind of died when you left the room."

"Is that why you decided to go through my things and steal my drawings?"

"No. I'm really sorry about that. We didn't think it would do any harm. Allison saw that you'd left your sketchbook and started telling me about the drawings you were doing. When she showed me the sketch you did of her, I was so jealous I almost bit her. But then I saw that it wasn't just her. You made everyone you drew look good. That's why we posted the pictures."

"Well, no real harm done, I guess. I just like to draw."

"I'll bet you've drawn Lissa, too, haven't you." *If only she knew!* "Tony, I'm not blind and I won't betray your secrets unless you are being a real jerk to someone I care about. I just want to know how it works—and if I stand a chance of being included."

"Bree, we've only known each other for like five days. In that time, you held onto my arm like you were afraid I'd vanish, you showed up at my competition a thousand miles away, you got naked in my hotel room, and…"

"… and I washed your smelly jock strap." All right. It was pretty ridiculous and we both started laughing so hard a flight attendant stopped to offer us a soft drink so we'd quiet down. "A little pushy, aren't I?" she sighed. "Sorry."

"I think we'll be friends, Bree. But don't push anything else. You don't know how complicated life is for me and how moody I can get. Just understand that, even though I'm not ready to share everything about me with you, I'm not trying to hide things from anyone and I'm not going to be a jerk to someone you care about. If I'm lucky, I'm not going to be a jerk to anybody else—whether you care about them or not."

"Okay. But I tell you what. I'm going to have a party in a couple of weeks and I want you to bring all your girlfriends with you."

"Hmmm??"

"The whole posse. I'll sort out who's who on my own."

"You're incorrigible."

"I hope that means irresistibly sweet and sexy."

———◁◆▷———

Lissa and I stepped out through the secure gate area to find our own little welcome home dance in progress. It consisted mostly—okay, entirely—of Melody bouncing up and down and squealing as she ran from one of us to the other and back. Finally, we were all three wrapped in a hug that was undoubtedly the focal point of the whole concourse. At least it was the focal point of the little redhead who was following behind us.

"Aren't you glad to be home, too, Brianna?" I heard Sam's voice and chuckle behind me. We all turned to see Bree just stopped behind us with her mouth hanging open. "I'll just pick up my bag," Sam continued, excusing himself.

"Bree, you remember my *girlfriend*, Melody, don't you?" I introduced casually. Bree's eyes shifted uncomfortably from Melody to Lissa and back.

"Oooo. I remember," Melody squealed. "You're the *really* friendly cheerleader from SCU. Welcome home!" Melody swept a surprised Bree into a hug and turned so she was facing me and I could hear her when she spoke softly in Bree's ear. "You and I have to talk, girlfriend. There are rules around here."

"I don't know what you're talking about," Bree bluffed. "I just went down with my dad to watch the competition." Melody flipped out her cell phone, held it close between the two of them and showed the phone to Bree. The redheaded cheerleader gasped and looked up at me. Her face was about the same color as her hair. "We'll talk later this week, 'kay?" Melody concluded.

Bree nodded her head and squeaked a barely audible, "Please?" It didn't take a rocket scientist to figure out what had just happened. Melody must have shown her the picture I sent on Friday night of Bree and Allison making out naked by my bed.

"It's all right, honey," Melody soothed. "Let's just delete it together, right now. I just wanted you to know that Tony and I don't keep *anything* from each other." She tapped her screen and I saw Bree heave a sigh of relief. Melody quickly held her phone out at arm's length and snapped a new picture of the two of them. "Look!" Melody showed me. "Don't we look like besties already?"

"Come on, Brianna. Let's go," Sam said, returning with a duffle from baggage claim. Bree turned to go with her dad but then turned back to face us, smiling.

"Don't forget to tell *everyone* about the party in two weeks," she said. "See you!"

"You are a wonderful evil genius," I laughed at Melody when Bree and Sam had gone.

"Oh, you should have seen her face when you showed her the picture," Lissa added.

"Yeah. It's probably going to strike her—right about now— that if I had the picture, you must have taken it and it's still on your cell phone. And then she'll figure out—about now—that Lissa probably has it on her phone, too."

"If I promise to have you two back for class Monday morning, can I steal you for the rest of the weekend?" Lissa asked. "I was so turned on last night during our telephone game..."

"My overnight bag is in the car," Melody said. "You'd have to throw me out on the freeway to keep me away."

---◁◆▷---

IT WAS A calm Monday. Surprisingly, I had no difficulty staying awake for Dr. Bychkova's lecture and slide show. I got my paper back, too, and I didn't do badly on it. If I needed to, I could skip the last one now and still be okay. Instead of my racquetball workout Monday afternoon, Lissa took me over to SCU to the sports therapy room. I was introduced to a couple of student trainers and Sam came in to talk about rapid rehabilitation and getting me back on my feet. They put me in hydrotherapy for twenty minutes and then dumped me into an ice bath for another twenty. While I was still shivering, I was wrapped in a thermal blanket and the guy mauled my back with what felt like a sledge hammer for half an hour. Yeah, it was just his hands, but he was really strong. I came out of an hour and a half in the team room feeling better, but exhausted. Lissa came to the dorm with Melody and me after supper and we all snuggled into the big bed in my room together.

I think Melody and Lissa may have fooled around a while, but I was so drained after my therapy that I drifted off to sleep. How sad is that? Two gorgeous naked babes, who I love with all my heart, fool around with each other next to me and I go to sleep! *Sick, man.*

In the morning, Lissa kissed us and headed for work after making me promise to go back to the sports therapy room in the afternoon. I'd be going there every afternoon this week—a fact I noted in my Daytimer.

Melody and I had been sitting in Fundamentals for a little over half an hour Tuesday morning, trying to decide what we were doing for a final project, when I saw the secretary from Dean Peterson's office come into the classroom. She handed something to Doc and after looking at it he said, "Melody Anderson, you are needed in the Dean's office. Please go with Miss Stevenson." Melody looked at me with questions all over her face, but I had no idea what was going on. Class continued, but I was pretty distracted thinking about why Melody would be called to the Dean's office. She was a better student than me, so maybe they were offering her some double degree opportunity, too. It was about forty minutes later that Miss Stevenson came rushing in again. She went straight up to Doc and after a moment he looked up at the class and said, "Class dismissed. I'll see you Thursday. Tony Ames, come with me."

I jammed my books into my bag and barely caught up with Doc halfway down the hall. I was having difficulty keeping up with my gimp ankle, but I managed to keep him in sight as I limped along. He stormed out the front doors and across the street to the administration building. *Oh my god! The mural.* That's all I could think. Could it have been damaged? Were there vandals? As we entered the building we could hear heated voices arguing in the hallway. When we were close enough, the first thing I heard that I could make out was Melody screaming, "I will not!"

We rushed into the hall to see Dean Peterson and two security guards with Melody and a woman who could only be her mother.

"If you ever want to see another cent of my money going into tuition and donations for this college, that pornographic monstrosity will be painted over right now. Give me a brush and I'll do it myself."

"What?" Doc bellowed as we came down the hall. He looked like a bull charging a red cape as he descended on Melody's mother. "How dare you talk about a work of art like that? The Vandals had more respect for Rome than what you suggest. This is a work of beauty and I will stand guard here around the clock to protect it if I must."

"You!" she met Doc's charge head on. This was a formidable woman. "Are you the man who painted a naked picture of my daughter? You've made her a lust-object in front of the entire school. What kind of man treats children like this? You should go to jail. How did you get her to model for this? Did you offer her a better grade? I've heard of men like you. Predators, all of you!"

"Mother! I'm nineteen. I signed a model release and I'm proud to be in this work of art."

"You are a child. I didn't want you to come all the way out here in the first place. You should have stayed home where we could keep an eye on you. You don't know anything about life and what you are doing."

"Madam, you are insulting a young woman and a student of this college," Dean Peterson broke in. "In this state and in all the rest of the United States of America, a person who has reached the age of eighteen is legally an adult, capable of making her own decisions and of executing contracts. And I guarantee you that, if you withdraw your support for your daughter at this institution, I will personally find scholarship funding for her to continue her studies here."

"What kind of school is this? Parents send their children to a small school so that they will be protected, not exposed to abuse and exploitation. I'll sue the entire institution and bring the authorities in to force the removal of this painting."

I'd just decided a few days ago that I had to take control of my life, hadn't I? What does a guy do when his girlfriend is being threatened by her mother? I was angry, but anger was all I could see in this hallway. This could be really bad. I had to change the game plan. I had to do something that would stop this nonsense before irreparable damage was done, either to the mural or to Melody—or even to her mother. I took a step forward and placed myself between Mrs. Anderson and Melody.

"Mrs. Anderson, may I speak with you for a moment?" I asked softly.

"And who are you?"

"I'm the artist who painted this picture." I could see her eyes bulge and I was afraid she might literally explode.

"You exposed my daughter to a student? A boy her own age?"

"Melody and I worked out the details together. No one else in this room can actually even identify that it is her in the painting. I'd just like to talk with you for a minute."

"I'm sure I have nothing to say to you."

"That may be true, ma'am. But if we start out this way and can't try to understand each other, it's going to make the next fifty years really difficult on all of us."

I have to give the woman credit. She stayed on her feet for almost ten seconds.

Twelve

I CAUGHT Mrs. Anderson on her way to the floor and settled her gently. I didn't attempt to revive her. I figured everybody could use the peace and quiet for a minute. I turned her over to Miss Stevenson and while she and one of the security guards tended to Mrs. Anderson, I took the opportunity to wrap Melody in my arms and surreptitiously text Lissa. "Dealing w/ Mel's Mom. Not good. Available for lunch?" I got a message back almost immediately. "Ready in 20 min. Say where." I comforted Melody and whispered to her.

"Do you love me, Melody?" She nodded into my shoulder. "Will you let me help?" Another nod. "Think of a place to have lunch with your mom and text it to Lissa. Can you do that? That's all you have to think about. Don't let anything else upset you. We love you and we will never let anything bad happen to you." She reached up and gave me a quick kiss then turned her back on the action while she got out her phone.

Miss Stevenson was giving Mrs. Anderson a sip of water out of one of Doc's stock of water bottles. I decided that if I was ever going to take control of the game, this was the time. My lover needed me, but she needed her mother, too. I knelt beside Mrs. Anderson and quietly took over from Miss Stevenson. I helped her to her feet.

"I'm sorry this has been so hard on you," I said. "Melody loves you so much; she'd never intentionally do anything to upset you and I guess I stumbled into it with both feet. I hope you'll be able to forgive me." I turned Mrs. Anderson to face Melody. Mel's back was still to us and she was talking on the phone. "Look at her, Mrs. Anderson. You must be so proud to have a daughter like Melody. She's beautiful, kind, smart. She's everything that I love. And I understand why you are upset about the painting." I turned her toward the wall to look at what I'd painted. Every time I looked at it I nearly cried. There was just something about it. But I knew what I had to say.

"There just is no way that I could capture that beauty and kindness with my brush. I really tried. I poured all the love in my heart into that painting, but just looking at her standing there and then looking at the painting, I can see how far short I fell. I'm so sorry I couldn't do better."

Melody's mother was silent, maybe for the first time since she arrived at the college today. I think that for the first time she actually looked at the painting and she began to see what I was seeing.

"It's just so... intimate," she whispered. "It's so hard to see my daughter grow up and not be my little girl any longer. I never wanted to think of her in... that kind of way. I just want to protect her. She is so precious to me."

"We're artists, Mrs. Anderson. That doesn't mean we're libertines. It doesn't mean we don't love. When I caught Melody and Lissa in that pose, I knew what it meant to be in love."

"You caught them? You mean you didn't put them like that?"

"No. We'd just finished making love and I turned and they were there, just like that. It was so beautiful I sketched it right there."

"You were…? Here?"

"Oh, no! Haven't you ever had an experience that was so intense and beautiful that every time you closed your eyes you could see it again? I painted this from memory." I heard a quick intake of breath behind me and had the impression it was Doc. He was the only person that wasn't in my line of sight.

"And my little girl was… with a… woman?"

"*We* are with her and she is with us. You want to meet her, don't you? She's having lunch with us."

"She's very pretty."

"Oh, more than that. She loves Melody like you wouldn't believe. Every time I see them kiss my heart nearly bursts. It just overflows with love and passion."

"Are you a poet, Mr…? I'm afraid I don't even know your name."

"I'm Tony Ames and I'm not a poet. I'm just in love with your daughter, Mrs. Anderson."

"And this other woman?"

"And with Lissa. My dad calls it a *ménage à trois*. Are you familiar with the term? It means a household of three."

"Your parents know about this?"

"We introduced them this past weekend. Melody has been so excited about introducing us to you, but a little frightened about how you'd respond. I'm sorry I spoiled it with this painting."

"It's not… not really awful. You are obviously very talented. But it's… it's… I can't bear to see my daughter in such an intimate setting."

"Parents are never supposed to see their children like this, are they? I think it's a shame. It's not there to titillate or make people uncomfortable, but what parent wouldn't want to know how happy and peaceful her daughter was. We should be able to share that with our parents, don't you think."

"I suppose... I... that makes some sense. You are a very well-spoken young man."

"I can only speak from my heart. My father told me this weekend that when I left for college he and Mom vowed that they would love who I loved and respect the decisions I made in my life. I think that works in every direction, don't you? I love Melody and I vow to love who she loves, and that includes you. There's never really just two people in a relationship, even if they are a couple instead of a *ménage à trois*. There is always your family, the family of your partner, your children, your parents and siblings. It seems that when we fall in love, we isolate ourselves when we should be reaching out to embrace the loves of our loves. Lissa and I love Melody with all our hearts, and we want to love you, too."

I'd tried to keep my voice calm and low key while I talked to Mrs. Anderson, but I wasn't going to mislead her. Talking to my mom and dad this weekend had helped me to see how deep our family ties go. I gradually understood that my depression was causing me to raise barriers between my parents and me when I should have been building bridges. I was determined to start off as right as I could with Melody's family. And Lissa's, too.

"Perhaps we should go to lunch and meet the rest of the family," Mrs. Anderson said softly. "Tony. Will you help me talk to Melody?" I nodded.

"Sweetheart," I said. Melody turned around and looked at me with my arm around her mother. I smiled at her. That was all it took. Melody rushed to us and wrapped her arms around both her mother and me and hugged us fiercely. "Your mom wants to meet Lissa. Where are we going for lunch?"

———◁◆▷———

I WATCHED MELODY and her mom as I hobbled down the street behind them. Lissa and Melody had chosen well. It was still early for lunch at Becky's Café, so there wouldn't be a crowd, and it was just far enough off campus that there wouldn't be many kids there during class break. The food was light and genteel—not too expensive, but not fast-food, either.

Mrs. Anderson had shrunk away from her rage and as soon as she apologized to the Dean, Doc, and Melody, Melody wrapped her in a hug that showed me there was genuine affection between the two. I was afraid for a while that it wasn't going to happen. I couldn't fathom what had really set her off. She just didn't seem like the kind of person to fly off the handle like that, but once she did there was no way to back down. I wondered how I figured out how to defuse the situation and whether it would last when we added Lissa to the mix.

Mother and child is a more explosive relationship than any other, in my book. Maybe Lissa would have insights that would help us out. I didn't remember the battles between my mother and me. Dad told me about them the summer after I graduated from high school. It seemed that when I was around three or four I went through a phase where I'd blow up at anything. Mom was at the end of her patience and between the two of us, we could go from "I love you" to a nuclear explosion in two sentences.

Dad said he was worried that we'd build up long-term resentment for each other and that he had to intervene. But he didn't join our confrontations. As soon as he heard the explosion, he would sweep in on me from wherever he was in the house and get down on the floor at my level and hug me. He'd just keep saying, "I love you, son," over and over until I calmed down. Then he'd turn and do the same thing with Mom. He never criticized us or joined the argument. He never took sides. He just put a different feeling in between us. Mom would wrap me up and say, "I love you," and we'd all calm down. It wasn't long that as soon as I blew up, Mom wouldn't wait for Dad. She'd just wrap me in her arms and say, "I love you."

I guess it worked. I've always felt secure with both Mom and Dad and as I learned to express my feelings better the blow-ups lessened and eventually just stopped altogether. Dad told me the whole story the night I announced my decision to go to PCAD. I knew Mom didn't want me to leave the state, but I was just as bull-headed as ever. Before we had a chance to really discuss it, though, Dad pulled us both into a hug and said, "I love you." Then we all knew it would be okay.

———◁◆▷———

MRS. ANDERSON STOPPED short as she entered the restaurant, looking straight ahead at Lissa. She was frozen in place. I heard her whisper under her breath, "Oh my god. The painting. I thought she…" Lissa looked up from the menu to see us coming in and the smile that she gave us lit up the entire room. Melody rushed to her and gave her a kiss on the lips. It wasn't an erotic, tongue-filled, passionate kiss, but it lingered long enough to make it clear that this was a kiss between lovers, not just a couple of friends meeting for lunch. "No one can be that beautiful," Melody's mom whispered. I didn't wait to correct her, but stepped up to collect my own welcoming kiss.

"Mom, this is my girlfriend, Lissa, and my boyfriend, Tony. Tony, Lissa, this is… Mom," Melody officially introduced us. Lissa stood and held out her hand.

"It's so nice to meet you, Mrs. Anderson." I swear there were tears in both their eyes when Mrs. Anderson took the offered hand and then pulled Lissa in for a hug.

"Please. I'm afraid I've got off on a bad foot. Call me Alexandra." I saw Melody raise an eyebrow at her mom, but she didn't say anything. Alexandra faltered and then turned to embrace me as well. "What am I saying? No one calls me Alexandra. I'm just so new at this. It's… it's… overwhelming. I'm Lexi. I expect you to use the same name my friends do." We sat and Lexi just stared at the three of us. A waitress brought the rest of us menus and we made a production out of looking at them. Lissa recommended a dish and Lexi thankfully put down her menu and said, "That would be lovely." The waitress took our orders and we had an awkward pause in which no one knew what to say.

"Mom, I'm sorry this all came as such a surprise to you. I've been trying to figure out when I could tell you and Dad. We wanted to all be together and not do it over the phone. I know it has to be a shock, but you know me; I never do anything the easy way."

"Oh, Melly, honey. I'm sorry I reacted so poorly. I flew out here to see you. You said there was a painting and I thought I would surprise you and spend a few days while I was… and then the picture… and the boyfriend… and the girlfriend… and your father…"

"Mom, what?"

"Harold's left us, Melly."

"What?" Melody's face was filled with disbelief.

"No. I promised myself I wouldn't do that. It's just so hard. He hasn't left *us*, Melly. He's left *me*. Your father still loves you dearly. Don't ever doubt that. You are his pride and joy. He never wanted to hurt you—or me either, for that matter. But you know your father. We've been slipping away from each other for a long time. This year, without you to hold us together, we just stopped trying. I'm sorry for the way I behaved this morning, for surprising you, for being so awful to your friends. My emotions… it's like going through menopause all over again. I went out of control. Please forgive me, baby."

Melody was stunned and tears were tracking down her cheeks. Lissa was closest and pulled her into an embrace as I raced around the table to catch her on the other side. I saw Melody reach out with her hand and understood instinctively what she wanted. I moved slightly so that I could encircle Lexi, too, and Melody caught her hand.

The three of us were so happy together that watching Melody and her mother suffering was unbearable. Sure, Lexi could say what she wanted about the marriage slipping away over time, but to actually let go of it must be terrible. It sure got me thinking; would Lissa and Melody and I face the same thing one day? Would one of us slip away, or would the others turn their backs on one? It was heavier than I could bear to think about and my own tears were near when the waitress set down our food and then hurried back with fresh glasses of water and napkins for all of us.

Lunch was subdued. We all dried our eyes and ate in relative silence, skirting the issue of the parents' separation. Lexi asked about school and asked Lissa about her job. It seemed she knew some people in the fashion industry in New York and there was a common thread for them to talk about while we all let the news soak in and began erecting protective barriers around the wounded hearts.

After lunch, Lexi said, "I had better go back to the Dean's office and apologize, and collect my bags. I just left them there when I was out of control."

"Dean Peterson is exceptionally understanding," I said. "I know from personal experience. We'll all go together."

"Where are you staying?" Lissa asked.

"I thought I would just check into that little hotel near the campus, but perhaps I should just go back to the airport. It was silly of me to intrude like this."

"Nonsense. Please come to stay with us," Lissa blurted out. Then she clapped a hand over her mouth and looked at Melody with a terrified expression on her face. It wasn't about the invitation; I was sure of that. It took me a second to figure out what had panicked her. I looked at Melody over her mother's head and mouthed, "The kids!" Melody understood and took matters into her own hands.

"Mom, we'd love for you to stay with us. We haven't sorted out all the living arrangements yet, but Lissa has a spare bedroom in her lovely home. There's just a couple of things you'll need to understand before you go there with us."

"I assume you are all sleeping together," Lexi sighed. "If you are truly a *ménage à trois*, then of course you sleep together. Frankly, if I were twenty-five years younger I'd have my hands all over your partners, dear." That got a little chuckle from all of us, but Melody wasn't finished yet.

"You'd have to stand in line," she laughed. "But there is one other little thing you should know about. The children." Lexi's breath caught and I thought for a bit that I'd have to pick her up off the floor again, but she recovered quickly.

"You mean I'm a grandmother?" she exclaimed.

"Well, there's no biological connection. If you're insisting on that, you'll have to wait a long time, I'm afraid. But Lissa's got two little boys who we all adore and I'm sure they'd love to have someone other than Tony read stories to them tonight. His rendition of *Red Fish, Blue Fish* is getting a little old. Are you ready for that?"

"Melly, life is a whole series of things we aren't ready for. I want to be a part of your life. Tony said his father told him something this weekend. Tell me if I don't get it right, Tony. 'I will love who you love and respect the decisions you make in your life.' But I'll always be here when you need me." She looked at me for confirmation. I nodded.

"I left off that last part," I said, "but my dad said that, too. We need our family and friends. I discovered that the hard way this year. Let's go get your bags and go home."

Thirteen

"**I KNOW YOU** wanted to be face-to-face, Mel, but I think you should call your father. Don't let the injury fester, and don't let him find out about us from someone else—especially not your mother," I said when we got to Lissa's house. The boys were still out with Molly, so we had a little time to get Lexi settled before the tornadoes arrived. She decided to lie down for half an hour while she could. That's when I made the suggestion to Melody.

"I don't know if I can. What do I say?"

"Do you love your dad, sweetheart?" Lissa asked. Melody nodded.

"We've always been so close. He paints a little, too, and wanted me to go to art school. I just can't believe…"

"So tell him that you love him. Everything else will follow." We all sat on the big bed and Melody called her father. As soon as he picked up, Melody launched in before he could say anything.

"Daddy, I love you." We couldn't hear his side of the conversation. Lissa and I were content to just be with Melody and support her.

"She's here with us.— Daddy, is this as hard on you as it is on her?— Yeah, I thought so. Is it really twenty-five years?— I just wanted to tell you I love you and that I understand. Well, I don't understand—not completely. But I know you and Mom are adults and that not everything is can be clear to a kid, no matter how old I am." I scooted around behind Melody and let her lean back against me as she talked. Lissa curled up beside her and just petted her hand.

"Daddy, I know there is a lot going on and there never seems to be a right time for anything. But I've got to introduce you to some very important people. I wanted to do this in person, but since Mom is here and has met them, I need to introduce you, too." She put the phone on speaker and held it out in front of her. I heard the shutter click and saw a picture of the three of us curled up on the bed on her cell phone.

"I'm sending you a picture, Daddy. I want you to meet my boyfriend, Tony Ames."

"Boyfriend? I'm so happy for you, baby. It's nice to meet you, Tony."

"Thank you, Mr. Anderson. It's nice to meet you, too."

"I have the picture. You are a nice-looking young man, Tony. Treat my daughter well. Who else is with you? There's another beautiful woman in this picture."

"Daddy, I want you to meet my girlfriend, Lissa."

"Hi, Mr. Anderson. Thank you for the compliment."

"It is well-deserved. Any friend of my daughter is also a friend of mine."

"No, Daddy. Lissa isn't just my friend. She's my *girlfriend*." There was a silence on the phone.

"Then Tony is…?"

"*Our* boyfriend, Daddy."

"Well. That is a bit much. Is your mother there? Put her on the phone, please." His voice had become crisper and decidedly less friendly.

"She's taking a nap right now. It was a pretty emotional morning."

"Is she… okay? I mean with all of this?"

"She's adapting. Will you, Daddy?"

"Right now I want to rush right out there and protect you from… from whatever it is. I'm not happy, Melody. You're too young."

"We all know that we're young and that people change, Daddy. You and Mom have just shown us that. But we're together, in love, and happy. Doesn't that count for something?"

"I'll withhold judgment. I worry about you, especially now… Lissa and Tony, don't hurt my little girl, do you understand?"

"We do," I said. "We hope you will also take that advice. Please, come out for a visit soon."

"I can arrange for you to stay in my house," Lissa continued. "Just give me a couple days' notice." We heard the front door open and Drew and Damon's voices called out as they ran down the hall.

"Oh yeah," Melody laughed. "You have to meet your grandkids."

"Melody!"

"Relax, Dad. We aren't married… yet. But you'll love the boys, believe me. I know you always wanted a boy instead of a frilly little girl," she teased.

"Don't you *ever* think that! I knew I was going to have a daughter the moment I found out your mother was pregnant and I could never have been happier." His voice got softer and I could hear a little teasing slip in. "Still, a boy might have been easier right now." Maybe the guy wasn't as bad as I'd assumed. If he could withhold judgment, so could I.

"Mommy, Meddy, Tony!" Drew and Damon screamed as they piled onto the bed with us. Melody snapped another arms-length photo with all of us crowded together in the picture.

"Here's the whole family, Daddy. I need to go now so I can play. I love you!"

"I love you, too, baby. I love you, too."

———◁◆▷———

DINNER WAS CHINESE carryout and a bottle of white wine. The boys were scrubbed and 'Meddy's Mommy' read *Fox in Sox* to them. There's something strangely unifying about Dr. Seuss. We were all from different parts of the country, but the non-sense rhymes had been an important part of growing up. We got the boys tucked in and the house was quiet once again.

"Tony," Lissa said, "You missed therapy today. We shouldn't let it go any longer." Lexi's head shot up.

"Are you seeing a psychiatrist?"

"Mom!"

"I'm sorry… I mean…" Lissa managed to swallow her wine without choking on it. I'm not sure how she managed.

"Physical therapy," I explained. "Not that I don't need any other kind, but this is for my ankle. I injured it in a racquetball tournament this weekend."

"An athlete artist?"

"Ironic, isn't it, Mom? I spend all of high school dodging the jocks and then I end up with the only student athlete in my entire college. It must have been my destiny." She sighed melodramatically.

"And you got two for one," Lissa laughed. "But I'm serious. We need to get you into the hot tub, do the stretches, and ice before bed."

"Yes, coach," I said as I stood. "Melody and I have classes at nine tomorrow, so I may not see you before I take off, Lexi. You'll stay for a few days, though, won't you?"

"Well, one or two. I don't want to wear out my welcome. Do you need a babysitter while you work, Lissa?"

"Molly will take the boys tomorrow after school. She's my nanny. But you are welcome to either hang out here at the house or come downtown with me. Or if there is someplace you'd like to see, I could drop you off on my way to work. We can talk about it in the morning. Now mister, get to the tub."

I started down the hall with Lissa supporting me in an exaggerated show that just meant she got to have her arm around me. Just before we entered the bedroom I heard Lexi speak to Melody.

"Oh my. How can you compete, Melly? She's just so intensely beautiful."

"It's not a contest, Mom. Come on, I want to show you something downstairs." We passed out of range of hearing them as they went to the lower level—the space where Melody and I had our easels and artwork. Mmm. If Lexi was upset about the painting in the school hallway, I wondered what she'd think after she saw the paintings on my easel downstairs.

Or the one that was on Melody's.

———⊲◆⊳———

THE BEST PART of my physical therapy was that Lissa and I were both naked. Other than that, it pretty much just hurt. The ice was almost unbearable and the heat of the spa was higher than we'd ever had it. I was looking for anything to distract me and Lissa kept pushing my hands away from her breasts and pussy while she worked on me. With good humored laughs, but firmly, anyway. I finally asked, "So how do you think Melly's mom will react to our paintings downstairs? I hope she hasn't started flinging paint around," I said.

"Melly? Don't tell me you're adopting Lexi's pet name for her."

"Naw. It is cute. Personally, though, I like Drew's name better. 'Meddy pway wid me.' 'Meddy, color.' 'Meddy hug me.' Your boy is serious competition for me."

"Well, the way Damon has been hanging all over you, I guess she deserves *some* attention. You've both been wonderful with the boys. Are you sure…? I mean… Isn't it too much for…? Oh shit. I don't know what I mean."

"Lissa, are you asking if our love for you and our willingness to be with you are lessened because you come with two of the greatest kids I've ever met? Are you worried that we'll leave you because we can't handle the boys?" Lissa looked at me and there were tears in her eyes.

"We didn't even tell your parents I have children. I thought Melody's mother would run for the door when she found out. How can you take on so much responsibility? How can I ask you?" I held out my arms and Lissa melted into them. The timer ran out and the jets in the spa went silent. I held her close to my chest and felt her sob quietly.

"We have to correct the situation with my folks," I said. "They need to know. I always thought that I'd someday be a father. It scared the bejeezus out of me. I thought I'd be stuck in a factory someplace trying to earn enough to pay for their shoes and my faceless pregnant wife's doctor bills. Or that I would become a teacher and face rooms full of resentful teens who I forced to draw arcs and lines until one finally showed some talent. My idea of children was that you had to give up your dreams to have them." Lissa quieted in my arms. The bathroom was still warm and steamy from the tub, but it was quiet save for a little splash if I moved my hands.

"Since I met Drew and Damon, I've felt something different. I saw how much of a responsibility kids are. It's hard! But for the first time, I've also seen how much joy there is in our family. It's selfish of me, I suppose, but I know we… you… aren't financially strapped and the boys are well-cared for. That takes away some of the burden I used to feel when I thought about having kids. I still wouldn't go out and start a brood at this age, but having them come along with the women I love is fun. And I know you have something with them I can never have, but I want to be right there with you, as much as you will let me. And I know for a fact that Melody feels the same way because we've talked about it. We love who our love loves, not only for her sake, but because we are a family."

Lissa pulled herself up to kiss me softly, then more passionately. I felt myself stirring beneath the surface of the water where I was pressed against her thigh. She felt my growing tumescence as well and touched me with her fingertips.

"I want us to be a family, Lissa. Do you think my dad knows a word for 'household of five'?"

"I think you just used it." I felt her hand more aggressively on my shaft. "Family."

"Make love with me, Lissa."

"Just a second." She stood and stepped out of the tub, grabbing a towel. I started to get out as well. "Just sit on the edge for a minute." She opened the medicine cabinet and took a small plastic bottle from the shelf. She dried her pussy and handed me the towel. "Dry yourself off." I did as instructed and she poured a dab of gel from the bottle onto her fingertips and smeared it thoroughly around and in her center. Then she used a little more and stroked the length of my shaft. The silky feeling was incredible.

"This is just slightly less water soluble than our natural juices. It's a lubricant that will make it easier to make love in the water." With that she stepped over to straddle me where I sat on the edge of the tub with my feet in the water. She lowered herself onto me and then pulled me toward her until we were able to sit in the water facing each other, enjoying our coupling.

We were quiet in our lovemaking. We've had some pretty intense sessions together and with Melody in the past few weeks. But this time, we just looked at each other as I gently moved her up and down my erection, buoyed near weightlessness by the water. There was a definite difference between the artificial lubrication near her opening and the more natural hot liquid deeper inside, but it was an incredible feeling. I dipped my head and caught her right nipple between my lips and it hardened as I tongued it, eliciting a plaintive moan from her. She leaned forward enough to lick at my right ear and I thought I would come on the spot. We lifted our heads together and kissed again, long and deep and filled with the desire to be one with each other—to find some way to be even closer than we were. I wanted to share her tongue, her eyes, and the very breath that escaped from her lips when I plunged deeply into her.

I ran my hands across her shoulders, her breasts, and her back. I gripped her butt as I lifted her and pushed her back down onto my hardness again and again. Our lips locked together and we each moaned our orgasms quietly and intensely into the other's mouth. We held onto each other and just sat in the cooling water while our breath returned to normal. She kissed me again and then looked into my eyes.

"We've all met your parents and Melody's parents," she said. "I think it's time you both met the boys' father." It was the first time I'd heard her mention Jack Wade not as her ex-husband, but as her sons' father. Somehow that was significant.

WHEN WE WALKED out of the bathroom, Melody had her knees pulled up to her chin, facing away from us in the middle of the bed. Her bare shoulders were shaking with silent sobs. Lissa and I both rushed to her and held her from either side.

"Melody, sweetheart. What is it?" I asked as I spooned against her from the back. She clutched Lissa to her, unable to stop sobbing.

"You… you… must hate me." That was a surprise. What had Lexi told her? Why was she so upset that Lissa and I were in the bath together? It just didn't make sense.

"How could we hate you, love?" Lissa whispered. "What is it?"

"My… my… family. They were so horrid to you. Even when Mom said she accepted us, she still tried to make it look like I was just hanging on to the two of you and that you were just being kind to me."

"She said that?" I growled.

"She talked to Dad when she got up from her nap. He told her it was all her fault. Now she thinks she is a failure as a mother. I yelled at her again. And I called Dad and yelled at him. I'm a terrible person."

"Shhh… shhh. You are not a terrible person, and we love you like crazy. We would never hate you and you aren't a hanger-on."

"Third wheel, Mom said. She said you'd leave as soon as you learned to ride a bicycle."

"That bitch! I'm sorry, Melody, but I'm going to go have a talk with her." I rolled off the bed and stood up.

"Don't leave me, Tony! Please, just stay here with me. Please hold me." I couldn't deny her plea and crawled back in beside her. Inside I was seething. I thought we'd come so far. I was seriously considering whether Lexi might be bipolar. For now, though, Melody needed me here and here was where I'd stay. I'd drive her mother to the airport tomorrow morning and tell her to go away. *Damn, that woman!*

I just kept hold of Melody and had my arm wrapped all the way across Lissa as we lay there and comforted her.

Being in front of Melody and facing her, Lissa had easy access to Melody's face and lips. She gently dried her tears and placed kisses on her nose and eyelids. It almost made me cry to watch her love Mel; it was so beautiful. Soon their lips were together and as they lost themselves in each other, their tongues played and their hands began a timid exploration of each other. Their caresses looked like two feathers touching, they were so light and soothing.

I watched.

I've been around the Internet enough to know that having two girls together is a huge male fantasy. I had it myself and then I became one of the few for whom fantasy became a reality. The reality was so much better. *Oh my god.*

Lissa and Melody had been together without me. Melody and I had been together without Lissa, and Lissa and I had been together without Melody. But whenever we were all three together (and awake) our sexual discovery had included

129

all three of us. The male fantasy pretty much requires him to be involved.

But I'd never been present while Lissa and Melody made love without me. Yes, I was there. Yes I was turned on. I just didn't want to intrude on the incredible connection between my two lovers. So I just lay there—close enough to be brushed by the errant hand or hair—close enough to feel the heat rising from their bodies—close enough to smell their arousal. I watched.

It was beautiful. I saw them give each other what they each wanted to receive. I saw them explore their breasts and pussies, but also their shoulders and backs. I saw their eyes connect and hold. I saw them each sink into the other's awareness so that not only touches, but even thoughts turned erotic.

When Lissa moved over Melody and began kissing her way down our lover's body, Melody didn't fight for equal pleasuring, but simply relaxed and received what Lissa gave her. Receiving without trying to control and give back was something I don't think I'd ever witnessed. Melody didn't try to reverse the roles and go down on Lissa. She just let Lissa give her all the strength and love that she could.

When Lissa had reached Melody's treasure, they grasped each other's hands on the side nearest me and Melody moved them over until they rested on my upturned palm. The three of us were tied together and I could feel the electric jolt when Melody gasped out her climax, then gasped again as Lissa drove her instantly toward another peak. A long, drawn-out syllable of ecstasy accompanied the third orgasm, never loud enough to leave the room, but so intense that it filled every corner.

Melody relaxed back into deep sleep, going limp beneath Lissa's hand. Eventually Lissa stirred and pulled herself up to lie alongside and slightly over Melody, kissing our lover's shoulder before she, too, slipped into sleep.

I pulled the sheet up to cover us. That's when I saw the slight movement near the door. Lexi stood leaning against the frame. She was sobbing silently, looking at the tableau on the bed. The flash of anger that I felt was quelled by the look of utter loss on the woman's face. It was the agony of defeat. I knew it well.

I carefully slid out of bed and wrapped my towel around myself. She didn't move as I approached her, eyes still fixed on the lovers. I put my arm around her shoulders and she leaned into me, tears still streaming down her cheeks.

"I thought he'd take me back if I just brought her home," she whispered so softly I could barely hear her. "What was I thinking? How could I sacrifice her happiness for a false hope? She'll never forgive me."

I didn't know yet if I would ever forgive her, but Melody needed her family. As much as I wanted to hate Lexi and her husband, I wanted them to accept us more.

"You should kiss her goodnight and go to bed now," I said softly.

She looked up at me for confirmation and then went to the bed. She petted Melody's hair softly, careful not to wake her sleeping baby. I watched as Melody whimpered a little and held her mother's hand to her cheek. I don't think she really woke up. Lexi kissed the top of her head and then walked past me. I heard the door to her room close down the hall.

I got in bed behind Lissa, wrapped my arm across both my lovers, and went to sleep.

Fourteen

I **WOKE UP** sometime in the middle of the night. Maybe 'woke up' is too strong a term. I floated up out of sleep far enough to be cognizant of my erection pressed between Lissa's thighs from behind. She floated with me and shifted just enough to guide me into her. For a long time, we drifted in and out of sleep as we made tiny movements, never sure if we were dreaming or awake. A feeling of deep contentment washed over me as I pressed my face against her shoulder and felt her nipple harden against one hand and Melody's against the other. I'm pretty sure I came, but I sank back down into my dreams, still intimately connected with my lover.

When the alarm rang, my eyes snapped open. Melody was closest to the alarm and fumbled with it. My cock was still nestled up between Lissa's nether lips.

"Mmmm," Lissa moaned, wiggling her hips into my stomach. "What a nice way to wake up… and to sleep." Melody, having succeeded in silencing the alarm rolled back toward us.

"Lissa sandwich," she said. She kissed our lover, her hands flitting over both of us. "Oooo. What's this down here?" Her exploring hand found where we were still semi-connected.

"Just leftovers," I said. "I had this most amazing dream and then I woke up to a dream come true."

"Mmm. Let's go back to sleep and all dream it together," Lissa moaned.

"Do we have to go to class today? I'm still exhausted." Melody stretched and sat up. Seeing those beautiful shoulders rise and the line of her arm flowing into her outthrust breasts as she stretched caused a twitch in my cock, but I knew it was just a salute. I reluctantly pulled away from Lissa and sat up. She moaned as she rolled to her back and put an arm around each of us.

"You might get away with cutting, but I've got to stay awake during Art History this morning. And I need to talk to Ms. Brock this afternoon about all the Concepts classes I've missed. She was a little sarcastic Monday about how pleased she was to see me in class."

"And I have to visit the Rosewood store this morning," Lissa said. "We're looking at a new line and I want to go over how the merchandise will fit into our display space."

"Fun! I want to do that," Melody said. She leaned in to kiss each of us. "Do I smell bacon?"

"Mmm. Your mother, unless the boys are cooking," I said. "She must have beaten us to the kitchen this morning." Melody's mood soured a little. We took our turns in the bathroom and wandered out toward the kitchen together. Lexi entertained the boys at the breakfast bar while she cooked at the stove. We all paused to listen. Melody stiffened a little, but Lissa and I hugged her between us. I could feel some of the tension drain out of her.

"My mommy is the best mommy in the whole world," Damon affirmed.

"Really? Who says?" Lexi asked.

"My daddy says so." Lissa was a little startled at that and began to move into the room. I held her back to listen some more.

"Do you know what I think?" Lexi asked. "I think your mommy and daddy have the best boys in the world. Do you want another pancake?"

"Mickey Mouse!" Drew shouted, holding out his plate. We took that as our cue to enter the kitchen.

"Mommy!" the boys called when they saw us. "We didn't wake you up." They were still in their pajamas and had syrup all over their faces.

"No honey, you didn't wake us up. Are you having fun with Mrs. Anderson?"

"Mickey Mouse!" Drew affirmed again.

"Mom, are you making Mickey Mouse pancakes? Can we have some?"

"Of course, dear. Lissa, I hope you don't mind that I commandeered the kitchen. When the boys came out I thought making them breakfast would keep them from disturbing you too early. There's fresh coffee."

"No, of course not. I love it when people are at home in my kitchen. What are Mickey Mouse pancakes?" Lexi showed the three connected pancakes that made a mouse face with blueberries for eyes, nose, and mouth. "How cute!"

"You were up early," I said casually.

"Still on East Coast time, dear," Lexi said pleasantly. "I had a lot to think about this morning." Melody tentatively hugged her mom from behind and we all gathered around the breakfast bar. There weren't enough stools to go around, but it didn't make a difference as we leaned against the counter and drank our coffee. When Lissa announced that it was time for the boys to clean up and get ready for school, Melody jumped at the opportunity to take them to wash their sticky faces and hands. Lissa and I poured another cup of coffee and sat with Lexi.

"Tony, thank you," Lexi started. Lissa raised an eyebrow, but I declined to respond with more than a nod. "Lissa, I don't know how to say I'm sorry in a way that you can believe after my behavior yesterday. I promise I will do my best to make it up to all three of you." She hesitated and I could tell that she'd made a difficult decision. "I don't want to lose my daughter. I don't understand how you can be in the relationship you are. It is so foreign to me. But if you are happy, I don't need to understand. My marriage failed. You three are so beautiful together that I have I have to accept that Melly is okay. I'll do my very best. I won't interfere or try to drive you apart. I'll even..." She had trouble going on. "...even defend you from Harold. I'll try. Just, please let me be part of your lives. I'll do better. I promise I'll do better."

What could I do? I just gave her a hug and said, "I have to get ready for class. I'll be out in a few minutes."

"Would you like to visit one of my stores with me this morning?" Lissa asked. "It will be much better than hanging around the empty house all day."

We would make this work for Melody's sake. Somehow.

———————◄◆►———————

WE MADE IT through the week. Lexi was true to her promise and worked hard at mending her relationship with Melody. She followed Lissa to various stores on Wednesday, went to classes with Melody on Thursday. She met our friends and even sat for a portrait—fully clothed—for our Live Painting class on Friday.

I'd like to say that I painted her with love and affection and that when she looked at the painting she could see herself through eyes that saw all the good in her. I can't. The painting was barely passable. I still harbored too much resentment and anger. Melody's portrait of her mother, however, brought the woman to tears.

I had a light workout on Friday, the first time I was allowed back on the courts. I worked entirely on serves so I wouldn't be running, stopping, and starting frequently. My ankle was feeling much better, but after the workout it was still pretty sore. Lissa sent me straight for the training room at SCU where one of the student trainers worked on me for about an hour and then wrapped my ankle so that I could walk to dinner.

Melody had packed clothes for me to change into before we met for dinner. It was dressier than anything I'd worn since school started. She'd selected a pair of khaki slacks, pale blue oxford shirt and my one and only navy blue blazer. Still, instead of going straight to the restaurant, I caught a lift to my dorm room and changed out of my sneakers and into my brown dress shoes after I dug them out from under the bed and behind my dresser. I was running late, so—feeling like a real adult—I called a cab and was delivered to the restaurant.

Fifteen

CARMINE'S CUCINA is a nice Italian place with a noisy, family-style atmosphere. Jack Wade had taken care of reservations and managed to get us a booth in one of the quieter areas of the bustling restaurant. This was a big deal. Not only were we managing the new and somewhat fragile relationship with Melody's mother, we were adding Lissa's ex into the mix.

Of course, I was late and they were all seated. Melody jumped up from her chair at the end of the booth and planted a hot kiss on me as soon as I approached the table. Lissa slid out of the booth and as soon as my lips were released from Mel, they were captured by Lissa. Then she turned to the table and introduced me.

"Jack, this is our boyfriend, Tony. Tony, this is Damon and Drew's dad, Jack Wade." I noted with pleasure that she didn't introduce him as her ex, but as the boys' dad. Jack and I shook hands. He was about the same age as Melody's mom—maybe just a little older. He was a nice-looking guy, reasonably fit, but definitely showing his age. There was nothing either antagonistic or overly friendly about his handshake. It was the completely neutral grasp that you might expect of two business men being introduced. I didn't know if I'd ever be friends with him, but something in me definitely wanted to earn his respect.

"I feel like I already know you," Jack said. "Last week the boys went on and on about how I should read Dr. Seuss like Tony does. I may have to take lessons. How long does this Dr. Seuss phase last, anyway?"

"I'm not sure," I answered with a grin. "I think I'd outgrown mine by the time I was in high school, though." Jack groaned.

Apparently, I'd arrived at the restaurant too late to order. Food just started arriving along with a bottle of wine. The waitress looked skeptically at me as she was placing the wine glasses on the table. I waved her off. "I'm in training."

"I'm the designated driver," Lissa jumped in. "None for me, thanks."

"Oh come on," Melody said looking at the waitress. "Do I look like I'm old enough to drink? Just serve the old folks."

Our waitress laughed and thanked us for making her job easier. She was cute. Her dark brown hair was curly, chin length, and was streaked with blonde so she almost looked like a tiger. I couldn't make out the exact shade of brown but with the pink restaurant lighting and dancing candlelight on our table, I knew exactly how I'd paint the highlights in her dark tresses. She wore a scoop neck top that hung open dangerously when she leaned over the table to explain the gnocchi, cuttlefish and bean salad, and beet salad with pistachios. I felt a little pinch on my thigh and looked over at Lissa who was grinning at me mischievously. Busted. A guy can't get away with anything. But the food was great!

"What are you studying, Melody?" Jack asked as we helped ourselves to the food.

"My first year has been taken up with general studio classes and 2D design," Melody responded. "If all goes well, when I have my portfolio review I'll be admitted to the textile design program."

"Another member of the fashion industry," Jack laughed looking at Lissa.

"Sort of," Melody agreed. "I love dressing Lissa up like a doll. But it's really the fabric side that I'm interested in and it goes way beyond wearable fashion. I wanted to bring my loom out, but you can't carry it on the plane. A little big."

"Well, maybe you can shop for one around here. I could keep an eye out if you'd like," Jack offered.

"That would be wonderful!"

"How about you, Jack," Lexi asked. "What do you do for a living?"

"I'm happy to say that I'm officially retired. I do a little consulting on the side, primarily working with the parents of young talent when they come into the agency. These kids come in—sometimes just eight years old—and it's amazing what their parents expect. We get everything from people who only want their kids to work during spring break to those who expect their kids to be the primary wage-earner for the family. The agency calls me in about once a month to meet with difficult parents and explain to them what the life is really like."

"What about the boys," I asked. "Do you have plans for them to start modeling?"

"Not if I can help it," Lissa broke in.

"I think Lissa and I agree that we won't intentionally introduce the boys to modeling. I won't object if they come to me and ask if they can try it, but offhand I'd say they have too many other interests. You are more likely to influence Damon into becoming an artist."

"Me?" Jack just nodded. I felt a hand on each leg stroking me gently and looked at each of my lovers. I smiled to let them know I was okay. Actually, I *was* okay. The thought that I could influence Damon and Drew's lives was a new concept to me and I found that it wasn't at all unpleasant.

"Speaking of talent, have you seen the mural painting that Tony did of our girls?" Lexi asked. I was a little worried about where this could lead. She'd been trying hard not to be critical of us, even though I knew she was fighting her nature at times. But since the meltdown on Tuesday, we hadn't actually spoken of the painting. It was the subtlety in her question, though, that impressed me. With just a few words, Lexi had positioned herself and Jack as parents with Lissa and Melody as "their girls." I wasn't sure how this was going to play out. But Jack really surprised me.

"Lissa gave me a tour of it this morning. She said I needed to know what I was getting into tonight." I had no idea that Jack had seen the painting. "I don't know much about art, but…"

"…you know what you like?" Melody and I concluded for him. We'd heard the old adage so frequently that we automatically supplied the end. Fortunately, everyone at the table laughed.

"Well, yes; there is that. But I also know enough to listen to what people who do know art have to say about it. I went back to look at it again this afternoon after Lissa went to the gym."

"You did?" Lissa asked. "Why?"

"I took Ben Bowers with me." My heart started beating in my throat. Ben Bowers is the art critic for the *Times*. That might not seem like much in a town like ours, but he was highly respected in art circles and had written critiques of work all over the world. He could be a scathing critic or a word from him could make the career of a new artist. *Damn!* Why had he brought an art critic to see a piece of student art? I grabbed both Lissa's and Melody's hands under the table and squeezed so tightly that they used their other hands to pry my fingers loose a little.

"Okay." I finally managed to breathe out and gasped another lungful of air in. "I guess I'm ready. What did he say?" Jack smiled at me.

"I asked him to write it down for me so I could get the words right," Jack said. He reached in his pocket and unfolded a typewritten page to read from. "*They should take a saw and cut this piece out of the wall on which it was painted.*" Jack looked up at me and smiled. I was stunned. The best work I'd ever done and the first critic who sees it hates it. But Jack smiled and it wasn't the vindictive smile that I expected. "I'm playing with you, Tony. Relax."

"He didn't say that?"

"Oh yes, he did. But I read it out of context. Let me give you the full notice. *The mural as a whole is a lovely collage of scenes. The flow from focal point to focal point is the obvious work of a master. But one vignette stands out from the rest. This segment is the only thing people who visit will see as the rest of the forty-foot-long mural fades away by comparison. They should take a saw and cut this piece out of the wall on which it was painted. It deserves a place of prominence in a museum without the clutter that surrounds it. Obviously painted by a different artist than the rest of the mural, we can look forward to seeing future works from a student whose art will far surpass that of his master.* I think that puts it into better perspective, don't you?"

I was speechless. Melody's mouth was hanging open and as Lissa reached to pull me into a hug she shot a chiding look at Jack. It was Lexi who broke the silence.

"Does this Ben Bowers know what he's talking about?"

"Ben and I go way back," Jack said. "He's one of the foremost art critics in the country. He writes a column for the *Times* on the local art scene, but his critiques of major exhibitions around the world are syndicated in over 100 different newspapers and magazines in a dozen languages. Praise from Ben is something you can take to the bank."

"My!" Lexi beamed at me. "I'm so proud of you, Tony." My relief at what Jack and Ben had said outweighed my surprise at Lexi's outburst. It didn't go unnoticed by Melody, though, who beamed at her mother and hugged me again.

The rest of the meal went by pleasantly in typical slow Italian fashion. An hour and a half later we were sipping cappuccinos as a small band started gathering on the restaurant's little stage. Tables nearby were moved back into more crowded spaces as the dinner service ended and people started coming in for drinks and music. They started off with some big band numbers, reset for the piano, drum, and bass trio. I could tell this was going to be a great end to the evening as the dance floor started to fill. Jack asked Lexi if she would dance with him and she blushed as she accepted his offered hand and he led her away from our table.

"You could dance, I don't mind," Lissa said to Melody and me. Melody looked at me expectantly.

"I'd love to," I said.

"I hear a but…?"

"You have a very nice one."

"Come on."

"No. The truth is practice was kind of hard on my ankle and I'd rather not dance on it," I confessed. "I took a cab to get over here instead of walking. But why don't you two dance?"

"I don't see any other girl-girl couples on the dance floor," Lissa said.

"Maybe you'll inspire something." I leaned in conspiratorially and they leaned in next to me as I whispered. "I saw a girl-girl couple last night and it certainly inspired me. They were the two sexiest women I've ever seen and they were dancing in bed right next to me. I'd be happy if I could wake up every day of my life to that sight. But right now, I'd love it if my lovers danced together vertically as well." I got kissed from both sides and slid out of my seat to let Lissa out as she and Melody headed for the dance floor. They were exquisite. Melody was just over chin height to Lissa, the same as she was to me. Her dark mahogany tresses formed a counterpoint to Lissa's short golden hair. They had a little difficulty sorting out who was going to lead, but Lissa guided Melody effortlessly. I was going to have to take some dance lessons. This looked like too much fun.

My view was temporarily blocked by another nice view in the form of our waitress leaning over the table to put two drinks down. The lights were low, but I could make out every detail of her bright red bra. She stayed there a little longer than strictly necessary as she made herself busy straightening the coffee condiments on the table. Then she slowly straightened and smiled at me.

"I thought sure one of those two was your girlfriend. Does their absence mean you are unattached?" She was just flirting. *Just flirting.*

"No, afraid not. It just means I've got a bruised ankle and can't dance right now."

"Oh, too bad. So which one is it?"

"Which ankle?"

"Which one is your girlfriend? They're both smokin' hot."

"Both of them."

"Yeah, both of them. But which one is *it*?"

"Both of them," I repeated. I looked her in the eye and smiled. The color was rising in her face and her nicely displayed upper chest was nearing the color of her still-exposed bra. She took a couple of shallow breaths.

"Oh shit! Oops… sorry! I just… wow! That just isn't something I see in here every day. Wow. Uh… your… dad, I guess… ordered the drinks, by the way. I wasn't trying to put the make on you. Well, not *just* trying to anyway. I think I'll go take a break now. Flag down one of the other girls if you need anything else." She backed up, almost tripped over the table behind her, and scurried to the bar. I looked around the dance floor again and when I spotted the girls, Lexi was dancing with them to a light jazz piece that gave the three lots of room to move as the crowd of dancers thinned. Suddenly Jack was sliding into the booth opposite me.

"Wooo! Lexi is a wild thing when she cuts loose." He pushed one of the glasses across the table to me. "Courvoisier. I want to have a drink with you and this is a small one. Just sip." I took a sip and it burned my mouth and my throat, warming me all the way to my stomach. After I got over the initial shock, the aftertaste in my mouth was surprisingly pleasant. "Tony, I want to give you a word of advice, man to man. And before you jump to conclusions, it isn't about Lissa. I'm scarcely in a position to give advice on unusual pairings—or tri-ings, if that's a word. Lissa's a grown woman, no matter how cute and young-looking she is. She wouldn't choose partners lightly."

"What were you suggesting, then?" I asked.

"Bob promised me that he wouldn't print the critique that I read you. He wrote it in a personal letter of recommendation. You can have it, but I wouldn't show it around until you really need it. He'll review the piece before the school's open house exhibition in two weeks, but it won't picture you as outshining your teachers. It will be a good review, but I talked to Bob about how some of his words could actually create hard feelings and make your situation harder rather than easier."

"Thank you. I was a little worried about how Dr. Henredon would respond. His work is really good."

"Yes, it is. But Tony, no matter how Bob phrases his praise, people coming to visit the piece will be able to see the talent. You are going to need an agent. Don't accept any position, job, contract, or offer until you have a certified agent look it over and negotiate on your behalf. I've been in the business for a lot of years and I've seen young talent come in after having signed an agreement when it's too late for an agent to help. There are a lot of people out there willing to exploit you if you let them."

"You want to represent me?"

"No. Even if I weren't retired, my expertise is in modeling, not art. I can introduce you to a couple of possible agents if you'd like, but it won't be me and it won't be anyone from the agency I work with. I won't have any potential conflict of interest in helping you. You're welcome to talk to me, but I hope you'll talk to me as a friend and as an influence on my children. I'm offering you that friendship whether things work out long term for you and Lissa and Melody or not." Jack looked me straight in the eye when he spoke. He was, indeed, talking man to man with me. There was no condescension, jealousy, or manipulation in what he was saying. I nodded.

"Thank you, Jack. Lissa has spoken to me about your sense of honor and the fact that you are a caring person. I appreciate it. I know you said you weren't giving me advice about Lissa, but would you mind answering a question for me?"

"Shoot. I'll answer if I can without betraying any confidences."

"Why did you and Lissa split? I get the impression that it wasn't entirely her idea." Jack smiled and took another sip of his cognac. He glanced over to the dance floor where the three women were moving off toward the restrooms.

"It was mostly my idea, in fact," Jack said. "Lissa is fiercely loyal to those she loves. I've known her since she was a baby. I'm her uncle, though not related by blood. Marrying her would have been tricky if we'd attempted to do it in the U.S. After Drew was born I was afraid she would shrink into her little world as a housewife and mother and in twenty years—about the time I was ready to die—she'd realize what a terrible mistake she'd made and I would die alone. I looked in the mirror and for the first time I let myself see my reflection openly and honestly. I'm more than thirty years her senior and those years will seem like more and more as time accelerates me into old age. Divorcing Lissa was terribly selfish of me. It was the only way I could think that she would continue to love and care for me into old age as her uncle, father of her children, and one-time guardian. I won't die alone."

"You still love her, don't you?"

"With all my heart, Tony. So much so that you'll never have to worry about me interfering." We raised our glasses in a silent toast to each other and polished off the cognac just as the ladies returned to our table. They sat, but began gathering up their things, preparing to leave.

"So, what did you decide?" Lissa asked.

"Huh? Did we decide something? About what?"

"The waitress, silly," Melody piled on. "We're dying to know if we have number nine to add to the future Tony models list." I laughed. All right. If they were going to tease…

"Oh, it was nothing really. She wanted to know if you two were exclusive with each other or if you dated around. I gave her your phone numbers."

"You didn't!" I laughed. Melody pinched my chin between her finger and thumb and scowled, leaning close to me.

"Just wait till we get you home, young man." She grinned impishly.

"Melody," Jack said. "I've just asked Lexi to take in the sights of the city by night with me. Do you mind if I borrow her for a couple of hours?" Melody looked at her mother in surprise. Lexi refused to meet her eyes.

"Well, okay, but what's your curfew, Ms. Anderson?" We all noticed that Melody had changed her title. For all her embarrassment, however, Lexi responded in kind.

"Would one be okay? It's a special night, after all. I'm leaving for Boston tomorrow afternoon." She sounded like I imagined Melody would have when she was dating in high school. Melody looked at Lissa and me as if to get our agreement. Lissa couldn't stop giggling. Melody looked at her phone to check the time. It was just after ten-thirty.

"Well, since it *is* a special occasion, I think we could extend curfew till two. Most of the clubs don't close till then. But don't you go getting drunk and miss your flight tomorrow." By this time, we were all laughing and headed for the door. Our waitress was still at the bar, so I tugged Lissa and Melody to a stop in front of her and then leaned in. I spoke just loudly enough so that the two could hear me.

"They say they'd consider adding you if you can pass the tests," I said. Both Melody and Lissa punched my arm. The waitress, however, grabbed a beer coaster and scribbled on it quickly and handed it to me. On the back it said, "Wendy" and her phone number. There was a heart drawn next to it. She waved as we left.

Jack and Lexi said goodnight as they headed to Jack's car. As soon as we were out of earshot, both Melody and Lissa started tugging at me.

"That was so cruel," Lissa said. "That poor girl thinks we're… What *does* she think we are?"

"You know you are going to have to call her now," Melody added. "And I'm going to write the script. You are so going to get punished when we get home."

"I have some ideas on that matter," Lissa added. "And we should safely have three hours before your mother catches us again."

"Again?"

"She saw us Tuesday night," Lissa said. "I saw her out of the corner of my eye and then Tony was so sweet with her. She kissed you goodnight and then left." Melody touched her cheek and I remembered Lexi cradling her cheek in her hand as she fell asleep.

"I thought that was a dream," Melody said. "A beautiful, wonderful dream."

Sixteen

It didn't seem like I'd been punished until I had to get up to go to Pilates on Saturday morning. Just getting out of bed was punishment enough, but Lissa pointed at the keys to the car and said to be back by noon, then she and Melody snuggled back into bed. There was no sign of Lexi. I assumed she'd returned last night. Molly had stayed with the kids at Jack's house. This morning it was just me making coffee and eating toast. I got to the club in plenty of time and then the Pilates instructor worked my ass off manipulating muscles that I hadn't worked in a week. I was still sore from my light workout Friday afternoon and in spite of feeling more energized, the Pilates hadn't eased my pain. I dragged myself into the steam room and dozed in the heat and moisture.

I got showered, rewrapped my ankle, and took another anti-inflammatory. I looked almost human when I returned to pick up everyone for the trip to the airport. That's more than I could say for the three women who dragged themselves out to the car. After an emotional goodbye at the airport security line, Lexi was gone and I looked forward to life returning to normal—whatever that was.

⸺◅◆▻⸺

It was a crazy hectic week. We got the official invitation to Bree's party on Monday. She was going all out. "*Welcome Pacific*

College of the Arts and Design student and Intercollegiate National Racquetball competitor Tony Ames to Seattle Cascades University at 8:00 p.m. at Coach Sam Jacobson's house. Refreshments will be served, but no alcohol or drugs will be allowed on the premises. Attire is semiformal (cocktail dresses, jackets and ties). A special contest will be held to guess the identity of Tony's girlfriend. Film clips and sketches from the USAR Intercollegiate National Championships in which Tony was the bronze medalist will be on display."

"Holy shit! What's with the big deal?" I asked as we looked over the invite. "I thought Bree was just having a party for a few friends. This looks serious."

"Maybe I shouldn't go," Lissa said. "I'm not sure I want to be in a contest to identify Tony's girlfriend, especially if Bree is running it."

"It's okay, darling," Melody said. "I worked out the details with Bree before she sent out the invites. There won't be any danger of our relationship being exposed. I talked to Coach Jacobson as well."

"I don't want my girlfriend selected by a vote," I said. "I'm pretty happy with the ones I've got."

"They're not voting, they're guessing. It will be fun."

"If you say so."

———◁◆▷———

MY PRELIMINARY PORTFOLIO review did not go well.

Art History and Art Orientation would have final exams. Fundamentals, Concepts, and Figure Painting had final projects. I was supposed to be able to show my progress through my portfolio and then the review committee would determine if I should continue on my current course of study or if adjustments should be made. They would be the final arbiters of my grades. My committee comprised Professor McIntyre, Dr. Henredon, and Abe Ardmore, the chairman of the Studio Arts Department. My preliminary review was with my advisor, Professor McIntyre. Hers was the only class for which my final project was complete as she had agreed to take my concept sketches and finished work on the mural as my final painting.

"Tony, your portfolio doesn't show anywhere near the progress you've made this year. Your presentations for Fundamentals are unspectacular. You are lacking significant examples from Visual Concepts, and you have nothing at all from your Art Orientation class. Frankly, if this were your final review, we'd reduce all your grades except Life Drawing/Painting a letter grade across the board."

"A letter grade?" I was stunned. My final review was scheduled for next week since I'd be missing the last week of school for National Singles. "What do I need to do?" I was near panic already. Losing a letter would mean that I positively wouldn't make a B average for the semester.

"You need to complete your portfolio in a professional presentation format. It needs to show progress from your earliest work in each class to your latest work. You should have been maintaining this portfolio all through the year, Tony. This is sloppy work. Just in case you've mislaid it, here are the criteria that were handed out during orientation *last fall*."

"I'll fix it," I said, taking the sheet. How did this become such a big deal? Damn, I hate this fucking school.

"Oh, and the student exhibition opens a week from Friday. With the splash you made with the mural, you should really have more than one piece in it. Your choice. But we need all the pieces you'll be exhibiting by end of day Wednesday."

"Thank you." I left her office feeling stunned. I knew I needed to add more to my portfolio, but I didn't expect her to come down so hard on me. Shit, if I lost a letter grade in every class there's no way I'd qualify for my scholarship. I headed back to my room to start gathering stuff up.

"DAMN IT, MELODY. Stop it! This is serious. If I don't finish this and get it right I won't even be able to come back next year." I had piles of material spread out all over the bed and was redoing one of my portrait sketches. It was an early sketch and wasn't anywhere near my best work.

"I don't get it. You've done all the work. Just put it in the portfolio."

"Do you know how much they count portfolio review?"

"Yeah. Thirty percent of grade. So what did she say?"

"She said my Fundamentals presentations were so-so, I was missing significant pieces from Concepts, and didn't have anything from Art Orientation. If it was my final review they'd knock a letter grade off everything except Life Drawing/ Painting." There, that ought to let her know how serious this was. I let it sink in with a smirk. I wasn't expecting the blow-up that was about to happen.

"So why the fuck are you redrawing a sketch for Life Drawing from last semester?"

"I saw it and it needed work."

"It didn't need work. Nothing in Life Drawing/Painting needs work. You've got that class nailed. Why the fuck aren't you pulling out your Art Orientation stuff and your Concepts stuff? Geez, Tony! Wake up!"

"And I suppose you've got everything in perfect order." I yelled back at her.

"Yes. There's nothing spectacular in my portfolio like there is in yours, but it shows the progress I've made this year. It's not that big a deal."

"Maybe for you it isn't. You're a perfect student. I'm a crappy student. I can't do the work with you trying to have sex with me all the time."

"Fine. I'm catching a bus out to Lissa's. You can just sit here and screw yourself for all I care. Call if you ever get your head out of your ass."

--------⊲◆⊳--------

I SPENT TWO painfully lonely nights alone in my dorm room with my portfolio spread out all over everyplace. I let the final paper for Art History go. I'd have to survive on what I'd done. It wasn't in the portfolio review.

I called Lissa and Melody a couple of hours after she left and apologized to both of them.

"For what?" Melody asked.

"For being a general ass," I said.

"Not too general," she responded.

"Okay. Then for being a specific ass. I'm sorry."

They forgave me, but we agreed that I needed the time to focus on school and they couldn't help but be a distraction. We'd all get back together Friday. Melody sat with me in Fundamentals on Thursday and we kissed at lunch and made up. It was all I could do to not beg her to come back to our room.

I went to the Concepts lab and Ms. Brock just waved me over to where the projects had been set during the semester.

"I wondered when you'd finally show up to do your portfolio photos. Your projects are over there somewhere."

I found them and did a series of digital photos from the earliest project to the latest—the sculpture that I'd done out of clay. It was a little damaged, but it didn't take long to fix the sags and get it back in order. I sorted through the photos on my computer and loaded the best on a thumb drive to take to Kinko's and have printed on photo paper.

My most recent presentations for Fundamentals actually weren't bad. They certainly showed that I'd progressed in my understanding of the assignments and in my presentation skills. I just hadn't put them in the portfolio yet, so I spent a late night at the library fighting for time on the color printer to pump out the selected presentations at thirty cents a page.

Art Orientation was the toughest. I'd considered the work in that class to be pretty much throw-away stuff. It was hardly more than doodles. I went searching through sketchbooks and the papers stacked on my desk until I had a pretty fair collection. I organized them from worst to best, hoping that no one would question what the chronological order was. I had no idea.

By Friday, my portfolio was about as good as it was going to get. It was hard to believe that every student had to go through portfolio review in art, juries in music, or performance in dance and theater. You could tell in the hallways that everyone was uptight. I saw a couple of kids come out of professors' offices in tears. Probably getting the same message I had. Yeah, we were all adults, capable of managing our own lives, but when you were faced with a professor ripping you a new one, you were just a kid.

I breathed a sigh of relief when we all sat down for lunch on Friday after Life Painting. Topic of discussion: What was everyone wearing to the party Saturday night? I'd listened to arrangements to borrow shoes, dresses, or makeup from each other and the merits of going braless or using an underwire shelf bra under a strapless dress. I excused myself to go to my Friday workout.

It was the first time I'd seen Lissa all week and my whole day improved the minute I saw her. We stole a couple of minutes to make out before we got on the court. I had to adjust myself in my shorts before I could serve. All of a sudden, going without sex for a couple days seemed like an eternity.

"I'll be so glad to have you in our bed tonight," Lissa whispered in my ear. "I can't satisfy that girl all by myself!" We laughed and started my first real scrimmage since my injury. It felt good. I worked up a sweat and my ankle was feeling strong.

Lissa cut it short because she didn't want to risk reinjury. I headed over to SCU to use the sports therapy room. I had a pretty good routine over there now and I'd met a bunch of guys in different sports. It seemed like the baseball guys were all in as bad shape as me. The trainers were working on arms and backs and I saw both pitchers with icepacks on their shoulders. I finally got my turn in the hydrotherapy bath and was just relaxing when someone splashed water in my face. I spluttered and looked up to see Bree and Sonia standing on either side of me.

"Hey! What are you two doing in here? This is the guys' locker room."

"This is a sports therapy room. It's coed. You'd better not be naked in there," Bree laughed trying to look through the bubbles in the tub. Thankfully, I wasn't, but I wasn't keen on her trying to find out, either.

"No. You just surprised me. I forgot this isn't the club. Everything is separate over there. So what brings you here? Need therapy?"

"Why? Do you want to massage my sore muscles, Tony?" Bree asked.

"Bree, behave. We just came over to make sure you remembered the party," Sonia supplied.

"I couldn't forget it. It's all the girls have been talking about. By the way, which *is* better if you are wearing a strapless dress— underwire shelf bra or braless?"

"I know which I'd do," Bree said. "But if you wanted to find out, you'd have to go exploring." She pushed her chest forward over the edge of the tub. Not to be outdone Sonia did the same thing on the other side.

"What do you think? Braless?" she asked.

"Um… I'm not that good a judge."

"Well, you're only using your eyes, dummy." They both wiggled a little more and I was really blushing, not to mention stretching my trunks in the bath.

"We have so much fun planned for tomorrow night," Bree went on. "We're going to see how many ways we can embarrass Tony."

"Great. I think I'll stay home and watch the Fishing Channel."

"What? Golf too fast for you?" Bree kidded. "If you don't show up tomorrow—on time—the entire football squad is going to hunt you down and drag you there. And getting physical with them is nowhere near as much fun as getting physical with us."

"Girlfriend," I said weakly. "Remember? Girlfriend."

"Just make sure you bring them all. We'll even have a few extras to choose from just to make sure you have a good selection."

Great. I had five dates for the party Saturday night already. There was no way I was going to get there on time.

Seventeen

S ATURDAY MORNING, after Pilates, I was delegated to pick up Sandra, Amy, and Kate and then *ordered* to drive all five girls to the mall for a beauty treatment. Yeah, I make it sound like I was really put upon, but just having those five in the car with me… Well, the temperature was rising. The teasing kept me red in the face.

When we got to the mall, Lissa sent me to her store and told me to ask for Rose. Rose would dress me. I was not to ask about prices since the purchase was going on Lissa's employee account and Rose knew the limits. I would not be allowed out of the house tonight unless every item of clothing on my body was new. Well… they would let me wear my good shoes as long as they were freshly polished. I dropped them off at the mall's shoeshine stand to have a professional job done.

When Rose was done with me, I went to QuickCuts and got my hair trimmed. The gal who cut my hair talked nonstop and wanted to know all about my date tonight, where I was going, and who I was taking. When I told her that I actually had five dates for a big party tonight she almost shaved my head.

Accidentally, of course.

Instead, she called one of the guys who worked there over and told him I needed special treatment. That made me nervous, but this guy was more of a traditional barber than a hair dresser and he wrapped a hot towel around my face and then proceeded to give me a shave.

"Howard, he has five dates for a party tonight."

"So, you want me to give you a shave or just slit your throat now?" he asked.

He actually used one of those straight razors you see in gangster movies just before somebody gets their throat slashed. I didn't breathe for twenty minutes. The result, though, was that my face was baby smooth and felt pleasantly tingly. I left a big tip for the two of them.

After four interminable hours at the mall, I was hungry, cranky, and loaded down with boxes of clothes for both me and the girls, including a new pair of slacks, a sport coat, and my shoes. The jacket was a deep maroon and was actually a pretty good match for the SCU school color. The shirt, tie, slacks, underwear, and socks were all chosen to match "the ensemble," as Rose kept referring to it. I even picked up a new pair of black loafers to go with the gray slacks.

Back home, I fixed a sandwich as girls in various stages of dress and undress ran from bathroom to bedroom to bedroom to bathroom as they got ready for the evening. Eventually, they all moved into the master bedroom to do makeup and put their dresses on. I was told to use the guest bath to shower and dress. I'd been waiting in the living room for forty minutes wishing Drew and Damon were there to read to when I was told to get ready to meet my dates. Well, I had a little surprise for them as well thanks to my collusion with Lissa. Only she knew what everyone was wearing and she'd stocked the refrigerator with flowers to match each girl's dress.

It was worth the wait.

———◁◆▷———

KATE CAME OUT first. I might not have mentioned how exotically beautiful Kate is. She hides it at school wearing bib overalls and a t-shirt with her hair pulled back in a ponytail. She's a couple inches shorter than me, which would make her taller than everyone else but Lissa. She wore a purple dress—her favorite color—cut about four inches above the knee. Her open toed heels raised her to eye-level with me and showed off her purple toenail polish. I was used to seeing her hair pulled back, but it was piled high on her head in a ballet dancer's bun that highlighted her facial features. I'd never asked Kate what her ethnic background was. Her surname is English or German, I think, but the vision in front of me was anything but. Having her hair piled on top of her head accentuated her long bare neck—and shoulders—and back—and cleavage… *Damn!* She couldn't have cut that dress any lower and been legal in most states.

I'd never seen her legs before. I mean naked. I mean in a skirt. *Shit!* She was wearing high heels and her bare legs were… awesome!

"God, Kate! You're gorgeous!" I couldn't think of anything else to say, though I was still just staring at her. She walked up to me like a model on a runway and then turned to walk back by the fireplace and stood facing me. Then she opened a piece of paper and read.

"Your dates this evening will arrive in order of seniority, newest member of the posse first to first member of the posse last. We've dressed for the occasion. Purple is for passion, royalty, bravery. It is the color I have chosen for our first date. You may kiss me now, but don't mess up my lipstick… too much." Kate was blushing and I was guessing that she hadn't read what Melody had written before she was sent out to face me. However, I wasn't going to pass up this opportunity. I stepped in front of her and looked into her deep brown eyes.

"Kate, I am honored that you would consent to be my date this evening." Melody had written the script for me, as well, and I'd taken the time to memorize it. I surprised Kate and pulled a flower from behind my back. The purple orchid accented her dress and makeup perfectly. I tried not to embarrass either Kate or myself as I pinned the corsage onto the limited fabric that was available, but she didn't seem to mind the backs of my fingers pressed against the soft flesh of her left breast.

"Decided braless was the right choice?" I asked with a bit of a smirk.

"I don't own one," she answered. Well, that confirmed that. I wanted to leave my fingers where they were, but I decided I'd better move on.

I leaned in to kiss her softly and she held her lips against mine without moving away. They were soft and slightly open and I fought the urge to press between them with my tongue. When I pulled back, she stayed in the same position with her eyes closed and the exposed portion of her chest rising and falling deeply. When it was apparent that I wasn't coming in for a second helping, she straightened with a sigh and looked into my eyes, smiling. She was going to be hard to resist. In fact, I wasn't sure I wanted to. A month ago I'd hardly noticed her. Tonight, I couldn't take my eyes off her.

She turned away from me and I saw a little bell on the mantel. She took it down and rang it and then moved aside.

Amy walked in. *Damn, she cleans up nice.* She was wearing her version of the LBD—Little Black Dress. It was cut directly from the choker collar down beneath her armpits, leaving her shoulders bare. Her long, dark brown hair fell straight to the middle of her back and her brown eyes were lined darkly. She had impossibly long eyelashes. The dress was skintight down to the middle of her thighs and then flared out in a ruffled edge. In a way that only Amy could pull off, the finishing touch was black patent leather army boots. She paraded into the living room, sashayed up to me, paused, executed a perfect turn, and walked away from me to stand in front of the fireplace and face me. She, too, unfolded a sheet of paper and proceeded to read.

"Black is the darkness of your soul, the mystery hidden within, the place where the sun doesn't shine." She stopped reading and looked back down the hall. "Geez, Melody! Did you really make me say that? I'll kill you!" I heard giggles down the hall. She turned back and read through the rest of her script silently, determining whether she was going to read it out loud. Apparently, the rest wasn't so bad, but as she read, she adlibbed. "It's the color I've chosen for our first [and probably last] date. I'm your second date tonight [since all the rest of them have already undressed in front of you]. You may kiss your date [but keep your damned tongue in your own mouth]." She puckered up her lips tightly, closed her eyes, and thrust her face forward. She yelped when I touched her chin and her eyes shot open.

"Amy, I am honored that you would consent to be my date this evening." When I showed Amy the red sweetheart rose that I had for her, though, her whole attitude softened. It was a little awkward pinning the flower on because I'm right handed and in order to hold the flower in place over her heart I had to pin it with my left hand. I was extremely conscious of the fact that I was pressing against her left breast as I struggled to get the flower pinned on. There was a little color rising beneath Amy's skin.

"Uh… you know I'm a lesbian, don't you?" she said when I'd finished. I nodded.

"Yeah. Me, too. Girls only. Doesn't stop me from appreciating your… um… beauty," I said.

She slammed her lips against mine and pulled my face hard against her with her left hand. I kept my tongue to myself, though I was sure I felt hers brush my lips. When we separated, I wiped my lips, checking for traces of lipstick and bruises. Amy reached to the mantel and rang the bell, then moved over to stand beside Kate. In spite of the fact that she's got almost no butt, she managed to swing it pretty enticingly. I turned in time to see Sandra coming down the hall from the bedroom.

The strawberry blonde's dress was fire engine red. It had a scoop neck over a generously cut bodice. The skirt was full, but was pulled up on the left side and tucked into its belt so it was below her knee on the right and upper thigh on the left. Her hair was done to match the dress, all swept up off her neck on the left and hanging below her shoulder on the right. Sandra has lots of curves—most of them in the right places—and she pulled off sexy to the max. When she swings her hips, you'd better duck. She marched up to me, looked me in the eyes, and licked her lips. Then she spun around and walked back to the fireplace. I was wondering when the girls had practiced all this runway stuff and decided they must have waited until I was in the shower. Lissa had to have coached them on their model walk. They acted like professionals. Sandra opened her note and started reading in a dramatic voice.

"I'm your third date tonight and I'm red. Red is for fire, lust, and emergency vehicles. [So if your heart stops, I'm your paramedic.]" She grinned toward the hallway. "I've chosen red for our first [Mmm, let's call it second…] date. I'm girl number three tonight and you may now lay one on me." I was pretty sure that wasn't what the end of the message said. I approached her and she closed her eyes and opened her mouth, tilting her head toward me. There was nothing demure about this offer.

"Are you going to kiss me or eat me?" I asked. Her eyes popped open and she started to pout, then she saw the pink carnation in my hand. It brought a quick smile to her lips and she thrust out her chest for me to pin the flower on. The scoop neckline made it easy to get a grip on the fabric and insert the pin through her corsage. "You opted for a bra, I see," I chuckled.

"Honey, these babies don't go anywhere without support."

"Oh, I don't know about that," I said. While her eyes shifted to Kate and Amy, I leaned into her and gave her a nice soft kiss.

"Hmm," she sighed. "I hope that's not the only kiss I get tonight."

"I hear the whole football team will be at the party, so I wouldn't worry if I were you." She slapped my face, but did it so lightly that it was just a tap, then turned for the bell and walked over to join Kate and Amy. I turned to face the hallway and watch a goddess approach.

Lissa's cocktail dress… I could hardly see it for looking at her eyes. It was a cream tunic that flowed as she walked and clung to her curves when she stopped. In her spike heels, she was easily four inches taller than me and her bearing was so regal that I couldn't help myself. I knelt on one knee and bowed my head to her, my script forgotten. No matter how she might have instructed the other girls on how to move like a model, Lissa walked in owning the place. Well, she did own the place, but… *Fuck!*

The dress wrapped up over her left shoulder and plunged halfway to her waist after it crossed her right breast. I wanted to stop her right there and paint the diaphanous folds the way they draped and clung to her body. She stopped before me and held out her hand. I took it and placed a kiss on the back of her fingers. She pulled me to a standing position and then without waiting for a speech, just bent her head and kissed me.

Really kissed me.

When she stood away from me, parts of my body were following her. She stood at the fireplace and faced me, but without reading anything she rang the bell and looked toward the hall.

Another goddess appeared.

Melody's dress was a perfect match for Lissa's, but in a teal that accented the dark mahogany tones of her hair. The fabric swished around her and if her walk was not as professional as Lissa's, the brightness of her smile made it unnoticeable. I knelt again. She came to me and I kissed her fingers as I had kissed Lissa's and Melody pulled me up into an embrace. I realized that she was wearing a flat sandal that emphasized the difference in their heights. Melody drew me to her and the kiss she gave me sent chills down my spine. When she pulled away from me, she whispered, "I love you," and went to join Lissa. Instead of standing next to each other to say their lines, though, my two girlfriends turned and gave a kiss to each other that was every bit as steamy as the ones they had given me. There was more than one gasp from my left where Kate, Amy, and Sandra were standing. The two girls parted and turned toward me.

"We're your last date tonight," they said together.

"Cream is the color of my skin, the texture of silk, the warmth of flesh," Lissa whispered, just loud enough to be heard by everyone in the room. "I've chosen to wear cream on my gazillionth date with Tony and Melody."

"Teal is the color of my lovers' eyes," Melody said. "Its depth knows no limit like the love we share. I've chosen to wear teal on my gazillion-and-oneth date with Tony and Lissa." I had tears in my eyes as I stepped toward them. In one hand I had a simple sprig of baby's breath to pin on Lissa. In the other hand the blue bell flowers of freesia for Melody. I pinned on Lissa's flower and then Melody's, noting with satisfaction that both had chosen the braless look—and feel.

"Melody and Lissa, I am honored each time you consent to be with me. I love you both."

We moved forward together and all three kissed. This time I know all three of the other girls gasped. It was probably a first for any of them to see.

"I feel like I'm a bridesmaid at a wedding," Kate said.

"Ah, but you're dancing with the groom tonight, sweetheart," I said. "Let's go to the party before Bree sends the football team after me."

Eighteen

"**READY-DOWN. HUT!**" Five very large linemen stepped forward as if to crush me when I walked through the door at Bree and Sam's house. Before they could take another step, five extraordinarily beautiful young women stepped in front of me. The football players came to such an abrupt halt that one actually fell over backward.

"Now that's what I call an impenetrable line," Sam laughed from nearby. "Welcome to Seattle Cascades University, Tony!" The line scrambled back to their feet and stepped forward to offer their arms and escort the ladies to the welcome table. Obviously Bree had set up the guys for exactly this purpose. She and Sonia approached and each grabbed an arm and led me into the main room of the house where music was playing and people were dancing. There must have been 100 people there. As we were walking in, I saw that each girl had a card with a number on it and they made a big show of displaying it to everyone we passed.

"What's with the numbers?" I asked.

"All the girls have numbers. That's how the boys will vote to determine who Tony's girlfriend is. We're just walking through and campaigning. The guys took your dates to get their numbers. I'm betting none of them get a single vote."

"That's not fair," I said. "No one here knows them."

"Don't worry," Sonia added, "as soon as they are seen with you, someone will put two and two together and they'll figure out the girls they don't know are the ones that came with you."

"By the way, you already know I'm an all-natural redhead because you saw the evidence in Tempe. But did you notice the halo tattoo I've got on the inside of my left thigh? I just love it when you kiss it."

"Bree!" I was a little surprised at hearing this little detail.

"Take notes, honey," she said. "You need to remember what every girl says or you'll give away the truth."

"You know how I love it from behind," joined in Sonia. "But there's one place only my boyfriend gets to go." I was shocked. I'd never done any of that before. I didn't know what to say. "You'd better remember what we tell you," Sonia whispered in my ear. Then she licked it!

"Oh Tony, you're here!" A perky Asian girl about as big as my left thumb jumped up and kissed my cheek, deftly shouldering Bree out of the way. "I was so worried you wouldn't get here," she continued, holding her card up for people to see. At about that time, Sonia was dislodged from my other arm and a drop-dead gorgeous black girl who towered over me took my arm and planted a wet kiss on my left cheek.

"Oh baby! Thank god you finally got here. These jocks have been hitting on me all night. Let's hit the dance floor and show them how you please your baby." I noticed they were both holding their cards up as we walked toward the dance floor.

"If I'm your boyfriend, I should at least know your names," I said quietly.

"I'm Rachel," said the little Asian girl. "I'm a gymnast, but since we don't have a gymnastics squad at SCU, I play with the cheerleaders. I can bend over backward and look out between my own legs. I'm so flexible you can put me in just about any position you want." She giggled. I was beginning to get the message. This was going to be a fun night.

"My name's almost the same as yours," said the girl on my left. "I'm Tonya, women's basketball. I'm tall enough that I don't have to stand on a phone book to do you standing up." I laughed as all three of us made it to the dance floor. We started rocking out, but it didn't take long before two more girls cut in on Rachel and Tonya who both kissed me again soundly before they parted. Inside of an hour, I'd danced with at least twenty girls. I was thankful that there was no alcohol at this party because I'd never have remembered half of what they told me. Each girl carefully gave me only one important "fact" about herself, usually having a sexual innuendo or promise attached to it.

My five dates each got a minute with me, too, and they each included one sexual innuendo. "You're a country boy, Tony. Don't you love riding horses? For me, going bareback is the only way to do it." Kate said the line so casually and straight that I turned and stared at her. Then she blushed and kissed me quickly on the lips. I noticed she didn't stop holding her card out, no matter how embarrassed she got.

"Only one thing I can tell you, honey," Sandra said. "Remember how big my nipples are? I've got something between my legs that's about the same size." Sandra moved my hand down onto her butt with the same hand that her number was held in. The girl was amazing.

"I can lick my nose with my tongue," Amy said to me. "You know what that's good for, don't you?" I choked on the coke I was drinking.

169

"You know, Amy, I hope you win, tonight. I think you are the only girl here I feel safe with."

"Hey! I'm a lesbian; I'm not dead. I'd swallow your cock whole if it meant I could get into Melody's panties."

I was with Amy and Lissa together—a situation I think they contrived—when Lissa leaned in and whispered in my ear, "Just tell them you know how to melt the Ice Queen." I laughed to hear her use the nickname that people called her on the circuit. "Besides," she continued, "it's true."

A few minutes later, Melody bit my ear and then said, "Just remember, I posed naked for you and it's my ass that decorates the admin building hall." She kissed me hard on the lips. She grinned and winked at me while she held her card up for people to see.

I'D NOTICED THAT the guys at the party hardly ever spoke to me, but everywhere I looked, several were watching me as they moved from girl to girl. It was around 10:30 p.m. when I was herded into Coach Jacobson's office. All the guys who could fit in the room were in there and I was pushed down into the desk chair. Then Tim Kost, the basketball captain, started with the questions.

"So Tony, about your girlfriend, uh… what's her name?" He made like he was going to tell me something significant, but it was obvious that he wanted me to give a name.

"Which one?" I asked back. All the guys groaned.

"So I saw her out back with Deke," one of the football line said. "I wasn't that close, but she was leaning over the porch railing and he looked like he was having some kind of seizure." The guy who spoke made an obscene movement with his hips. I laughed.

"Oh man. Sonia does like it from behind. But I don't mind. There's certain depths only her boyfriend gets to plumb."

Then the questions started flying. The guys had all talked to each of the girls to find out what their secret was and would toss out a situation, ask a question, or name a girl. I had to give out the correct bit of information that showed I was intimately familiar with the girl. I suspected that nine-tenths of everything I heard that night was made up, but every once in a while, someone would make a buzzer sound to indicate that he knew different than I did about the girl in question and she would be eliminated. I thought I did pretty well. My mouth was dry, though, and I needed a Coke before I could answer another question. Bree yelled from the doorway that time was up and everybody had to cast their votes. I escaped and made my way to the refreshment table in time to get a few shrimp off a Costco tray and some kind of skewered thing with a spicy sauce. It was the first time I'd managed to get to the food since I got there.

Now that was odd. All evening long there had been one or two women hanging off of me. Now there weren't any near. They were around, sure, but no one was paying any attention to me. I could breathe. I looked around nervously, though, trying to spot each of my actual dates and especially my girlfriends. Sandra was out dancing with two huge linemen who were competing for her undivided attention. Amy was near a window and Tonya was towering over her and leaning in rather intimately. Amy didn't seem to mind at all. Kate was with Tim and looked like she was having fun. Lissa was talking with Sam as if she was one of the "adults" at the party and talking to the kids was beneath her. It took me a while to spot Melody. She was being blocked by a really good looking dude who was definitely in her personal space. I finally placed the face. He was one of the pitchers I'd seen with an icepack on his shoulder. Melody looked uncomfortable. When the guy bent down to kiss her, I broke a land speed record moving toward them. Tim was a step ahead of me, though and before the sound of Melody's slap died, Tim was between them. He spoke quietly to the guy and waved me away. The dude threw up his hands in disgust and marched away. Tim came over to talk to me and I noticed that Melody had headed toward the bathroom with Kate.

"He's a jerk," Tim said flatly. "Don't worry, though. There's a few of us in the know and we've been watching out for your dates. Sorry I didn't get there quicker."

"Hey, thanks for stepping in. I guess I'd have blown the contest if I'd tipped everybody off that Melody is my girlfriend."

"Hey, I didn't know that! I should go change my vote," Tim laughed. "Only I think it's too late. Here comes Bree with the hermetically sealed envelope."

I heard a coach's whistle blast out and everybody turned to look at Sam. Bree stepped up beside him and called me over to join her.

"Okay, everybody's dying to know who Tony's girlfriend is," Bree announced. "Well, here I am." She kissed me. Mercifully, she kept it brief, but still… "Okay, okay. This isn't about who Tony's girlfriend *really* is, but about who you all *think* she is. So the results are right here in this envelope and the winner gets to be Tony's date for the rest of the party." She made a big show of opening the envelope and blowing on it like they do on the Oscars. She pulled the slip out of the envelope and held it up. She scowled. "This can't be right. It says number seventy-one. Sonia, do we have a number seventy-one here?"

"No way, baby," Sonia called back. "There's only forty-three girls here according to our official log."

"Well that sucks. Who stuffed the ballot box with seventy-ones?"

"I did," said a sultry voice across the room. A tall, lean, and totally stacked brunette in a floor-length, low-cut evening gown glided across the floor holding up a ridiculously large 71 in front of her face. I joined in the laughter figuring this must be two midgets doing a clown act or something. Then the number moved and I realized what I was seeing.

"Allison? What are you doing here?"

"Tony!" She rushed to me and definitely planted a hot kiss on me, pushing those bodacious boobs into my chest. She pulled back and started in on her spiel. "Oh Tony, after that night in Tempe, I haven't been able to think of anything but you. I couldn't eat. I couldn't sleep. I just had to come back to you, darling. I'm through with Arnold! I promise I'll never leave you again."

"It looks like we've got a winner," Bree shouted. "Folks, Allison Perkins of Kansas State University, Intercollegiate Women's Racquetball competitor. Tony, it looks like we've found your girlfriend."

About the time Allison had said she was through with Arnold I'd recovered enough to realize this was an elaborate joke and that suddenly all attention was off of the five women I brought with me to the party. I couldn't help myself. I hugged Allison and told her how happy I was to see her.

"WHAT'S NEXT?" ALLISON asked as people left. It was close to midnight and the party was breaking up. People had been leaving steadily since the big reveal. It was time for me to take my dates home.

"Slumber party!" Bree squealed.

"I think that's my cue to take my ladies home," I laughed. "We'll see you tomorrow, though, right Allison?" There were a lot of looks from girl to girl before anyone answered.

"Yeah. You'll see me, I think," Allison grinned. There seemed to be an awful lot of laughter at some secret joke.

"Late lunch," Melody said, still giggling. "See you all… um… later."

The party had been a blast. I'd had a limitless supply of beautiful women hanging on me all night long, each plying me with a sexy secret. Then true to the contest rules, Allison had become my special date for the rest of the party and we'd had a blast dancing and telling people about the sketches of the tournament that were displayed near the TV. Frankly, I was horny as hell. I couldn't get my crew home quickly enough and get my two girlfriends into bed.

Was I surprised!

Nineteen

ABOUT TEN MINUTES after we got in the door, while I was still trying to tactfully suggest that Lissa loan her car to Kate so the others could return to the dorms, Bree pulled into the drive and three more squealing girls came running into the house. I looked at Bree, Sonia, and Allison.

"What are you guys doing here?" I asked. Okay, it was after midnight and I was a little slow on the uptake.

"We told you," Bree said. "Slumber party."

"Here?" It was clear that I'd been left out of the planning for this entire evening.

"Everything's downstairs, girls," Lissa said.

As everyone was trooping downstairs I heard someone say, "Truth or Dare and there's only one boy in the room!" I stopped at the top of the stairs and looked down, not sure if I wanted to descend into this pit of pheromones. I felt hands on my arms pulling me back from the brink. Melody and Lissa guided me back toward the bedroom.

"Yes, we are going to party," Melody said.

"And yes, you are invited," Lissa joined, "but it's not what you think."

"Well, for that matter it might not be what they think either," Melody laughed. "We haven't arranged an orgy, Tony. There's only four tits and two pussies you get to play with in this house tonight."

"As long as they're the ones in this room, that's all I want," I said. Melody and Lissa both kissed me and started getting undressed. I hurried to get out of my clothes and into bed, only to see the girls putting pajamas on.

"We can't go to a slumber party naked," Melody said. "At least not at the beginning."

"Come on, you," Lissa said. "Get your PJs on."

"I don't have any pajamas."

"Sweats," Lissa said. "It's only for a little while and then we'll come back up. Watching you at that party with all those girls fawning over you got me all worked up."

"Me too," Melody chimed in. "I almost regret inviting everybody over. Come on. Let's go down and have a glass of wine before they drink it all."

I followed Lissa and Melody downstairs in time to see all the rest of the girls gathered around the corner I used as a studio. My daybed and drapes were still set up and there were several of my sketches and paintings tacked to the walls. On the other side of the room, Melody's studio was set up and an equal number of her sketches and paintings were posted.

"That's it! That's it!" I heard Sandra squeal in the crowd and saw a camera flash go off. "That's just the pose in the painting."

I edged into the group with Lissa and Melody and looked at the daybed setting. Kate was stretched out on the bed in a very good imitation of the pose I'd painted in the mural. *God!* She was beautiful in a little pajama shirt that buttoned up the front and shorty pants. I'd seen her legs for the first time earlier in the evening when she wore her party dress, but what she was exposing here was all new territory. A camera flashed again and Kate saw us standing with everyone around.

"Do me next, Tony?" Kate husked. I wondered how many glasses of wine she'd had already.

"Oh you know me, Kate," I said ignoring her double entendre. "I only paint nudes."

Never in a hundred years would I have anticipated what quiet, demure, shy Kate did next. She sat up and pulled the curtains over her legs. Then, moving only her right hand, she calmly unbuttoned her pajama top and let it fall off her shoulders to the bed behind her. *Oh my fucking god!* I knew Kate was a beautiful and exotic looking girl, but she captured something in that pose being partially exposed that I hadn't even considered before. There was a casual seduction in the way she looked over her shoulder at me that just stopped me cold. She was uncovered from the waist up with the drapery caught around her elbows.

I felt a hand in the middle of my back pushing me forward and someone shoved my sketchbook and graphite into my hand. I sank down on the floor right there and started to draw. Kate's hair was falling out of the dancer's bun she wore to the party and it hung over her eyes. I didn't realize how long her almost-black hair was. The purple polish on her nails just screamed out at me as her left hand was draped off the back of the cushions she leaned against. The one partially exposed breast was enough to make me want to see the rest of her. She had a slightly oval areola and small nipple that was hard and prominent perched on a perfectly rounded breast that faded in a smooth arc to her tummy. There was a natural path from the valley of her breasts, down across her sternum and plunging into the darkness of her navel. It continued in fine dark hair until it disappeared beneath the waistband of her shorts.

I whispered, "Wait. Don't move," as I got up to rearrange my drapes, taking the opportunity to look more closely at her. I pulled more fabric down until it created great waves of material all around her, being careful not to let it occlude the shape that I'd already laid in.

I didn't want to stop and Kate's eyes never left mine. I kept filling in more detail when I returned to my seat on the floor. The concave where her pelvis stood out from her thin frame. The folds of the fabric piled around her. The individual strands of her hair. The depth of her eyes. The nonchalant smile. I took as long as possible, just so I could continue to stare at this beautiful creature. Eventually, though, I had to say it was finished and stood up.

Kate snatched her pajama shirt and suddenly turned beet red as she buttoned up her shirt.

"I can't believe I just did that," she whispered. "Oh my god. I can't believe it."

"Yeah, that's right where I lost my virginity, too," Melody said taking the drawing to Kate. "Well, I didn't exactly lose it. I sort of wrapped it in a bow and made a present out of it." The girls laughed.

"Yeah," I said. "Only without the bow."

"Me next, Tony."

"Me! I want a picture."

"No it's my turn."

I couldn't keep track of who was talking, but apparently they thought I was going to sketch everyone tonight. No way!

"I'm not a fucking factory, ladies," I called out . "That pose just happened to be right. I can't manufacture those one after another. Believe me, I've got nothing against seeing each and every one of you naked in my studio, but I can't do any more tonight. I haven't even had a glass of wine yet."

There were generally disappointed noises, but someone handed me a glass of wine and Bree said, "How about a fun little slumber party game before poor worn out Tony has to go to bed?"

My sense of foreboding skyrocketed.

———————⋖◆⋗———————

"ALL RIGHT," LISSA said. Several very sexy games had been suggested. "First of all, Tony, relax. Melody and I have completely agreed on this game, so all you have to do is enjoy it."

"You see," Melody said, "all our friends here are lonely and a little scared of the dark. We're all going to be down here in this big room all by ourselves tonight and we just want a little kiss goodnight."

"You wouldn't deny us a goodnight kiss, would you?" Bree asked. "I mean here we are, all in our jammies, ready to be tucked into bed and we just want one little kiss."

"Each," Sonia hurriedly added. "Think of poor Allison, Tony. She came all the way out here from Kansas to see you. You wouldn't make her go to bed without a goodnight kiss, would you?"

"And you practically made love to Kate for the past half-hour," Amy said. "But you haven't even kissed her. Just one little goodnight kiss. Please, Tony?"

I could see that I was going to be bombarded like this until I gave in and since Melody and Lissa said they'd agreed, who was I to deny these poor girls a goodnight kiss? It's not like it was unappealing.

"Okay," I said. "One little goodnight kiss."

"Each," repeated Sonia.

"Each," I agreed.

"Oh. There's just one thing, Tony," Lissa said. She stepped up to me and held out a black scarf. "You get to be blindfolded. Your hands have to stay behind your back. And you have to guess who just kissed you after each kiss."

Oh. *Oh crap!* I thought I'd just give a little friendly peck and be done, but this was going to be difficult. Lissa moved behind me and tied the blindfold on my face. *Dang!* She was good at this and I couldn't see a thing.

"Okay, girls. Line up. No talking and once you've had your kiss, get back in the line where you were. Oh yes. And the bell. Where's the bell?" Someone rang the bell I'd heard several times earlier in the evening. "There's a strict time limit," Lissa continued. "No longer than one minute per kiss."

A minute? As in sixty seconds? That was never long enough with Lissa or Melody, for sure, but you could do some serious damn kissing in a minute. I wasn't going to get away with a peck on the cheek.

"Okay. Hands behind your back, Tony. You can only use your mouth. Ready, girls?"

I stood there silently for what could have been an eternity but was probably ten seconds. Then I felt a presence closing in on me before I felt lips on my lips. It started softly, but there was a tongue probing at my mouth in no time and as I opened my mouth a bit to respond, I was nearly devoured. There was almost no lip involved in this kiss at all. It was all wide open mouth and tongue probing as deeply into my mouth as it could reach and enticing me to follow it. The kiss was so active that I was getting tired by the time the bell rang and she pulled away.

I shifted my weight around a little because I could tell I was becoming aroused.

Ah hell. They had to know I was going to get aroused doing this. I was keeping my hands behind my back and if they all wanted to look at my hard-on, I wasn't going to stop them.

"Who was it?"

"Um… that would be Sandra. Yeah. Most definitely Sandra."

"Aww!" I heard from my left. "I knew I should have stood on a chair!" Everybody laughed.

"Okay, next," Lissa said.

There was no hesitation or osculatory foreplay with this kiss. The girl walked up to me, put both hands on the side of my head to position it where she wanted it and mashed her lips against mine. Her tongue probed my mouth in quick darting motions that led me on a chase around both our oral cavities. On top of that, she'd moved in close enough that her chest was mashed against mine and I was sure she could feel my cock pressed into her thigh. She kissed with a single-minded determination that blew my socks off. It wasn't like it was loving, or wanton. It was pure, raw oral satisfaction. When the bell rang I was gasping for breath.

"Damn!" There was a lot of laughter. "I guess… I think that was… maybe Allison?" There were a few titters, but no one was letting the cat out of the bag. "Could I have a drink of water?" I asked. A moment later I had a cold bottle of water in my hands and took a long drink. That last kiss pretty much sucked all the fluid out of my body. After I'd cleansed my palate, I set the bottle down and returned to my receiving position with my hands behind my back.

The next kiss was tender and playful. There were soft lips and plenty of tongue. But there were also teeth, nipping at my tongue and lips. There was a moment when my lower lip was sucked into her lips and pulled out before she let go and returned to a passionate and intense lip lock. This wasn't a kiss, it was foreplay. Just before the bell, she ground her pelvis into my cock and I thought I heard a whimper through the kiss.

There was no doubt in my mind whatsoever. As she pulled away from me I whispered, "I love you, Lissa." Then I announced to the room, "That was definitely Lissa."

There was another round of "awww" and "oh that's so sweet." Hmm. No one seemed surprised that I'd know Lissa's kiss that well. Had we told everyone here? Well, maybe they had. There was no way eight girls would be here for a sleepover and not know the three of us were together. I took another quick drink and got ready for round four.

The next girl was like an instant replay, right down to the whimper at the end of the kiss and the crotch grind against my cock. *Shit!* Did they do that on purpose? Would Lissa come through the line twice? No that had to be against the rules, or there was no point in the game. But, damn! Now what was I going to do. I started going through the list in my head in order of height. If you put Sandra at the shortest end and Lissa at the tallest, where did this girl fit? Well, definitely at the tall end. So who else was at that end? There'd be Lissa, Allison, Kate, and Amy. On the short end going up, Sandra, Melody, Bree, and Sonia.

Damn it! Had I misidentified Lissa? Then I thought of Kate, mimicking Lissa's position on the daybed while I sketched her. Kate. That had to be it.

"Kate," I said at last. There was silence. Before I knew it my head was being pulled down into another sensuous kiss.

I'd never considered before just how incredible kissing was. Oh, I loved it, no question about that. But how often do you get a chance to compare and contrast the kisses of eight different women in a row? This kiss made me smile. It was just soft and dreamy and sensuous. The tongue play wasn't aggressive or hungry, but a natural extension of the lips. I just wanted to live in this kiss and I was really disappointed when I heard the bell.

"I love you, Melody," I called after the girl. That brought a round of laughter, but there were no comments. I grabbed a drink and awaited the next round.

The next kiss was tentative—almost shy. I felt like a fifteen-year-old at a school dance. I was painfully aware of my erection and was trying not to bump it into her. Her first taste of my lips was soft and hesitant. She pulled away as if tasting the feeling to see if she liked it. The next was a little firmer, but still that underlying current of explore and remember. There was the tiniest lick across my lips. Instead of pushing my tongue out to meet her, I just let my lips part a little to give her access. She seemed to like that and pressed forward, but before we got too engaged, the bell rang. My heart was beating a thousand times a minute. Geez! I did not want that kiss to end. I was standing there thinking that next time we'd have more time. Then I realized I had to put a name to the kiss. There were only Sonia, Bree, and Amy left. Amy would sure never kiss like that. I just had a feeling that Bree wouldn't be so hesitant and this girl felt a little taller than the short redhead. It had to be...

"Sonia?" I said at last. God, I hoped it was Sonia.

The next lips that found mine were dry. They were soft, but there was no indication that she was interested in anything more than a little peck. This had to be Amy. I decided to have a little fun and quickly ran my tongue across her lips. She jumped back with a little squeak and then stepped away. I chuckled.

"Sorry, Amy," I said with a chuckle. That got a good laugh.

Well, that only left one more girl—Bree. I decided that here I was blindfolded and couldn't be held accountable for my actions, so I might as well just enjoy this last kiss. And boy did I!

It was a confident kiss. This girl knew what she wanted and was determined to get it. Her lips were passionate. There was no hesitancy in mashing her tits against my chest or grinding her pussy against my erection. Her arms went around my neck and her tongue came into my mouth. It swept across my teeth between my gums and my upper lip in a move I instantly recognized. *Oh my god! I made a mistake.* A big one. I had to break off the kiss myself because I was about to come in my sweats. I was pretty sure there was already a wet spot on the front from all the pre I'd been leaking since the second kiss, but this was seriously dangerous.

"Mel…?"

I was gasping and couldn't catch my breath. I didn't even try to guess. I just stripped off the blindfold and stared into Melody's eyes. Before she could say anything, I pulled her to me and kissed her again. By the time I let her go, she was gasping for breath as well.

"Don't think I'm *ever* going to forgive you for that, mister," she growled in false ire. "If you had called out 'Bree' after that kiss you'd have slept alone tonight. You just might anyway." I pulled her to me in a hug.

"I love you, darling. I don't know how I got fooled."

"Well, that wasn't the only one."

I looked at the lineup. Each girl was holding a sheet of paper with a name on it in the order that I'd identified them. But only two of the names were with the right girl. I was correct with Sandra, but was blown away by the fact that Amy was standing next to her with a sign that said "Allison."

"That kiss was you?" I shrieked. She grinned.

"What? You thought lesbians couldn't kiss?"

"I am seriously considering converting," I laughed. I looked down the line to Sonia who was holding up Amy's name. "You were, so…"

"Um…I kinda have a boyfriend," Sonia said. "I don't think he'd be too happy if I was French kissing another guy. It was nice, though."

I was relieved to see that I'd guessed Lissa right. If I'd screwed up both my girlfriends, I would have to leave in shame. Of course, it was Bree who had kissed me with such tender passion that I thought it was Melody. What surprised me most, though was that it was Allison who had so carefully mimicked Lissa and that soft tentative kiss that made me want to go on forever was… Kate. She was still looking into my eyes as if I'd never stopped drawing her. *Oh my god.*

"Okay, girls. Tony kissed everyone goodnight, now he has to go to bed," Melody said.

"Hey, aren't you coming?" I asked.

"Not yet," Melody said with a twinkle in her eye. "Lissa and I promised the girls a bedtime story, and believe me you don't want to stay for this one." I had a feeling I was going to be embarrassed again.

"Go on to bed, darling," Lissa whispered as she kissed my cheek. "We'll be up soon."

I did as instructed—brushed my teeth, drank about a gallon of water, and slipped naked into our bed. I was thinking about all the different, wonderful kinds of kisses I'd just experienced when I drifted off to sleep—a haunting pair of deep brown eyes still gazing into mine.

Twenty

I WAS HAVING a wonderfully delicious and naughty dream.
Bree and Allison followed me to the big bed after passing me around to be kissed soundly by an entire harem of beautiful girls. Hands were running all over my body and my cock was fully erect and ready to explode. My lips were being covered with kisses. Tongues played in my mouth and dared my tongue to chase them.

And then I felt lips on my erection. Lips and tongue and warm silky depths of her mouth taking me in. Bree and Allison faded away as I watched Kate with her dark brown eyes looking up at me as she made love to my cock. I was near. I tried to warn her, but I wanted her so badly that...

Impending orgasm brought me out of sleep and I opened my eyes with a moan. The room was dark and silent save for the little slurping noises around my cock.

I jumped away in the bed, scrambling out of her hands, coming fully awake as I shouted out, "No! Can't! Girlfriends... Melody... Lissa. Please stop!"

The bathroom door opened and in the light I saw Lissa rush into the room—coming toward the bed.

"I'm sorry," I said. "I didn't know... I didn't mean..."

The covers were being pulled back as Lissa pulled me to her in a hug. Pulled me against her beautiful breasts that I'd just betrayed. Melody finally struggled out from under the covers at my waist looking at me with surprise and disappointment on her face.

"Was I that bad?"

"Melody! Oh my god. I thought…" I couldn't go on. I just reached for her and pulled my two beautiful lovers into my arms. My lovers. Not Bree or Allison or Kate. My heart began to slow down but I was still having trouble catching my breath. "Oh god… I thought it was…" I stopped, not wanting to say what I thought. "I was dreaming. I had a nightmare."

The two girls petted and soothed me with words like 'there there' and 'it's okay'. But I knew it wasn't really okay. Yes, I'd been passed from girl to girl for a kissing contest and I was hyper-aroused when I went to bed, but I shouldn't be fantasizing about other girls when I had the two most beautiful women I'd ever known hugging me from either side and sharing my bed every night.

"I sure didn't think I'd give you a nightmare waking you up like that," Melody pouted. "What was I? A giant anaconda swallowing your prick?"

"No you were…" Maybe it was stupid of me. It was only a dream. But it had been so real that even with my arms around my girlfriends, I was still shaking. I softly kissed Lissa's breast, against which my face was still cradled, and then squeezed Melody up toward me so I could kiss the top of her head. "I dreamed I was cheating on you," I whispered.

Both my lovers pulled away from me and turned to stare me in the face. I'd done it. I was so ashamed.

"You were having a nightmare that you cheated on us in your dream?" Lissa asked. A smile played across both their faces as they looked at me and then at each other. "Oh, Tony. Is it any wonder that we love you so much? Only a man who loves us like you do would interrupt a blow job because he was dreaming it was someone else!" Both Melody and Lissa started giggling. It was obvious that they just didn't understand.

"But it was so real. It wasn't just that I was having a fantasy, I thought it was really happening."

"Well, that's because you were giving me a tonsillectomy with your cock," Melody laughed. "That part was real. Now I want to know about the rest of this cheating dream. It wasn't Bree, was it?" There was just a hint of menace in that question.

"No," I answered quickly. "At least, not at the end. It started out with everyone. Do you two know what you did to me tonight? I just had eight mind-blowing kisses from eight incredibly beautiful women who were competing to see... I don't know... it seemed like they were competing to be like you two. To *be* you."

"Well, that was certainly the case with a couple of them," Lissa agreed. "But it was all in good fun. We thought you'd get a charge out of it and then we'd come upstairs and benefit from how turned on you'd be."

"Well, I guess you were right about that. If I hadn't fallen asleep..."

"You should have seen how Allison watched Lissa kiss you," Melody broke in. "That girl was definitely taking lessons."

"I thought she'd join us at one point," Lissa laughed. "I could feel her breath on the back of my shoulder. She was determined that she'd get you to say she was me."

"She's a quick study," I snorted, finally beginning to relax. "For a while I was panicked that I'd just told someone else that

I loved her and that you were the second kisser. Then I thought about how…" I wasn't sure I wanted to go there, but I decided to plunge ahead. "…how Kate was imitating you on the daybed while I sketched."

"That was incredible," Melody said. "I've always liked Kate, but she seemed so distant from everyone here. She is seriously hot. I knew she was going to pull something."

"Well, I thought maybe she was the one trying to imitate Lissa. Then when she really did kiss me…"

"Did you see the wet spot on her pajamas?" Lissa giggled. "That girl has a serious crush on you."

"Huh?"

"All the girls down there are our friends," Melody explained. "But there are really only two that I'd go any further with—Kate and Allison. Ever since Kate watched you paint, she's been in awe of you."

"And…" Lissa said, but halted. She glanced away with a little smile.

"Yeah," Melody continued. "I saw that."

"Saw what?" I asked.

"Saw Kate kiss Lissa goodnight when we came upstairs. We all had a little smooch-fest downstairs after Lissa and I finished our story, but most of them were just little cheek kisses or girl kisses. Kate's kiss was serious."

"Ahem," Lissa cleared her throat and raised an eyebrow at Melody.

"Yeah. Both of us," Melody said.

"Kate? Kissed both of you?"

"Oh yes," Lissa breathed.

"It wasn't inappropriate…"

"…but it held promise."

"I think I'm getting hard again."

"Want us to go get her?"

"I could just close my eyes." That got me a little slap on the shoulder, but I was close to being smothered by kisses and Melody was leaving a trail of them down my chest on the way to resuming what I'd interrupted. By the time she had me fully in her mouth, I had my mouth full of a very juicy Lissa.

Mmm. I guess girls have fantasies, too.

———◁◆▷———

WE SLEPT IN Sunday morning. When I woke up, I was snuggled between my lovers and wouldn't have moved if it weren't for my full bladder. It had been a highly charged night filled with doubts and unusual stimuli, but in the light of morning I could see that I had exactly what I wanted lying next to me. I wormed my way out of bed. Watching Lissa and Melody was like watching the wake behind a passing ship. They just flowed toward each other into the space I'd vacated. In a second, you couldn't tell I'd ever been in the bed as they were wrapped in each other's arms, still sound asleep. I was so much in love it hurt.

After I'd finished in the bathroom, I decided not to disturb the vision of tranquility in my bed. Instead, I padded to the kitchen to make coffee and surprise them. As I was on my way out the door, I saw our pajamas and my sweats on the floor and was reminded that there were six other women asleep in the house. I pulled on my sweatpants before I emerged from the bedroom.

The house was quiet, so I grabbed the Sunday paper from the front steps and relaxed at the breakfast bar with my coffee. I'd just finished "Dilbert" when a hand caressed my shoulder and there was a light kiss on the back of my neck. I smiled, then was startled when Allison stepped around me and reached for a cup to pour herself coffee.

"You done with the comics?" she asked.

I smiled and handed them to her. She was still in her version of pajamas which consisted entirely of a short nightie and bright blue bikini panties. I admired her shape—the musculature of her legs was sharply defined. She hadn't done well in the Intercollegiate, but she was definitely a strong athlete. She wiggled her butt at me and laughed.

"I'm still going to get a finished drawing out of you before I leave," she said, "so you'll get to—how'd you put it last night?—see more of me."

"Oh, you're terrible," I said, leering at her. "I still can't believe you came all the way out here for this silly party. But I'm glad you did. It's really great to see you. And you took off without me getting your contact info."

"That's sweet. Bree took it and *promised* she'd give it to you. But I didn't come just for the party. Didn't you know?"

"Uh… know what?"

"I'm working out with you this week to prep for National Singles. Lissa said you needed more variety in your training and she couldn't coach while she was playing. She didn't have enough good players to challenge you so I volunteered."

"What about school? You aren't cutting out are you?"

"We're in the middle of an agricultural area. Spring semester finals are next week, but I don't have a single class with a final, so I'm free as a bird. I'm not going to summer quarter. I start my summer job in two weeks."

"So I'm going to play with you this week?" *Shit! I didn't mean to say it quite like that.* She poked her tongue between her lips and held it between her teeth as she looked at me. It was a very sexy look.

"I certainly hope so," she said coyly. I didn't want to press this issue. I was definitely going to have to watch myself if Allison was going to be around all week. Fortunately, two more of the lovely beauties from downstairs appeared in the kitchen doorway.

"Coffee?" croaked Amy. I pointed to the pot. I needed to put another on and I filled the kettle to bring it to a boil. I'd forgotten there were so many people who'd want to wake up this morning. I'd have to make several pots.

Amy was the only one of the girls I'd seen last night who wore what I considered pajamas. They had full length pants and a short sleeved button shirt. Don't think they weren't sexy, though. The silky fabric clung to every curve on the girl—tightly enough that I could verify there was nothing under them but skin. She raised the pot toward Sonia and asked, "You?"

"Don't drink it," Sonia responded. She looked at me and smiled, pointing a finger at me. "Boys do *not* see me looking like this, understand?" I grinned and nodded. Her blonde hair was sticking out on one side. She had crib-face and her eyes were a little puffy. But Sonia is a classic Scandinavian beauty. I don't think you could make her look unattractive. The fact that her baby doll pajama top and matching panties exposed both her cheeks and her tummy didn't hurt.

"That's too bad," I answered. "Boys would be falling over each other to see you like this."

"Oh, you. Is there juice?" I pulled the various juices out of the refrigerator and pointed her to the cabinet with glasses in it. Then I watched as she stood on tiptoe to reach up into said cupboard. Her top rode even further up. *Wow! What an ass!*

Amy reached over from where she was standing and softly patted the ass in question. I figured fireworks would explode, but Sonia, glass in hand, just relaxed toward her and planted a firm kiss on Amy's lips.

"Morning," she said.

"Uh… I thought you had a boyfriend… you mentioned… last night… about kissing…" I stumbled in surprise.

"Oh, he wouldn't mind me Frenching a girl—just not another boy," Sonia smiled. "As long as I tell him about it afterwards."

"Great! The object of another male fantasy," Amy growled.

Four hands attacked my ribs and I jerked around to find Sandra and Bree trying to tickle me into fits. I squeaked a bit and ducked away from them, but not before Sandra pinched my ass.

"Fine!" Melody exploded from the kitchen door. "We can't leave him alone with six sexy girls for a minute!" There was a fit of giggling from the girls and Bree and Sandra both snapped to attention with their hands behind their backs as if nothing was happening.

The result of this action was to thrust two prominent bosoms into the fore. Sandra wore a flannel nightgown that came all the way to the floor, but by the way things continued to move after she stood still, I was forced to surmise that she wasn't wearing the support that her girls usually had. The t-shirt that Bree wore to sleep in barely covered her pussy and was so thin that her pointy little nipples were clearly visible. I was thinking about the trimmed patch of red hair that would probably be visible if she just stretched up a bit. I'd just poured two cups of fresh coffee for my lovers when another voice broke in.

"Do you have any tea?" Kate asked.

My head involuntarily snapped toward her at the sound of her voice. Unlike any of the rest of the girls, Kate's hair was neatly brushed and pulled back in her customary ponytail. She was wearing a t-shirt and her bib overalls, but barefoot. I was still drawn to her purple toenail polish.

"Hey. You got dressed," I said involuntarily. I hoped I didn't sound as disappointed as I felt.

"What? Didn't you see enough last night?" she asked. *Shit. Busted.*

"There's tea on the counter and mugs by the coffee pot," Lissa said. "Tony, be a sweetie. We're going to need more hot water. Please?"

"Yeah, I'm all about being in hot water," I said as I refilled the teakettle again. "If we're going to have all these girls living with us, we're going to need a bigger coffee pot and teakettle."

"In your dreams!"

"Live with you?"

"Not unless you grow a vagina!"

"Who said anything about them *living* with us?" Melody finally overrode the cacophony. "Don't get your hopes up. It was only a dream." I flushed at the allusion to my panicked awakening in the middle of the night. Yeah, but it had been a hell of a dream. I heaved a big sigh as though I was much put-upon.

"Well, that's a relief," I said. "I was beginning to worry that I didn't have a big enough Daytimer."

Twenty-one

THE MORNING was casual and no one other than Kate seemed eager to get dressed. The party wasn't over. I was a little worried because I'd thought of a few things I still wanted to pull together for my portfolio and I was counting on some time today to do it. Lissa put three frozen quiches in the oven and tasked me with frying up a couple dozen chicken breakfast sausages. She pulled a big tray of fruit out of the refrigerator and put it on the counter. No one made a move toward the dining room and we ended up all standing around the kitchen eating and joking. I endured several jabs about real men and quiche.

Thankfully, the girls cleaned up the breakfast mess in about five minutes and all retreated to the basement, leaving me alone with my project, which I spread out on the dining room table. I could hear various giggles waft up the stairs occasionally, but inside a little more than an hour, I was feeling good about the improvement over what Professor McIntyre had seen on Wednesday. My final project for Concepts was even looking good and I added it to my portfolio thinking that I'd review it one more time before I turned it in. I was looking it over when Lissa called to me from the basement.

"Tony. Do you have time to do another sketch for us? Just one, please?"

What the hell. I was caught up and pleased with my portfolio. There were eight gorgeous girls downstairs and with luck one of them would get naked while I sketched her. Why not?

"I'll be right there," I called down.

I used the bathroom and picked up my music player and headset from the bedroom. If I was going to do a serious sketch, I was going to have to block out all the giggling and laughing that the other girls would be doing while I was working. I couldn't count on them to be quiet through another whole sketch like last night.

I bounced down the stairs, scanning through my playlists and was all the way into the room before I realized all the girls were in the corner where Melody usually worked, complete with her lights turned on. I turned around and was faced by nine gloriously naked or nearly naked girls posed as if in the midst of a bacchanalia. Plates full of fruit were strategically placed. The daybed and my drapes had been moved into the corner, huge pillows were scattered on the floor and each girl was posed to create a delicious tableau.

Wait. Nine? My mind had jumped to the number before my brain had caught up. Kneeling behind the bed—apparently up on a chair to get the right height—Wendy, our waitress from *Carmine's* was offering a bunch of grapes to Kate, who was stretched out luxuriously on the bed. On either side, Lissa and Allison were poised, ready to serve, one with a ewer and one with a tray of bread and cheese.

Melody and Bree were positioned on pillows in front of the bed with their legs curled under them, looking at Kate's face. Just behind Wendy's left shoulder, Amy and Sonia were pressed closely enough together that their breasts were just touching and they were looking into each other's eyes. Sandra knelt at the head of the bed brushing Kate's hair.

I was speechless.

"Will this work, Tony?" Melody asked sweetly.

"Oh god, yes!" I practically shouted. "Let me grab my things."

"If you go grabbing your things, we all want to watch," Allison snarked.

"Yeah, yeah," I said, too engrossed in composing the scene in my mind to respond. "Are you all comfortable enough to hold those positions for a while? It could take me a bit to get all the… um… details in."

"We marked everyone's positions and took a reference photo on a timer. We should be able to take a break in half an hour and still get back into position," Lissa explained. "We've been working on this scene for an hour."

"Great. This is great. Sandra, I need you to shift to your left just a little. Can you do that?"

"Sure."

"Amy and Sonia, you are just a little too close to the other action. I want you lost in your own world. You have room to move farther back, don't you? Almost to the wall."

"Sure, Tony," Amy said. "And don't worry about us getting lost in our own world. We will be." There was a giggle from all the girls and heads turned slightly to watch Amy and Sonia scoot back and Amy reach over to peck Sonia on the lips.

"When I get to you, I'm going to want that little move, Amy. Remember it. Uh… the action pieces. Wendy… um… it's good to… uh… see you."

"It's probably the last time I'll ever flirt with a customer," she laughed. "Oh god, I can't believe I'm doing this."

"Could you straighten up just a little? From here it looks like you are about to fall over onto Kate."

"Sure." The move had the added benefit of bringing her breasts fully into view. Oh, what that red bra had hidden!

"Allison and Lissa, I'm most worried about you two. The position of the tray and ewer are nice, but it's hard to hold an action pose like that, even for gorgeous athletes. I think it should be a little more relaxed. Allison, lower the pitcher to rest it against your hip. Get it comfortable so it doesn't strain your arm. You are attentive and ready to serve, but not swinging the racquet yet."

"Got it. Gee, I had no idea this was so hard."

"Lissa," I continued. "Same thing goes for you about being ready, but not being in action yet. Here." I grabbed the table I'd used as a prop for the candle and fruit in my first drawing and moved it over next to Lissa, careful not to block the luscious curve of her ass with the cloth on the table. I moved the bread and cheese tray to the table and repositioned Lissa with her head up and just her fingertips resting lightly on the loaf of bread. I took the opportunity to trail my fingers down her back and across her ass.

"I don't think artists are supposed to touch the models like that, are they?" Lissa asked innocently. There was a quick burst of laughter and then everyone straightened back into their places and forced the smiles off their faces. Just three more people.

"Okay. Speaking of unnecessary touching," I said, moving to Melody and Bree. "You two are beautiful, but you look like you're afraid of each other. Sweetheart, scoot in toward Bree. I want your positions to be perfectly matched like you're twins in an interlocking puzzle. Bree, this leg out just a little more so

Melody can fit hers into the crook. Good. Cheat just a little this direction, Mel. Left hand on her waist. No, lower… on her hip. Bree, reach out with your left hand and take Kate's right hand. Rest them on the edge of the bed so you don't have to work on holding them up. Perfect."

I stepped away from the tableau to my easel. I put a twenty-four by thirty-six-inch pad of Bristol Vellum on the easel and looked back and forth between the scene and my paper. One more thing.

"Kate," I said softly. She looked up at me expectantly. I just repeated a gesture she'd used a few weeks ago, but in reverse. I pointed two fingers at her eyes and then pulled them back toward my own. She smiled. I swear, I've never seen a smile like hers.

"Okay, everybody relax into your positions. I'm going to take a new reference photo. Ready?" I clicked off about five shots from slightly different positions and then sat at the easel.

"Twenty minutes and then we'll take a break," I said. I put my headset on and pressed play. I slipped a pad of newsprint in front of the Bristol and tore through half a dozen warmup drawings in five minutes. Then I started getting serious.

IT TOOK THREE more thirty-minute poses interspersed with fifteen-minute breaks before I was satisfied that I'd captured what I needed. Kate's focus never wavered from my eyes. Everyone else was focused on her except Amy and Sonia. With just the nipples of their upstage breasts touching each other and Amy's lips on Sonia's cheek as the blonde looked up at her, they provided a counterpoint to the intense scene in the foreground. I looked back and forth from my sketch to the tableau as Adele crooned "Take It All" sexily in my ears.

I let myself simply take in the beauty of each girl in front of me and for the first time this afternoon I felt myself swell in my pants. I shifted my position a little to hide the tumescence and breathed a huge sigh.

"That's it, ladies. I don't know about you, but I'm exhausted." Everyone relaxed and started moving toward me to look at the drawing. I noticed that not one girl bothered to dress or cover up. In fact, as I watched them come toward me, Kate was still intensely looking at me with a little smile on her face. She stood straight and regal as she paused a few feet away and repeated our little gesture. Only this time, she pointed her two fingers at my eyes and then back not to her eyes, but to her breasts. *Oh, wow!* Then she giggled, blushed, and rushed to join the other girls pressing in around the drawing.

Everyone was very complimentary and I got a very personal, very naked hug from each of the nine girls. So much for hiding my erection.

"Tony, I know it's only three, but why don't you go get us refreshments from upstairs. There should be Bellini makings for ten. I'd send someone else, but you are the only one who's dressed."

"Yeah, I noticed," I sighed. They all giggled and Melody pushed my ass toward the stairs.

I don't get aroused while I'm actually painting. There's too much to focus on. I don't see tits, I see shadows and highlights. I see contrasts and colors. I see the light playing across hills and valleys, folds and drapes, foreground and background. But when I stop drawing and just look at the subject to enjoy it, it has a whole different impact. And yes, it's physically exciting. It wasn't a scene or tableau. It was nine unspeakably beautiful women displaying their naked charms for my benefit.

Twenty-two

WHEN **I** RETURNED to the lower level bearing two bottles of Prosecco, a bottle of peach juice, and the required ten glasses, the first thing I noticed was that no one had dressed. At least not in clothes. Melody had produced a dozen strips of fabric and the girls were busy draping them partially over their bodies, apparently making sure that their most delectable bits stayed exposed. The tableau setting had been rearranged and it looked like they were getting ready for another sketch. I groaned inwardly. I'd worked for two and a half hours on the last one and I couldn't believe the girls wanted to go through the agony of posing again.

The girls descended on me as I poured the Bellinis. Each one coyly took the cocktail and kissed me on the cheek, including Melody and Lissa. I poured my own and we raised a toast.

"Here's to all our new friends and models," Melody said.

"Here's to naked art parties," Bree seconded. Everyone laughed.

"No kidding," Sonia added. "I've never been to a naked slumber party before. If you're naked at an athletic party, you're in deep shit."

"There's only one problem," Lissa said. Everyone looked at her expectantly. "Someone here is way overdressed." Everyone turned to me. I know I got red. My erection hadn't completely died from the last round of getting kissed. It had been all I could do to keep my hands still.

"Ohhhh," I groaned. "Is this going to be another 'embarrass Tony' moment?"

"Just go behind the curtain like a good art model and get undressed. Then come back out here and we'll get you in costume," Melody said.

"These sheets are costumes?"

"You'll see."

I obediently went back behind the drapes and shed my sweats. That took about a second. I looked down at my cock. It didn't make any difference if it was up or down; I was going to be embarrassed. *Oh well.* I took another drink and walked out as casually as I could.

They didn't stare. Well, not all of them. At least not all at once. Melody and Lissa came over and held out a length of red fabric. They draped it over my right shoulder so that it hung down to the top of my right thigh. Like the girls, however, it didn't really cover anything. Everyone examined it critically and then Amy stepped over and pulled it down a little further until it came to about mid-thigh. I was a little nervous when Sandra approached with a pair of scissors, but she stepped behind me and cut off the back of the fabric at the same length as the front. I don't think anyone noticed that the whole time she was supposedly cutting the fabric, she had one hand squeezing my bare ass.

Two strips were cut from the scrap and Allison grabbed one to tie the sheet in a bunch at my shoulder. Kate brought the other one and put it around my waist. She was enjoying rubbing my skin front and back, too, and it was becoming obvious that I was enjoying it. Her nipples lightly brushed across my arm and my erection came to full attention.

"Hey Melody, does that thing ever go down?" Bree asked.

"Not if you don't fuck with it," Melody answered promptly. This elicited a bunch of groans, including one from me.

"Okay," Sandra said as she tugged me toward the rearranged daybed. "This is scene two." She pushed me down on the bed. For a minute I thought she was going to jump on top of me, but she restrained herself.

"I can't draw if I'm in the scene," I said matter-of-factly. Certainly they would see the logic of that statement.

"Are you totally oblivious to the fact that there are four other artists in this room?" Amy demanded. "Come on, Tony. We need a model for our portfolios, too."

"If you draw me with an erection, they won't let you enter it in the student exhibition, so just settle down, okay?" I laughed. Okay, I was on this side of the easel again. That's where this adventure started, if I remembered correctly. But the likelihood that my boner was going away anytime soon was pretty remote. After Sandra got me pretty much in place—facing the opposite direction that Kate had been—Allison slid her pretty ass in under my head. I was suddenly looking up at her very erect nipple.

"Get your tongue in your mouth, Tony," Lissa laughed. "Just because she kisses like me, doesn't mean she *is* me."

Oh geez! Things got harder, so to speak, when Wendy stretched out behind me on the bed and was propped up on various pillows. Her head was up against Allison, so her boobs were pretty much in my ear.

"Better view than last Friday?" she whispered.

"I'm finding it hard to believe you're here doing this," I answered.

"For real. I thought I was just kidding around and teasing a nice young guy while his girlfriend's back was turned. Then she calls me and says I need to do this. What could I say?"

"Which one?"

"Melody. She invited me over to see the mural you painted before she asked me to come and pose. Wow."

"Glad you came?"

"I haven't yet, but if you move your elbow a little, I might."

I looked up past Allison's boob at Wendy's face and both girls broke up laughing.

"Tony, no tickling the models," Amy said as she positioned Sonia. Sonia sat on the end board of the bed leaning across Allison's left shoulder so she could see me.

Finally, Kate got Bree settled in front of me in a mirror reflection of where she was in the first sketch. She was leaning on me with her arm crooked across my thigh looking directly up past my cock at me. When I looked at her she pointedly looked at my cock and then licked her lips. I closed my eyes and shook my head. Then the damn girl blew on me.

"Behave yourself!" I reproached her quietly. She just grinned at me.

After a few more minutes, the artists agreed upon where each person should be looking and the reference photo was taken. I was definitely going to get a print of that for my private collection.

"Hmm. Four artists. Five models. No waiting. The room is full," Lissa said. "I think that leaves me to go make arrangements for dinner."

"You can't get dressed, though," Melody yelled.

"Yes, dear," she laughed. "May I put a robe on when the delivery boy gets here?"

"I suppose, but you should check to see if he's cute, first," Melody teased.

"Or she," Amy yelled.

"Ladies, can we draw now?" Kate interjected. There was sudden silence in the room. I looked at the artists at work and wondered what our scene looked like through their eyes. Kate had positioned herself so she was looking directly at me. She glanced over at the other artists. Her eyes came back to mine and she made the familiar gesture once again. *Look at me.*

Somehow we made it through another hour-and-a-half of posing and sketching. I'd say it was boring, but really… I was lying back pillowed on two beautiful breasts with a third poised directly over me and a sexy redhead who was reminding me of her presence every few minutes by sending a short puff of air over my cock and balls. Said appendage finally deflated for about ten minutes during which time all the artists hurried to draw it while it wasn't pretending to be a flagpole.

When the drawings were finished, we all got to tour the results. They were pretty impressive. Sandra had a distinctive style. She loves to cover her coarsely textured paper with graphite and then use an eraser and tortillon to bring out the highlights. As a result, her images seem to appear out of the shadows. Her finished sketch was a real work of art. We were all impressed.

Melody and Amy both talk about how drawing isn't really their thing. They're both into graphics. But what they produced proved that good advertising still depended on good artwork. Melody's was a simple drawing with good detail that I was pretty sure she'd render in acrylics or pastels later. Amy had gone straight to bold watercolor markers and it looked like it was ready to put in a catalog. Kate's style is tightly controlled. She draws small things big. I'm sure that if she set her mind to it, she could make a drawing look like a photograph. The amount of detail she'd put in her drawing in the two hours we were working was astounding. And it was just my face. Not even my whole face. Pretty much just my eyes, nose, and forehead. It wasn't just a technical masterpiece. It really had feeling. I could imagine that when Doc saw this piece he might regret having chosen me for the mural instead of Kate. I studied the drawing for quite a while, just absorbing what she had done.

When I looked up, she was standing right beside me. She met my eyes and I sensed that she was waiting for what I would say. I must have looked a little worried.

"Kate, this is really good. Are you going to paint it?"

"No. I don't think so. I'm just going to finish it the way it is or use it as the basis for a charcoal and pastel."

"You should display it in the student exhibition. This will blow everything away."

"Well, not everything." I think she blushed, as if praise from me was something special. Hell, anyone could see how outstanding this piece was. We were going to have to get past the hero worship someplace along the line. I didn't know what else to say, and while I was thinking about it, my eyes absently traveled over the artist instead of the artwork.

God, she was beautiful. Her toga sheet was worn as a sash over her left shoulder. It passed between her breasts and was tied at her right hip. She'd tied a cord around it just below the knot so the ends hung straight down in a tight bunch along her right leg. Her breasts were firm and round, high on her chest with dark nipples and areolae that were slightly oval instead of perfectly round. Her black hair was pulled back in her usual ponytail, tied with a bit of gold cord. She was long in the torso and it seemed like it took forever to scan down from her breasts, past her navel, and on to her mound. Like so many of the girls, she shaved most of her pussy, but left a perfect rectangular patch of short black hair that was just as wide as I imagined her opening would be if I was licking it.

"Seen enough yet?" she asked softly. I looked back up to her eyes. There was a bit of color in her cheeks and I realized I'd been practically examining her.

"Not really," I said. "I want to draw you."

"I think you did. Twice."

"I want to do it again."

"Why?"

"I want to memorize you." As soon as I said it, I was afraid I'd gone way too far. What was I, an artist/stalker? Her breath was ragged as she inhaled.

"I don't think we can do that right now," she said. "We're supposed to be eating dinner." Indeed, there were cartons of Chinese food being opened and everyone had paper plates. Lissa made tea and everyone realized how famished they were after the day's posing and sketching. My stomach was growling as well. I turned with Kate to join the group at the table.

"Soon, Kate," I said.

Twenty-three

EVERYONE was finally gone. Bree drove Allison and Sonia back to her house. Wendy offered to give Amy, Sandra, and Kate a lift to campus. We'd cleaned up the trash and had a bag sitting by the garage door ready to take out, but the three of us were still naked, so we hadn't taken it to the garbage cans yet. It was a regular receiving line on the way out. Every single girl gave each of the three of us a warm kiss on the way out the door. Even Sonia laid one on me.

"What about the boyfriend?" I asked.

"I've been naked with you all day," she smiled. "Don't tell him."

When Wendy came to kiss me goodbye, she wrapped both arms around me and pulled me close for a long, sensuous kiss.

"I understand I missed this opportunity last night, so I just wanted to see what the big deal was." She ground her crotch into my persistent erection. "It *is* a big deal," she grinned.

It was Kate, though, that captured us. I was at the point where I could recognize her tentative but hopeful kiss as she pressed soft lips against mine and allowed her tongue to slip between them. It left me breathless. But as I watched, she gave Lissa and Melody exactly the same innocent but provocative kiss. By the time she was out the door, I was ready to burst.

"Oh, god! Women, I am so fucking horny! Nine beautiful naked women all day long. I've been hard for hours."

"Believe me, lover, *everyone* noticed," Lissa said.

"And do you know what they are all thinking now?" Melody asked.

"They are all riding home in their cars, quietly sitting in their little wet panties wondering which of us you are going to fuck first and how many orgasms we'll have before you're through," Lissa finished. With that, my two girlfriends wrapped an arm around each other and headed toward the bedroom, hips swaying in unison with their boyfriend panting along behind.

They walked straight to the bed, crawled up on it together, and stopped. They were pressed tightly together with just their hands and knees on the bed and their legs spread apart. I walked into the bedroom to see the most incredible display of ass and pussy of my young life.

"Tony," Melody said, "we love how you make love to us. We love how you always think of our pleasure and are slow and gentle with us. We love you, Tony. But right now we are every bit as horny as you are and all we want is for you to come up behind us and fuck us into oblivion." With every heaving breath, her hips swayed and as they did, so did Lissa's. Who was I to argue with what my girlfriends wanted?

I walked right up between Melody's ankles, positioned my cock at her entrance, and pushed. The feeling was almost enough to make me pass out. As I sank to the root in her hot, wet tunnel she raised her head and wailed her pleasure. Lissa caught her lips in a kiss, but it was difficult for her to keep the contact as every time I pulled out and slammed back in, Melody would move back and forth a foot with the impact. I was lost in the sheer joy of fucking. I loved Melody and treasured everything about her, but at the moment it was difficult to feel anything but the heart-stopping pounding as she repeatedly screamed out my name and Lissa's.

That was a reminder to me. I pulled out of Melody and she moaned longingly after me, but in a flash I was positioned behind Lissa and began to sink between her beautiful fleshy lips. Lissa is about seven inches taller than Melody, and from this angle it was easy to see that most of the difference is in their legs. Her butt and pussy were a good four inches higher than Melody's, but the different angle was no less pleasurable. Lissa took up the wail from Melody as I fucked her harder than I'd ever done before. We were animals in heat and none of us could think of anything but fucking.

I let my left hand trail down Melody's ass as I plowed into Lissa and soon I had two fingers plunging into Melody's hot box. And that set the stage for the rest of the night. I kept switching back and forth between the two hot women, savoring every difference that I could between the two. They brought hands up to each other's pussy and strummed their clits as I filled their vaginas. They only stayed upright by means of leaning against each other for support.

When I was ready to come, I pushed them both over on their backs, crawled between them and sprayed all over their tits and necks—something I'd never done before. We were wild and depraved. We didn't even clean off. I was still hard. They rolled toward each other and mashed their come-covered tits together. I leaned forward between them and used the juices as lubricant as I slid my cock into the crevice between their breasts. They fought mouth to mouth for my next load, which was not long coming.

I rolled to the side, finally too exhausted to keep going, though my cock hadn't received the message yet. Melody crawled up over Lissa and the two girls devoured each other. In seconds, both girls were screaming into each other's pussies as they climaxed again.

We showered. We soaked in the tub. We found massage oil and oiled each other until we were all slippery and sliding back and forth over each other in a full body-to-body massage. In the aftershock of our naked posing party, we couldn't get enough of each other.

————⊲◆⊳————

AT MIDNIGHT, FOUR hours after our guests departed, we were cuddled in a slippery, sweaty ball in the middle of the bed, so physically spent we couldn't move.

"How are we ever going to keep the next posing party from turning into an all-out orgy?" Lissa asked. "I thought they'd never leave so we could get in here and fuck!"

"If one more girl had ground her pussy against my cock, I'd have come," I confessed. "God, I was so primed I thought I'd explode."

"There were at least a couple who were hoping you would. What was Bree doing to you while you were posing?" Melody asked. "I thought we'd never be able to sketch your cock in a normal state."

"I was intimately cuddled with four naked girls. That *was* my normal state. Every time I started to go down, Bree would blow across my balls and then up along the length of my cock. The others kept trying to help things along as well. Wendy kept shifting just enough to rub her nipple across my ear and keep her wet pussy against my arm. And Allison had her hand on my butt through the whole sitting. Sometimes it was just sitting there, but if she noticed Bree was doing something, she'd start raking her fingernails down my crack."

"During one break, Amy and Sonia came upstairs to see if I 'needed any help,'" Lissa said. "They sandwiched me between them just to thank me for being such a wonderful hostess. A little hug would have been one thing, but they were both worked up and were getting me there, too, with their 'innocent' little rubs. I don't know where we'd have ended up if you hadn't called them back to pose."

That gave us all a moment's pause just to contemplate the scene.

"Hey," Melody broke into our thoughts. "I don't mind if you get it on with Amy and Sonia, Lissa. In fact, I'd kind of like to watch. Amy's been hitting on me ever since we met last fall, but she just doesn't do it for me."

"She said she'd swallow my cock whole if it would get her into your panties," I volunteered.

"Whoa! I couldn't believe the way she kissed you in the contest. She looked like she meant business," Melody said. "But the chances that you'd get a blowjob from Amy are slim to none, even if it *was* a guaranteed trip to my pussy."

"How about Wendy?" Lissa asked. "Her inhibitions dropped like autumn leaves once she got here this afternoon. And from our earlier talk, I don't think she's that much of a partier. She says she works most weekends and has a live-in boyfriend."

"Well, she and Bree definitely decided that the fastest way to Tony's cock was through me," Melody said. "They were on me like white on snow. I got a kiss on the ear or a nibble on the neck every time one of them walked by me."

"What gives with Sandra?" I asked. "She's always so forward and suggestive. I mean she even stripped to the waist for me and shoved her nipple in my mouth a few weeks ago. But she has to be the worst kisser I've ever known!"

"God! Have you ever seen such fat nipples? Don't be too hard on her, though. Keep playing hard to get and she'll be happy" Melody said. "If you ever returned one of her passes, she'd panic. I don't think she has much experience, no matter how big a game she talks."

"Did you notice that the little protrusion between her labia was almost the same size as her nipples?" I asked. "Talk about a mini-penis!"

"Okay, but what about Allison?" Melody asked. We were all quiet about that one.

"Look, Tony, when I asked Allison out here, it wasn't *specifically* for you to fuck her," Lissa said. "I thought it would be good for you to see someone else on the court this last week of practice before The Ektelon. She didn't do well at Intercollegiates, but she's a good player and it will shake things up a bit so you don't get too used to just playing me for hard contests. And she's a nice girl. That being said, neither Melody nor I is going get upset if you fool around together. She knows what the score is and she doesn't really have an agenda. If it happens, it happens."

"I'm not going to…"

"Don't make foolish promises, Tony," Melody cut me off. "I might even let her get into my panties, except I really don't think she's into girls. Too bad. They might not show, but that girl's got balls."

"Okay, I won't make promises," I said, "but I really have all I can handle in this bed with me right now."

"Unless Kate was available," Melody said.

"And that brings us to the elephant in the room," Lissa added.

Everyone accounted for except Kate. I felt my cock twitch at the very mention of her name. *Damn. Kate.*

"Kate is a problem," Lissa continued. "Kate is in love."

"With all of us," I said. Melody and Lissa nodded.

"Tony, we have to be careful with Kate. It's not that I think she's fragile, but she could interpret anything any of us do as a sign…" Melody said.

"I agree," Lissa said. "You could see it in her sketch. And Tony, we could see it in yours. I think your professor would call it 'connection.'"

"Yeah. That's his word," I affirmed. "She really came out of left field. Three weeks ago, I thought she was stuckup and aloof. A week ago, I still thought she was terminally shy. Now that I think about yesterday and today, though, I don't think I've ever seen anyone so vulnerable."

"It was her, wasn't it?" Melody asked quietly.

"What?"

"When you woke up in a panic as I was giving you a blow job last night," she continued. "It was Kate you were dreaming about."

"Shit. I didn't…"

"It's okay, Tony," Lissa said. "It's not unlikely that *I'll* be dreaming about her tonight. We just have to be really careful and make sure we are all in synch."

"Kate could become our lover," Melody sighed.

Twenty-four

"**T**ONY, let's play 'cheesey."

Oh crap! Not now!

"I'm sorry, Damon," I said to the boy standing behind me. "I have to work."

"Making pictures is work?"

"It's what I do in school."

"In first grade we *write*."

Well, that was true enough. But right now I was focused. That session Sunday afternoon was still fresh in my mind. I hadn't been able to think of anything else all day. I sketched all through Art History in the dark. At lunch, I ran to Daniel Smith and picked up five 22 by 30 inch sheets of 140 pound Arches Coldpress watercolor paper. I couldn't wait to start working on it. During Concepts, I spent the entire class trying out different light sources in my sketches and avoiding eye contact with Ms. Brock.

I was even distracted through racquetball practice. Allison fired straight games past me. I complained that I wasn't back to a hundred percent after my injury, but both Allison and Lissa knew that I was preoccupied. Allison was meeting up with Melody and Kate after practice, but Lissa and I had to get home right away, thank heavens. She didn't want Molly to have to stay late after having the boys most of the weekend, and I just wanted to get to my easel. I'd already taped up a sheet of paper and was beginning to lay in the sketch when Damon came downstairs wanting to play a board game.

"I can help color," Damon said. He reached for my paints and I caught his hand before the tubes of watercolor scattered on the floor. I spun on him.

"Damon, I'm busy. You can't help." *Geez, kid! Don't you know what a deadline is?*

Damon backed up and started for the stairs just as what I thought sank into my consciousness. *What a stupid fuck I am!* Of course the kid doesn't know what a deadline is. He's six years old. *Shit! I even have trouble understanding deadlines and I'm nineteen.* That's just too young to have kids.

Except Lissa was only nineteen when Damon was born. How the hell did she manage it? Sure Jack was there, but he had a job and Lissa was in school. Now I'm here. Lissa has a job and I'm in school and part of my family wants me—no, needs me.

I watched Damon back up toward the stairs. I had thirty-six hours to get this painting finished if I wanted it included in the student exhibition and my portfolio review. I could see it take shape in my head. I knew now exactly where I was going to have the light source, how I would cast the background figures into shadow. I was ready to paint.

But the truth was I didn't need to. I had adequate paintings for the exhibition. My portfolio looked good now. Why did I obsess about this shit?

"Damon, wait!" I said. I pulled off my headset and dumped my music player on my stool. I practically ran to him which set off a fit of little boy giggles and a desperate attempt to get away from the monster attacking him. I grabbed him around the waist and swung him up over my shoulder, tickling him as he came to rest in my arms. I set him down and he headed for the downstairs hall. I caught him again and lifted him.

"Damon, listen to me. Do you know what you and Drew and Mommy and Melody are?" He hesitated for a second while he considered my question.

"We're your girlfriends!" I laughed at him. That was a pretty simple way of putting it.

"Better than that," I said, hugging him. "You and Drew and Mommy and Melody are the most important people in the world to me. You're my family. I love you."

"Like Daddy?"

"Daddy's love is special, Damon. No one can ever love you like Daddy. No one can ever love you like Mommy. But I love you like Tony. So you know what I think we should do?" His eyes were big as he seemed to realize that I was very serious. He shook his head.

"I think we should play Parcheesi," I said. "'Cause this time, I think I can beat you."

I carried him squealing up the stairs and we got the game board.

<hr>

GAME. DINNER. CLEANUP. Bath. Story time. Tuck the boys in bed. Another story. It was nine o'clock when I went back downstairs and stood in front of my easel. Try as hard as I could, I couldn't recapture the feeling. All day I'd obsessed over what I was going to paint, moving into the zone. Now it was gone.

I felt Lissa before I heard her. Her hands were light on my shoulders. Her breath was sweet on my neck. I sighed heavily.

"I heard what you said to Damon," Lissa said softly.

"Hmm?"

"When I realized he'd come downstairs, I came to get him so he wouldn't bother you. I was just at the top of the stairs when I heard him burst out in giggles. And then you told him we were your family. I ran back to the kitchen so you wouldn't see me crying."

"Lissa, I'll tell you the same thing I told Damon. You and Melody and Damon and Drew are the most important people in the world to me. You are my family and I love you."

"You didn't have to interrupt your work. I know how important it is—you've been talking about it all afternoon. He's little. He'd understand."

"That's just it, Lissa. He's six. He *wouldn't* understand. I'm supposed to be an adult." I took Lissa in my arms as I tried to put my emotions into words. "Remember when we talked about whether I was ready to have kids as part of my life? I thought financial security and having Jack to share the responsibility would make it easy. But it doesn't take away *my* responsibility. I'm his mommy's boyfriend. That gives *him* a claim on me, too."

"I try not to make a claim on you, Tony," Lissa chided.

"You're right. You've done nothing but give. Lissa, honey, believe me; I'll survive my disappointment over not getting one more piece in the exhibition. I've got plenty. I wouldn't survive losing you and the boys and Melody."

We went upstairs and cuddled on the sofa. We decided to call Melody and find out how many girls she had in her bed. The answer was four. Amy, Sandra, Melody, and Kate had finished their projects and turned them in. They were already feeling like celebrating. Allison was certainly in the mood, since her school was out last week. So all five of them were camped in my room and sharing the big bed.

"Without the testosterone in the room, though, everyone has elected to stay clothed."

"I can't guarantee the same thing," I said. "I'm not getting any painting done anyway, so I might as well do some art appreciation."

"Darling, love our lover," Melody said. "Can't wait to see you tomorrow."

———◁◆▷———

DAMNED INSPIRATION. Now that I'd given up on doing the painting in time to have it in on Wednesday for the exhibition, the image kept flitting through my mind. I wanted to focus on Lissa, but my mind kept wandering off. I'd look at her nose or the curve of her lips or the valley between her breasts and sketch it in my head, flinging paint on the canvas—seeing the light as it would come alive. Lissa must have asked me the question three times after we made love before I came back.

"Tony, why don't you paint?"

"Oh, but I'm here with you. I don't want to leave you and go to a cold, unfriendly art studio."

"You may be here physically, but you aren't with me," she persisted. "Go down and work for a while. We can make love in the morning before work."

"I don't know how long it will take, Lissa. I have class in the morning and if I work all night, I won't be worth shit. I'm supposed to present my final Fundamentals project."

"Call your professor."

"It's after ten. I can't just call him."

"That man is more than a lecturer for you, Tony. He's a fan. Call him and tell him you need to reschedule your presentation for Thursday because you're painting. He'll listen."

"I don't know."

"Call." She produced my cell phone and I looked up his listing. I shook my head, shrugged my shoulders, and just pushed the call button. What was the worst that could happen?

A woman answered the phone.

"I'd… uh… like to speak to Dr. Henredon, please," I stuttered out. *Geez! I probably woke up his wife.*

"This is Dr. Henredon."

"Oh. I mean… I'm sorry… I was calling for Dr. Glenn Henredon."

"May I tell him who is calling?"

"Tony Ames." It was quiet on the other end of the line. For a long time. Finally, there was a click and I heard Doc's voice.

"Tony? What prompts this late-night call?"

"I'm sorry for disturbing you, Dr. Henredon. It's about my final project."

"Please don't tell me it isn't ready to present tomorrow."

"No, it's ready, sir. I'm not."

"Are you ill?"

"No sir. I'm painting. I… I'm sorry, this was a bad idea. I just didn't want to stop."

"Never mind," Doc said. "Now I understand. Will this piece be in the student exhibition?"

"If I can get it finished. It's pretty big."

"I've seen you do big. If you promise to present your project on Thursday, I'll approve your absence tomorrow."

"Thank you, sir. I won't disappoint you, sir."

"About that, Tony," he said. *Oh no, what did he want now?* "You did a fine job on the mural."

"Thank you, sir." He'd told me that about a dozen times.

"No one expects you to paint a masterpiece every time you face the canvas. Don't paint for the exhibition. Paint for yourself. It's what you do. It's why you came to PCAD. Paint because you can't do anything else, not because you need something for a portfolio or exhibition. Do you understand?"

"Yes sir. Thank you."

I disconnected and turned to look at Lissa. I couldn't believe it. I pulled her into my arms and kissed her, deeply and passionately. She melted against me for a few seconds and then pushed me away.

"Take that passion to the studio," she said simply. "Wake me later if you need a break."

Twenty-five

I WAS HIGH on adrenalin when I reached my studio. It's funny how now I considered the lower level of Lissa's house to be *my* studio. Mine *and* Melody's. We had each set up our stations with all the supplies we needed, including lights. We were spending four or more nights a week at the house and it had become the center of my universe.

I was worried at first that we were taking the boys' play space, but Lissa said she'd tried to get the boys to play downstairs, but everything kept migrating back to the living room. She'd finally given up and set the rule that all toys had to be in their room before stories could be read. As far as she knew, they'd never gone back downstairs again.

I worked from the sketch I created Sunday afternoon and laid out the framework for the painting on a sheet of watercolor paper. I'd bought five sheets, even though they were seven dollars apiece, because I was pretty sure I'd mess up one or more as I was trying to master the lighting for my scene. When we posed and sketched on Sunday, we used fill lights bouncing off the ceiling to highly illuminate the models. That way I was able to draw all the detail I could over the two hours that the girls posed. But now that I was ready to create a work of art, I needed to determine my light source and where the shadows would fall across their perfect bodies. When I chose a light source, I would have to deal both with the way it changed their curves and where their shadows fell. I couldn't have a light source that conveniently left no shadow across a part of a particular girl's torso that I especially wanted to paint.

It could be sunlight, moonlight, candles, torches, incandescent, or headlights. But all of the lighting information had to be added to the plain sketch. I could see it in my head. Therefore, I could draw it.

———◁◆▷———

MAHLER, SYMPHONY NO. 2. Paint on my brush, I attacked the paper in short bursts. Focal points, Doc had called them. Just a quick stroke to establish where the eye would be led. Six women focused on the reclining nude. The nude with her eyes fixed on me. Two unnoticed in the background shared a kiss. When the stunning vocals of "The Resurrection" in the last movement pulled at me, I could feel Sandra pulling the comb through Kate's hair, loving every strand it touched. There were only highlights scattered around the paper. The pencil sketch beneath was beginning to disappear.

Grieg, *Symphony in C Minor*. The room began to take shape. It was not what I expected. I thought it would be a dark medieval castle. Torches would cast deep shadows. But instead I found a Parisian lady's boudoir, pre-World War II. The men were off preparing for conflict—negligent of the women they would leave behind. The ladies entertained themselves in the rooms of Mademoiselle Katarina—a 1930s slumber party. A fire burned in the grate casting shadows where the light of a lone lamp did not reach. Cinnamon, crimson, and tangerine colored the skin of the serving girl nearest the fire—her hips lush and round, as anxious for what the night would bring as her mistress.

Schubert, *Duet Fantasy in F*. Just two hands on the keyboard as I highlight the red of Mademoiselle Brianna's hair, but soon a third hand reaches in, then the fourth. Sometimes discordant, nonetheless, the Melody plays off her twin's flesh with her subtlety. Matched in body shape and position, one races up the scale as the other descends. While both are fixed on the same object of their affection. A hand strays from one to the other. A leg touches at the crescendo. Fiery red highlights on one girl are reflected in deep mahogany shadows of the other.

I was listening to Liszt's "Csárdás Macabre" when I smelled the tantalizing aroma of fresh coffee. It was a delicate dance between two women fawning over their mistress. Sandra brushed her lady's hair while Wendy softly petted her arm, smiling at the reclining figure. The Hungarian dance with its forbidden parallel fifths creating both tension and passion. The two ladies danced in competition with each other for Katarina's attention.

I sensed Lissa behind me before I saw her. Perhaps it was the approaching aroma of the coffee. I smiled as I turned to her and welcomed her good morning kiss with the coffee. She mouthed the words 'I love you' to me and waved as she went back up the stairs to prepare to go to work. I turned back to the painting as I sipped the stimulating brew and picked up a hairline brush to add just a touch of deeper amber to the shadow between the cheeks of Lissa's most exquisite butt. Then I returned to other figures as the music accelerated into "Csárdás Obstiné" with its crashing arpeggio as Wendy's hand and eyes swept the beauty before her. Something in the back of my head was telling me that I'd just shared a passionate kiss and cup of coffee with the most delectable woman in my world, and had returned to painting without ever leaving my zone. She was a part of it.

———◁◆▷———

I CONTINUED LISTENING to my music as I ate a late breakfast. Lissa had left me bagels, cream cheese, jams, fruit, cereal, milk, juice, and more coffee when she went to work and took the boys to school and daycare. I moved around in my sweats and t-shirt as I ate and refreshed myself, listening and waiting. There was only one part of the painting left to do. I could see it and feel it, but I couldn't yet hear it. I ate my way through Ravel's *Bolero*, its utter sensuality washing over me to such an extent that I got hard while imagining the scene in front of me. Ever since that ridiculous movie, it has been a favorite lovemaking song for couples all over the world—probably long before that. But that was for couples. Watching nine naked beauties in my mind's eye—not only as they posed, but as they laughed and dressed in their even more sexy togas—added a whole new dimension to the raw sexuality of the piece.

But it wasn't what I needed.

I put my dishes and leftovers away with my eyes half-closed, swaying to the music—feeling their kisses—aware of their pussies pushed up against my straining cock. Living a fantasy that had been reality just forty-eight hours ago. My heart was accelerating as I returned to the painting. Waiting. Expecting. It reached its dramatic climax and then it was over.

But that's not life. If you only live for the climax, then what comes after is disappointing. The intensity of the peak left me yearning. Aching for the next.

And then, it was there.

Softly building with mixed atonalities, raw passion, subtle overtones, shyness replaced by forwardness, allure, and intensity. Gershwin's *Rhapsody in Blue*.

I painted Kate.

———◁◆▷———

A CUT FROM the orchestrated score of *Kingdom Hearts* was playing as I stepped back to look at the reference photo on the digital camera and my painting. It always surprises to me to look at a photo and then see what I painted. I don't paint from photos. I mean, really, if you've got the photo, why do you need a painting? But life, captured on canvas, is never what you see in a photo. At least, not what I see through my eyes.

The most obvious change was the setting. The photo clearly showed a room full of naked women, drapes hanging around that didn't quite reach the ceiling, and even flood lights that reduced the shadows. The painting was a lady's room in Paris. Just barely in the painting on the left, a fireplace burned brightly to take the chill off the room. The drapes on the tall window next to it were drawn, but a gap between the panels allowed late afternoon sunlight to streak through, painting a light stripe on the Oriental rug in the foreground. On the right, Allison had just come through an open door through which you could see a shadowy figure in the hall beyond—too dark to distinguish his features.

I'd switched Melody and Bree. I wanted Bree's colorful skin exposed, but also, having Melody closer to Kate seemed right. With Bree's hand held against Melody's hip, she was the very image of desire—trying desperately to get closer to her near-twin. Adoration showed in the eyes of Sandra and Wendy as the only ones other than Kate who were fully face forward.

I'd taken a liberty with Lissa, too. Her hand still caressed the bread, but her chin was lifted slightly. From her position, she could see beyond Kate on the bed and you could follow her eyes to the couple in the shadowy corner where Amy and Sonia had their tryst.

Just a touch more color on the rug. A highlight on the elbow.

The audience on the live recording began applauding. I bowed and pulled the headset off. The subtle shift of focus helped, but no one who looked could miss the connection between the artist and the center model.

The style was much more fluid than my mural painting. This was watercolor and was looser. Overall, there was less detail, but the play of color and light, the crispness of occasional details, and the composition of the piece would carry it with much more emotion than the more realistic acrylic wall painting could convey. Well, beauty is in the eye of the beholder, I suppose. I used a hair dryer to make sure the paint was completely dry. Then I packed things up, showered, and called a cab.

———◁◆▷———

"TITLE, SIGNATURE, AND model releases, if you please."

Professor McIntyre hadn't even looked up when I walked through the door. The paperwork for my exhibit entry was already complete save for the three things she asked for.

"I was afraid you weren't going to make it. Your girlfriends all came in insisting, however, that their pieces be arranged around yours as a suite," the professor continued.

"Girlfriends? All?"

"All four of them. I assume they are in your painting as well."

"Do you need to see it?" I asked as I nodded.

"Good question. Do I *need* to?" She looked at me and handed me the materials I needed for mounting the piece. Shit, how did the girls even know what size it was? The foam core was cut to the right dimensions, set to extend on all sides of the painting by about two inches. Since framing art like this is costly, students all exhibited paper drawings and paintings on foam core and fastened them with magnetic posts so no damage was done to the piece by using tape.

"You have about twenty minutes to get that mounted and get it down to the gallery for installation. I'll take a look at it later." She flicked her fingers at me in a gesture to get going and went back to her work. I was almost out the door when she called me back.

"Tony."

"Yes, ma'am?"

"Are you returning to school next year?"

"Yes, ma'am. Unless I'm not welcome?" I was afraid she was talking about my upcoming portfolio review. Oh man. If I didn't to qualify to return to PCAD in the fall, I was pretty sure I wouldn't be welcome at SCU either. Everything was going to hell in a handbasket. My heart started thudding in my chest.

"Good. I wanted to make sure," she said. "You are going to become a popular artist overnight. I wouldn't be surprised if there were multiple offers to buy some of your works after the gala Friday night. But you need a broader portfolio. Much of what you are showing is a variation on a theme."

"What do you mean?"

"The painting in your hand…" She gestured and I thought she wanted to see it, so I brought it back to her. She simply laid her hands on the portfolio as if a mystic. "I see a nude. Ah, several of them. And what is this? Drapes? Curtains and fabric hanging everywhere. A low-angled dominant light source—fire?—casts deep shadows. How am I doing?"

I blushed and nodded. All right. She had my style pegged. "What should I do?" I asked.

"You should focus your next term on bringing that incredible eye to bear on new subjects and experiences. If you don't, you'll end up being classed as a romantic portrait painter. You've honed your skill and your eye this year. Next year, you need to broaden your horizons. I have several suggestions regarding your classes next year. We'll discuss it at your portfolio review on Thursday. That will be all." This time she really was dismissing me.

Twenty-six

I WAS ABLE to concentrate on my racquetball Tuesday afternoon and beat Allison, though we both worked hard. I agreed with Lissa about the intercollegiate tournament not having shown Allison at her best. And I have to admit—I missed a couple of shots because I was watching the jiggling on her chest settle down. Maybe they don't make stronger sports bras.

"For heaven sake, Tony. You've already seen 'em naked. Can't you keep your eye on the ball?" she laughed at me.

"Geez, Allison. I'd never win a match if they didn't separate men's and women's. You are *so* distracting," I laughed right back at her. I'd been busted good and there was no way to pretend I wasn't staring.

"Thank god we don't have nude racquetball parties like I've heard some artists have. None of us would hit the ball," she said as she wiggled her butt at me.

"All right, you two," Lissa said, opening the court door and stepping in. "This is supposed to be practice, not foreplay. I think that's enough, today. Tony, why don't you get a shower and relax while I work out with Allison for a while."

"I'm cutting it short tonight, darling," I answered, giving her a kiss. "I have to go study for my Art History final tomorrow. I'm going to stay in the dorm tonight so I don't disturb anybody."

"Hmm. After Melody's little escapade last night, are you sure there'll be room for you in your dorm room? It's a big bed, but really…" Lissa waggled her eyebrows at me.

"I'm going to have one of those chain things installed on the inside of my door," I suggested.

"Like the one in the hotel room that you didn't use?"

"Oh yeah."

"Well, if no one else is volunteering, I'll come keep you company," Allison said. "It's an *awfully* big bed to be alone in."

"Appetizing as that idea is, I really have to study." I kissed Lissa and Allison stood next with her lips puckered. I stepped back a step and Lissa kissed her. Allison's eyes flew open.

"Oh!" she squeaked. "Every time I tell myself I'm not going to do that again, I get pushed off the wagon." We laughed and I gave her a quick peck.

"I'll call you and Melody later to say goodnight," I said to Lissa.

———◅◆▻———

I DID OKAY on my history final. Not an ace, but I won the point. I'd missed Dr. Bychkova's last Art History lecture while I was painting and, in a way, I was sorry it was over. I just wish the lectures hadn't been so boring. My final project in Concepts was done and Ms. Brock suggested again that I take her 3D class next year. That reminded me that I needed to slate time with my SCU advisor to set my schedule there for the fall.

Another practice. Allison changed her tactics and I spent most of the match staring at her behind in a pair of ultrashort shorts. The big thing about this workout, though… no, not that… Lissa had us play facing the opposite direction so the glass wall was in front of us. That threw me off my game more than watching Allison's cute ass did. Lissa said I needed to get used to playing the glass wall. Not easy, but it proved just as difficult for Allison.

I cuddled between Melody and Lissa Wednesday night and went to sleep before either of them had finished kissing me goodnight. What a party animal, huh? My Fundamentals final presentation was anticlimactic. I gave it, Doc said thank you, and called on the next student. Then I sat there and listened to eight more presentations before my last Fundamentals class was mercifully over. I handed in my Art Orientation paper and went to face my portfolio review committee.

You would think that by the time I got this far the portfolio review would be a breeze. Doc Henredon did a lot of nodding his head and saying, "Good." Abe Ardmore picked at every page of my portfolio. I swear, he even asked about my choice of photo paper for the pictures of the mural. Prof. McIntyre seemed to need to prove that she wasn't easy on me in front of the department chairman. Between the two of them, I felt pretty beat up by the time I got out of there with my suggested schedule for next fall. I noted 3D Concepts was on the list, but I was going to have to eliminate something in order to get my English and Science requirements in at SCU. This was going to be tough.

I took it out on Allison and Lissa during practice and they gave as good as they got. Lissa decided we weren't getting tough enough and this would be the last hard practice before Chicago, so we played cutthroat. In racquetball, only the server can score, so in cutthroat, the server is always playing against the other two players. When the server is side-out, the next player in rotation serves and plays against the other two. A game of cutthroat is usually to twenty-one and has to be won by two points. I hadn't worked so hard since Tempe. It was great. We called it quits at the end of an hour with none of us remembering what the score was.

When we finished the match, we hit the showers and an hour later three happy and refreshed people left the club. Outside, Melody pulled up in Lissa's car with two very happy, bouncing boys in the back.

"Mommy! We had ice cream!" Drew blurted out as soon as we got into the car. Lissa raised an eyebrow at Melody, who was laughing.

"Busted! You just can't keep a secret with little boys," she laughed. "Molly said they ate a good dinner, so we went through Dairy Queen on the way over to pick you up."

"Not that I couldn't have told by looking at their faces," Lissa said. She grabbed a sheet of paper towel from a roll in the back of the SUV and began seriously scrubbing each face. She licked a corner of the towel and used it to wipe some of the sticky mess off Drew's cheek. "Mommy spit cleans anything," she explained while the rest of us looked on in astonishment.

"Boys, this is Allison," Lissa said when they were reasonably clean and we finally got settled in the car. "Allison, these are my little terrors, Drew and Damon."

"It's nice to meet you guys," Allison said. "Mommy has told me so much about you."

"Are you our girlfriend, too?" Damon asked. That brought a silence to the car. Allison glanced at each of us with terror on her face. She swallowed and answered in a weak voice.

"I'm a girl, but I'm just a friend-friend."

"You can be *our* girlfriend," Damon persisted. "It's okay." He caught hold of Allison as she moved to sit beside Lissa in the third row seat and hugged her to his car seat. She smiled.

"Wow!" she said. "I've never had such handsome boy-friends. Or so enthusiastic!" She reached over to the other car seat where Drew was anxiously holding out his arms and hugged him, too.

I kissed Melody quickly and she headed home.

MELODY, WITH A little help from Molly, had pulled together a nice meatloaf and baked potato meal that was almost ready to come out of the oven when we got home. I read stories to the boys while Allison and Lissa had a glass of wine and put a salad together. Melody and I got the boys cleaned up a little more thoroughly and tucked them into bed.

It was after seven and I was starving when we finally sat down to dinner.

"Ah, the ultimate comfort food," I said. Her meatloaf was so good it melted my heart as I looked at her. Neither Lissa nor Allison had said a word, but chewed with a look of ecstasy on their faces. I caught Lissa's eye and we both jumped up and ran to either side of Melody. "Smooches for the cook!" I yelled as Lissa and I peppered her cheeks with kisses.

I looked at Allison and raised an eyebrow at her.

"It's really, really good," Allison said, "but I've sworn off kissing girls. Again."

"Oh, all right," Lissa said, "but you can't kiss the cock if you don't kiss the hen."

I didn't think she'd meant that quite the way it came out. Melody and I both looked at her, startled. Lissa blushed.

"I mean… that's… you know…" she sputtered.

"Oh hell!" Allison exclaimed as she rushed to Melody. "Pushed off the wagon again!" With that she planted a big kiss on Melody's lips and then ran back to her chair. I was sitting there and she almost sat in my lap before she realized it. Lissa was sitting at my place. Melody jumped up and sat in Lissa's chair. Allison looked at us trying to figure out what was going on and finally settled into Melody's chair.

"Musical Meals," Melody explained. "You're just lucky we didn't clear your place while you were distracted."

"Um… can I have my fork, please?"

We had a good laugh and passed each person his or her own plate of food and silverware. It was a game we'd tried once with Damon and Drew. The boys ended up in such hysterical laughter that Drew threw up, so we'd never done it again. But it was worth it just to see the look on Allison's face.

"Are there any other little games you play that I should know about?" Allison asked.

It turned out there was, but she was completely okay with joining the three of us in the spa for half an hour before we all went to bed. We're pretty casual about nudity together, but Allison had already seen that last weekend and wasn't nearly as uncomfortable getting naked with us as she was with the thought of eating from someone else's plate.

I don't know if she was expecting anything else, but after the bath, we all kissed each other goodnight and Allison went off to the guest room to sleep.

"It's too bad she's so uncomfortable about letting go and kissing women. She always enjoys it so much when she does," Melody said.

"Yes," Lissa responded, "I could have been persuaded to move over a little to fit her in the bed. But it looks like that privilege is going only to Tony."

"Wait, wait, wait," I said. "I'm not completely comfortable with the idea of all of us sleeping with someone else, let alone with one of us—namely me—sleeping with someone when the others aren't present. I may be engaged in a polyamorous relationship, but I've still got a heaping helping of Midwestern morals on my plate."

"Nobody's going to push anyone to do something he or she is not comfortable with," Lissa said firmly. "That includes any of the three of us or any guest we have in our house, right?"

"Right," we all agreed.

"Still," Melody said coyly, "I bet Tony wouldn't feel quite so reluctant if it was Kate instead of Allison, would you, sweetheart?"

I took too long answering, and both my lovers fell on me, kissing and giggling.

"Just think," Melody said as she crawled up above me and brushed my lips with her left nipple, "wouldn't you love to taste Kate's luscious little tit? Do you think she tastes different than we do?"

"Do her nipples get harder than mine?" Lissa asked as she nudged Melody far enough away to feed me her own stiff nipple. We both moaned as I flicked it with my tongue and sucked it into my mouth.

"When you dreamed of her, did she suck on you, too?" Melody asked, demonstrating the question by taking my left nipple between her lips and pulling lightly. I've never seen this explained in anatomy classes, but I am pretty sure there is a nerve that runs directly from my left nipple to the tip of my penis. I let out a bit of a squeal that apparently vibrated Lissa's nipple enough that she made a high-pitched whine that would have called dogs. Her nipple popped out of my mouth and in a second I could see the beautiful flower-like petals of Lissa's pussy descending toward my lips.

"Did you lick her, Tony? Did she flood your face and your tongue with her juices? Did she taste sweet and smell like the sky on a sunny day?" Lissa asked as she dipped her pussy toward my lips and my waiting tongue. I tasted her sweet nectar and smelled her fresh-from-the-bath scent mixed with the spicy aromas of her arousal.

My girlfriends had me on edge. What were they trying to do—filling my mind with images of Kate? Would her pussy taste this sweet? Her lips were incredible; would her pussy be as welcoming to my tongue? Was her black pubic hair as soft and lush as it looked? Were her labia as smooth as Lissa's? God! Why couldn't I get thoughts of eating Kate out of my mind while Lissa's beautiful and ready nether lips saturated my tongue?

"Did Kate make love to your cock with her mouth, Tony?" Melody continued the narration. "Did she wash your balls with her tongue? Did she squeeze your glans with her lips and nip at the underside of your big, stiff, beautiful prick? Could you feel her hot breath on you as she dipped to take your length in her mouth…" Melody's narration was interrupted as she demonstrated exactly the move she was describing, taking me deeper and deeper into her mouth. I felt Lissa reach down and flick my nipples with her thumb as she continued to glide up and down my face, sucking my tongue into her pussy.

I was panting. I didn't think I was going to last much longer. Between Melody's mouth on my cock and my mouth on Lissa, and all the things they were saying, it was too much. They were here with me, but they were filling my head with images of

Kate. Kate, whom I'd painted. They'd see the connection. They'd know. I was in serious lust, if nothing more. But so were they.

"Did you make love to her in your dream, Tony?" Lissa asked. The wet pressure of Melody's mouth left my cock and I thought I'd be able to recover for a minute—regain control.

"N-n-no," I gasped out. "I didn't. I wouldn't."

"Did I interrupt you too soon, darling?" Melody asked. I could feel her hand on my cock.

I licked Lissa from her clit all the way to her rosebud causing her to squeal out her delight and whisper, "More, more."

"Did I wake you up before she stroked the head of your cock against her clit, Tony?" Melody continued and I felt her rubbing me in her moist slit—rubbing against her clit. "Was it just before you put your cock at her opening? Her wet, slippery, welcoming opening with its little landing strip of soft black hair? Didn't you get to sink your thick, hard cock into her? Feel her part to let you into her secret depths?"

Melody was sinking down onto my cock. It was her pussy I was in, not Kate's. But the feeling was just so... so much I couldn't restrain myself. The instant Melody pressed down until she was sitting on my balls and I was pushed up against her inner walls, I exploded. I exploded from my cock and from my mouth at the same time. I'd never screamed during an orgasm, but I screamed into Lissa's pussy, vibrating against her clit, my tongue begging to get further into her channel. Screaming at the top of my lungs, over and over again as I pumped Melody full of my come. Hearing first Lissa and then Melody try to top my volume by screaming out their own climaxes. Then their mouths were locked together as they continued to moan their pleasure into each other and I had yet another spasm of pleasure shoot from my balls.

All this from a dream that I called a nightmare, so afraid that I'd betrayed my girlfriends that I couldn't breathe.

I hugged them. I cradled them in my arms. I whispered over and over how much I loved them. I kissed them. I petted them. All I could do was love them.

Twenty-seven

MY LAST CLASS of the semester. Everyone else had another week to go, but Lissa and I would be leaving for Chicago Sunday. All my finals were done. My projects were in. My portfolio had been reviewed, and I was ready for summer... after I played my heart out at National Singles.

There was quite a buzz in our Studio class. I think everyone was feeling the onset of summer. We didn't have a model as the class was working on finishing their final projects. Mine, of course, was painted on a wall in the admin building but I surprised Professor McIntyre with my new painting of Lissa in the bath. I liked it. The steam rising gave her an ethereal look. Melody and Kate were next to each other, supposedly painting, but frequently leaning in to whisper to each other. I kept sketching the two of them together on a small pad with an HB pencil. Everything is a muted gray when you use HB lead. I could give a quick flick with my thumb and a hard line would turn into a soft shadow. I loved how their faces looked together. One with soft English features and the other a more angular, exotic, but not quite Asian profile. Professor McIntyre was reviewing a student's work on one side of the classroom when Maggie Wright spoke up from the other side.

"Professor, how do we enroll for the nude painting parties?" There was a big laugh from the nineteen women in the class as I tried to find a hole small enough to crawl into. I was even more surprised by Professor McIntyre's response.

"Well, I understand that they are by private audition only, Miss Wright. And I might remind you that while your work during those sessions might be admitted for exhibition, the parties do not carry any academic credits."

"I'm taking names of next semester's candidates," Melody said. "One criterion is that you have to be willing to have your ass immortalized on a school wall. And, of course, the artist will have to interview the ass in question."

There was a riot of chatter and a number of voices yelling "Me. I want in."

"I think that is enough for today. In case you haven't seen it, our student exhibition was reviewed in this morning's *Times*. Some of you might be interested. There is a copy on the desk. Take whatever time you need to finish your project this morning, but officially, class is dismissed."

THE BOYS WERE excited, as well they should be. I was dressed in a tux and the boys each had a suit and tie on. I'd spent twenty minutes getting the little ties knotted. The three of us were escorting eight beautiful ladies to a gala opening tonight. I'd shown the boys pictures—fully clothed pictures, please—of all eight girls and let them choose which ones they wanted to escort. Each boy got two girls. Poor me. I'd be stuck with the other four.

I wasn't surprised that Lissa and Melody were the first chosen with a little dispute over who got whom. Allison won third place and was awarded to Damon who still insisted she was his girlfriend. Drew chose the last from the pictures I showed him. I was surprised.

"Why did you choose that one, Drew?"

"Pretty," was all the boy would say. Well, I had to agree.

The limo arrived that evening at seven and the six of us loaded in. Damon's escorts were in the car, he having won Lissa and Allison. Drew got Meddy and accompanied me to the dormitory door to pick up his other date. When the girls came down, I introduced them.

"Ladies, this is Mr. Drew Wade. Drew has asked for the honor of escorting Miss Amy Garnet to the Gala this evening. Amy, would you join Meddy as Drew's date this evening?"

"Why me?" Amy asked in surprise.

"Pretty," Drew answered.

"Honey, you may be the only boy I ever accept a date with. May I have your hand?" The two held hands and went to the limo to join Lissa, Melody, and Allison. I turned to Sandra and Kate.

"Miss Wells. Miss Holsinger. I'm afraid that leaves just me to escort you. May I have the honor of your company?" They each hooked a hand through my arm and we went to the limo. We picked up Bree and Sonia next. Sadly, Wendy had to work and couldn't come to the gala. The two cheerleaders were stunning. I escorted one on each arm to the limo and they hugged it like they'd never let me go. Bree stumbled a bit on the way to the car and I chided her about wearing heels that were too high for her. I explained that I would be escorting four ladies this evening and they needed to share. They were surprised that instead of Lissa and Melody they'd be joined by Kate and Sandra.

It was a little crowded in the limo with eleven of us, but Drew and Damon gladly took places on Allison and Melody's laps and Bree and Kate both managed to sit partially on me with Sonia and Sandra cuddled in as closely as they could get.

The Student Exhibition Gala is the equivalent of a spring Cotillion at PCAD. It is an excuse for everyone to get dressed up and act sophisticated. Ours was by no means the only limo hired for the night.

The plan was to spend an hour or two at the gala, looking at the exhibits and acting sophisticated, drinking fruit punch and discussing the relative merits of this or that bit of art. Then we'd pile back in our limo, and go hit one of the clubs down on The Ave. Jack had volunteered to join us at the gala and collect the boys to go home when they started to get tired. I didn't envy him the job because I could tell neither of them was going to be happy about leaving without his dates.

I wasn't expecting the splash we'd make with our entrance. People noticed the eight beautiful women first, then the three men escorting them. Damon and Drew absolutely ate up the attention as nearly everyone from our Life Painting class descended on us with congratulations for stealing the show. I was prepared to thank people for appreciating the mural and just let it go at that, but there weren't that many people in the hall looking at the mural. I couldn't figure out what all the fuss was about.

The admin building, with offices on the second floor, was also the building that housed the galleries and theaters. By having dance and theater performances in the same facility where art was exhibited, students got broader exposure to those who attended one event but wouldn't have come to another. The gala, starting at 6:30 p.m. would be a preface to the dance recital at 8:30. Many people would go from one to the other.

Being in the admin building, I expected the mural to get a lot of attention. Now that it was finished, it was truly a beautiful piece and I felt good that my contribution didn't stand out as being foreign to the work as a whole, no matter what Mr. Bowers' letter to me had indicated. As expected, there was a small but steady stream of people outside the theater who walked the length of the mural in both directions and nodded their appreciation.

It was inside the gallery that the surprise was waiting. There was a good-sized crowd gathered around a group of paintings and drawings titled *The Rhapsody Suite*. My watercolor of a Parisian boudoir with nine naked women was at the center. Displayed around it were four slightly smaller pieces that were different treatments of a male surrounded by four females. It was easy to objectify the artworks. We were just males and females, not a close group of friends and lovers. Arranged on either side were works by other members of the Life Drawing/ Painting class. They seemed to orbit around the central five.

Sandra's brooding graphite piece on heavily textured Strathmore drawing paper captured the entire scene in high-lights removed from the dark background. Melody captured a soft romantic scene in pastels on Grumbacher paper. I loved her style. She talked about not being a real artist and only being interested in textiles, but when she set her pastels on the page, it was stunning. Amy, of course, used markers on bright Bristol vellum and created an image out of the scene of five nudes that could have been used to sell baby oil if she wanted. It had a sense of whimsy that I found adorable.

As soon as I saw the fourth drawing, I could see why there was a crowd. It wasn't just for my watercolor. Kate's charcoal on soft gray paper was unlike anything in the exhibit. I looked myself in the eyes. She didn't include the girls in her drawing. It was just me—my eyes, nose, and forehead. When I looked at myself, it was more revealing than looking in the mirror.

"We know the artist of this watercolor creates an intense connection with his models. Here we see not only the connection with the central character, but he leads us away from her to the shadowed figures in the background. They are the story that is told in this painting, though the connection with the central figure is as intense and moving as the connection in the mural." I didn't know who was speaking to the small group gathered in front of the suite, but he seemed to know what he was talking about. I decided it wouldn't hurt to hear what he had to say.

Lissa leaned in next to me and said, "That's Bob Bowers."

"But the surprise—" Mr. Bowers continued, "—the beauty that is unexpected—is here in this simple work of charcoal. There is nothing simple about the talent shown here. Where the work in the large piece shows the artist connected to every character in his painting, this smaller charcoal shows not only a connection, but understanding. Look in the eyes. The artist shares the shadows of her model's heart. This is not only a portrait; it is a window into the soul. On their own, these are five fine pieces of art. As a suite, someone could own a legacy."

I couldn't have said it better. When I looked at my face in Kate's charcoal drawing, I could see the depression, the hope, the love, and the doubt. Standing where I was, I could even see the artist—Kate—reflected in my eyes. Beneath the eyes were the shadowy shape of two fingers, pointing to them. "Look here," they seemed to say.

I turned to Kate and kissed her on the cheek.

"Anytime you need a model, Kate," I said. "Anytime at all."

The End

Also by Devon Layne

(Now available as Kindle eBooks.
Print versions coming soon!)

The Model Student Series

Book One: Mural *(Now in Paperback!)*
Book Two: Rhapsody Suite *(Now in Paperback!)*
Book Three: Diva *(Paperback coming soon)*
Book Four: Triptych *(Paperback coming soon)*
Book Five: Odalisque *(Paperback coming soon)*
Book Six: The Prodigal *(Paperback coming soon)*

Erotic Paranormal Romance Western Adventures

Redtail *(Now in Paperback)*
Blackfeather *(Paperback coming soon)*
Yelloweye *(Coming in 2017)*

Visit DevonLayne.com for more books!